# TRACE EVIDENCE

# JOIN THE PACK IN ALL OF THESE THRILLING VIRALS ADVENTURES!

# TRACE EVIDENCE

KATHY
REICHS
and BRENDAN REICHS

SHOCK

SHIFT

SWIPE

SPIKE

PUFFIN BOOKS

PUFFIN BOOKS
An imprint of Penguin Random House LLC
375 Hudson Street
New York, New York 10014

This edition first published in the United States of America by Puffin Books,
an imprint of Penguin Random House LLC, 2016

*Trace Evidence* copyright © 2016 by Brennan NextGen LLC
*Shift* copyright © 2013 by Brennan NextGen LLC
*Swipe* copyright © 2013 by Brennan NextGen LLC
*Shock* copyright © 2015 by Brennan NextGen LLC
*Spike* copyright © 2016 by Brennan NextGen LLC

CIP data is available

Puffin Books ISBN 978-0-14-751920-7

Printed in the United States of America

1 3 5 7 9 10 8 6 4 2

Brendan Reichs and Kathy Reichs would like to dedicate this book to the loyal Virals fans all over the globe. Thanks for taking this ride with us!

You know who you are! We'd like to thank Arianne Lewin at G. P. Putnam's Sons and everyone at Penguin Young Readers Group, Krista Asadorian and the amazing team at Puffin Books, Don Weisberg at Penguin and Susan Sandon at Random House UK, who championed this series from the beginning, and Jennifer Rudolph Walsh and the tireless team at William Morris Endeavor Entertainment. You guys made it all possible. Many thanks!

# CONTENTS

# SHOCK

I stood outside on the curb, waiting.

Sweating, actually.

I'd worn a long-sleeved Red Sox hoodie and jeans, appropriate clothing for late fall in Massachusetts, but clearly too much for semitropical South Carolina. There'd been no time to change after stepping off the plane—unsure whether or not I was late, I'd hurried to baggage claim, dragged my two battered suitcases onto a cart, and then hustled out into the stupefying, unnatural mid-November heat.

And stood there.

Twenty minutes and counting.

Back home in Westborough, we'd be prepping the fireplace soon. Unpacking our winter hats and gloves. Not strolling around in shorts and T-shirts like these blond people surrounding me, radiant in their tanned, athletic perfection as they soaked in the morning sunshine.

*Home.*

The word seared my mind.

I had to stop thinking like that, since I didn't have one anymore.

*We.*

I had to stop thinking that way, too.

Unbidden, tears gathered in my eyes. I pushed them back, angry. Determined not to let my emotions overcome me. Not again. Not today. At least not where anyone could see.

*I have a first impression to make.*

Wiping my eyes irritably, I glanced up at an iron clock bolted to the concrete pillar beside me, just above the taxi line sign. Twenty-*five* minutes.

*Am I going to need a freaking cab?*

I slipped out my iPhone, then cursed softly as I remembered it'd run out of juice on my two-hour flight here. Forgot to charge, then one episode of *Scrubs* too many.

Anxiety crept in. Slowly and stealthily, like a jungle cat.

Everything about this place felt foreign to me. It was more than just the temperature. Scanning the pickup area, I spotted palm trees swaying in the breeze. Heard a symphony of chirping crickets. Complete strangers nodded as they strolled past me, smiling, in no particular hurry. Some even said hello.

This was *not* how people acted in Boston, the only city I'd ever known. That stuff could get you punched in the face.

Carolina.

Even the name sounded exotic to me.

What did I know about the South? I could count the number of times I'd left the Bay State on one hand, with fingers to spare. Maine. Vermont. Rhode Island that one summer when I was twelve. Familiar, normal New England locales, not so different from my central Massachusetts home.

But this place? I felt like I needed a passport. Westborough seemed a million miles away.

*Calm down. You can do this.*

The silent pep talk did nothing to ease my nerves. I was about to meet my father for the first time, face-to-face. A person Mom never told me about—not even his name—in all the years we spent together. A man who'd played no role in my first thirteen years of life, right up to the day of my mother's funeral, when distant relatives began whispering about what was to be done with me.

When everything I'd ever known was ripped from my fingers.

We had spoken over FaceTime, sure. Three times in the last two weeks, while the "arrangements" were being made. Christopher "Kit" Howard was to become my legal guardian. Honestly, he was the only realistic choice.

Other than my great-aunt Temperance Brennan.

How's that for a shock? Turns out, I'm related to someone famous, and never knew. She'd even offered to take me in, though we both knew it wouldn't work. The Fates had decreed that Kit Howard would parent me through my high school years.

So now I had a dad. I guess.

Whatever. Only four years until college.

That got me thinking about Mom again—the car accident, the doorbell, the sad-eyed police officer—but I shoved the raw memories away. After two weeks of mourning, I was desperate for a reprieve. My tears were spent.

Another gaggle of passengers exited the airport. They all seemed to have rides waiting.

Where was this new father of mine?

*How can you be late to pick up your long-lost daughter?*

As if in answer, a mud-streaked Mini Cooper raced around the corner. Tires screeched as the tiny car slowed, then lurched forward, cutting across two lanes to halt directly before me. A boyish-looking man with curly brown hair leaped from the driver's seat. He wore a Pearl Jam tee, khakis, and the panicked expression of someone who has no idea what he's doing, but is pretty sure he's done it wrong.

"Victoria?" he called across the hood. "Er. I mean, Tory? Tory Brennan?"

He winced as if he'd just made a second strike. Which he kinda had.

"That's me." Voice flat, trying to keep my roiling emotions in check. "Hello."

"Hi." Then he stood there, staring dumbly, as if he didn't know what to say next. Maybe he'd never gotten this far in his head.

I understood. There was no script for this scenario. No rulebook on how to greet a close family member you've never met before but intend to share a home with, effective immediately.

So we stared at each other. Behind him, a shuttle bus roared toward the exit.

"I'm Kit," he blurted, breaking the awkward silence. "I mean, Christopher Howard. Your father," he sputtered. Then Kit shook his head, as if certain he'd finally struck out. "It's nice to finally meet you in person," he finished lamely.

Spotting my bags, Kit shot forward. But he moved too fast, whacking his knee on the fender as he rounded the vehicle. Kit grabbed his leg, flushing beet red. A four-letter word curled his lips, but after glancing at me, he choked it back.

I suppressed a smile. This guy might be a total doofus, but he was clearly more nervous than I was. Which was oddly comforting.

"Sorry I'm late," Kit managed finally, still grimacing as he rubbed his injured limb. "Flight status said you'd be delayed an hour, but then it changed suddenly and you were already on the ground."

He dug out his phone and thrust its screen at my face, as if to prove his point. But the app was displaying the correct landing time, nearly a half hour ago.

"I mean, the stupid info changed. Without warning." Kit glared at the device as if it had personally betrayed him, then shoved it back into his pocket. "I should've come early anyway."

"It's no big deal," I said, trying to give him an out. "We probably made up time in the air. Airlines always get that stuff wrong."

He nodded in thanks. "Your bags. I'll get them."

Before I could warn him, Kit grabbed both suitcases and tried to lift them at once. But he clearly underestimated their weight. The first one dropped like a stone, nearly smashing his foot, while the second bag toppled the cart before slamming into the side of his vehicle.

For a beat, Kit simply stared at the carnage.

"Maybe one at a time?" I suggested. "And maybe open the trunk first?" Internally, I was debating whether I wanted to get into the car with this man. Kit needed to calm down *a lot* before he could safely drive.

"Right." Kit shook his head. "Trunk." He reached for his keys, then realized they were still dangling from the ignition. An exasperated look crossed his face.

Kit closed his eyes. Took a deep breath. Ran a hand over his face. Then his lids slid open and he gave me a wry smile. "I'm going to start this over," he said, meeting my eye directly for the first time. "Hello, Tory Brennan. I'm Kit Howard. And I'm very sorry I'm late."

He stuck out his hand. I shook.

There. Meeting my father, complete.

"I was very sorry to hear about Colleen," he continued in a gentle voice. "Your mother and I hadn't spoken in years, obviously, but I remember her well. She was a good soul. Kind. I'm heartbroken for you and her family. I know that doesn't make things any better, but I want you to know anyway. I wish we'd learned of each other under better circumstances."

His words surprised me. Unlike nearly everyone else, Kit hadn't flinched from addressing my mother's death directly. Nor had he tried to convince me that everything would magically be okay. I appreciated that. I couldn't handle any more ridiculous conversations that danced around the reality that my mother was dead, she wasn't coming back, and it was always, always going to hurt. My father, at least, seemed to understand.

Who was this man, who couldn't make it on time to our first ever meeting but communicated with me better than people I'd known my whole life?

"And I'm sorry we're strangers." Kit leaned back against his car, a touch of heat entering his voice. "That decision wasn't given to me, though I accept why Colleen chose the way she did. But I want you to know, it wouldn't have been this way had I known."

I nodded curtly. Looked away.

There was only so much honesty I could take right then.

"It's fine," I said in a level voice. "I don't blame you." Both mostly true.

Kit seemed about to say more, but must have thought better of it. Instead, he walked back around the car and popped the trunk. Only one of my suitcases would fit inside, much to his chagrin. After a bit of maneuvering, we were able to jam the second into the car's narrow backseat, but only at the expense of my legroom.

"Sorry about this." Kit was frowning at the clown car arrangement as he delivered his third apology of the morning. "First thing tomorrow, I'll trade it in for something bigger."

My hands flew up in protest. "Oh no! It's fine. Please don't give up your car for me."

"No," Kit said firmly, buckling his seat belt. "Should've done it yesterday. This thing doesn't work well for me anymore, either. Not where I live. Where we live, I mean. I get stuck in the mud once a week."

I almost didn't want to ask. "The mud?"

Kit turned the key. We both cringed as the engine squealed.

"It's already running," he explained needlessly. "The car."

"Yes." Slight pause. "Do you need a minute? Before we go?"

To my surprise, he laughed out loud. "So I don't drive straight into a bridge abutment?"

I snorted despite myself. "Something like that."

Kit ran a hand through his mop of curly hair. He kept the car in park. "Perhaps you've noticed that I'm a little nervous."

I grinned faintly. "A touch."

He chuckled, some of the tension leaving his shoulders. When he spoke again, it was as if we were peers. "Man, I have no idea what I'm doing. I've never even had a *dog*, much less a teenage daughter." His eyes were wide in disbelief. Then he started, realizing what he'd said. His head whipped toward me. "Not that I'm comparing you to a pet, of course!"

"No," I said quickly, not offended in the slightest. "I know what you meant."

He nodded in gratitude, but couldn't seem to stop talking without a filter. "I mean, my God! I'm going to be your . . . your *dad*. This is so . . . *nuts*. I'm in no way prepared for this job."

"Don't worry," I said in a soothing voice. Weirdly, I felt like the adult in the conversation. "It's not like I've had a dad before. There's no act to follow."

He gazed at me intently. "Do you want to call me that? Dad? Is that what we do?"

I stiffened. "Let's just stick with Kit for now. Okay?"

"Yes. Of course. Absolutely." He seemed to realize how he'd been rambling. "Tory, you absolutely *must* know that I'm happy you're coming to live with me. Thrilled. I refused to consider any other arrangement. I don't want you to think—"

"Kit."

"Yes."

I smiled, but my tone was serious. "I know. I heard, and can already tell. Just keep being honest with me. I like that better than you pretending to be some sitcom father."

He sighed with genuine relief. "That I can do. You're a smart kid,

Tory. I have no idea how to impersonate a dad anyway. Let's do the thing where we just act like ourselves, and go from there."

"I like this plan." A pause. "What was that earlier about mud?"

Kit shifted into drive. "Yes. Well."

He cast a furtive glance my way as we pulled away from the curb.

"How do you feel about island living?"

# CHAPTER 2

It was an uncomfortable ride.

Wedged into the passenger seat, I stared out the window with both knees pressed against my chest, lost in thought as we rolled through the unfamiliar terrain. The sun was a brilliant yellow orb hanging in a perfect Carolina-blue sky. As we crossed mile after mile of lush, grassy swampland—everything green and yellow and tan—I couldn't shake the feeling that my old life was slowly fading away, never to return. The idea made me sad.

Kit called this area the Lowcountry, and he wasn't lying. I didn't see so much as a steep hill as we crossed a dozen waterways and several large islands, headed for God-knows-where.

Seagulls and cranes. Green, brackish water. Swaying reeds. Crisp salt air.

So much of it was foreign to me. What was this place?

"Morris Island is . . . special," Kit explained as we crossed a low concrete bridge to a colorful seaside town named Folly Beach. The place had three stoplights, tops. As we cruised along the main drag, a limitless blue expanse appeared dead ahead.

We'd reached the Atlantic Ocean, but somehow weren't there yet.

"I thought Charleston was, like—" I waved a hand aimlessly, struggling for the right words, "—a *city*. You know? With lots of people, and stuff."

"Huh?" Kit shot me a confused look, then his eyes widened in understanding. "Oh! No. This isn't Charleston out here." He chuckled, turning left and heading north along the spine of a skinny barrier island. "I don't live downtown. Far from it, actually."

The ocean was to our right, mere yards away. I spotted open water on the left side of the road as well, beyond a triple row of vacation homes marching alongside the street. A mile farther up, the land thinned to a single line of houses. Then even those fell away.

"I live in a pretty unique place." Kit pointed to a sign announcing the end of the public road, but didn't stop, pulling through the final cul-de-sac, over its curb, and onto a shady strip of unmarked blacktop hidden from easy view. We crossed a bridge, then followed the pavement as it disappeared into heavy brush. "Welcome to Morris Island."

I raised an eyebrow. "There's nothing here."

"Not much, I admit." He was watching me from the corner of his eye, gauging my reaction. Which only deepened my unease.

Nobody had mentioned that Kit lived off the grid, beyond the end of the road, like some kind of hermit, or maybe a psychopath. And he was clearly aware of that fact.

"It's about where I work," Kit began, navigating the Mini through a maze of scrub grass. "You remember me talking about that, right?"

"You're a marine biologist. A professor." I knew that much. Not that he apparently lived inside a remote sand cave, or in a tent on some deserted beach, but it was something.

"For LIRI," he confirmed. "The Loggerhead Island Research Institute. I specialize in the sea turtles and dolphins that live and breed off the South Carolina coast. I study them. Treat them when they're injured. Generally make a nuisance of myself."

I nodded. Kit and I weren't close enough yet for me to tell him how cool I thought that was—and how much I wanted to do something similar—but it was true. Kit discussing his work during our phone calls had been the first thing that warmed me to him. Had helped me begin to truly consider the idea of a South Carolina life for myself.

"So this is Loggerhead Island?" I asked, eyeing the surrounding wilderness.

"No," Kit said quickly as we emerged from the high grasses into a field of low, scruffy sand dunes. "Loggerhead's a thirty-minute boat trip from here."

My shoulders slumped in dismay. "We need a *boat* to get home?"

"No, no!" Kit shook his head, rushing to explain. Then he pursed his lips. "Well, *yes*, actually. At times. But not the way you're thinking." He spun a finger in air. "This is *Morris* Island, where I live. I work at the institute, which is on Loggerhead Island, farther off the coast. My job is the whole reason I stay out here. It's easier to get to the lab and back."

I scanned the horizon anxiously. Hadn't spotted a man-made structure since we'd crossed the bridge. Panic bubbled up inside me. I gave my father a sharp look. "You have a house, right, Kit? With walls? A roof? Running water? I don't mind living in the sticks, but I'm not camping—"

He waved a hand to cut me off. "Yes, a house. And no, not alone. Look."

He pointed ahead to where a lonely building poked from the dunes. For a hot second I thought it was some kind of mansion, standing there all by itself—at this point, *nothing* felt off the table—but as we drew near, I realized it was a tidy housing complex.

There was nothing else around it.

"That's it?" Trying to keep my voice steady.

*This is the dictionary definition of "the middle of nowhere."*

"Ten units," Kit said cheerfully, pulling into a lot behind the building and pressing his garage door opener. The second door from the right began to rise. "Forty neighbors total. I'm Numero Dos. We are, I mean."

"Is there . . ." I craned my neck left and right, searching for any other sign of civilization. "Is there anything else?"

"Not on Morris." Kit maintained his peppy tone, but I could tell he was monitoring my reactions closely. "The rest of this island is protected as a nature preserve. No construction allowed. The state owns both Morris and Loggerhead, and built these townhouses for key staff working out at LIRI. Otherwise, there wouldn't be anything here at all."

"Nothing else." My spirits sank into my shoes. "Just this."

"And the best beach in Charleston," Kit retorted, still forcing cheer into his voice. "Morris Island is absolutely gorgeous, Tory. It'd be a travesty to spoil it with tourists and condos. We have the nicest front yard in America, you'll see."

"Yeah. Sounds . . . great."

*Dear God, can I get out of this?*

Kit sensed my obvious reluctance. "Hold on, I have an idea." Instead of pulling into the garage, he spun the Mini around and parked behind the building. "Let's take a look before we go inside, what do you say?"

I shrugged. "Look at what?"

"At why I choose to live here." Kit opened his door and stepped outside. Without other options, I followed suit, trailing him reluctantly around the corner of the building.

Then my breath caught.

*Wow.*

Before me, a rectangle of vibrant green grass stretched to a short slope, which tumbled down to a gorgeous white-sand beach below. There, gentle waves lapped against the pilings of a sturdy wooden dock that marched out into the ocean. A handful of small boats were tied up along its length. Beyond the pier, blue-green water stretched as far as the eye could see, rivaled only by the towering majesty of the cloud-dotted sky.

It was . . . spectacular.

The sun reflected radiantly off the water. Slow, lazy breakers rolled in like an advancing army. Seabirds flew in long formations, cawing and swooping, coasting on thermals before dive-bombing the waves in search of their next meals.

I felt something blossom inside me. A seed of contentment, opening. Taking root.

This was a place I could love. Where I could live.

Kit was watching me take it all in. "Like I said, living on the boundary has its perks."

I was about to agree when a door creaked open behind us. Then a buttery Southern voice practically squealed, "Is that her? Oh my goodness, let me see! Let me see!"

I spun to see an elegant blonde woman hurrying down the steps of Unit 2. She wore a snug yellow sundress and impractical heels. Blue eyes. Cherry-red lipstick. The woman was tall and thin, and undeniably beautiful. Yet I had a sudden impulse to turn and run.

Kit shot me a sheepish glance. "Okay, so I didn't get to tell you about my girlfriend yet. Her name is Whitney, and she was determined—"

The woman stopped as if poleaxed, her face cratering into a comical pout. "You didn't tell her about me?"

"There wasn't a good opportunity," Kit said, darting forward to snag her hand, trying to watch us both at once. "Tory's flight was early—"

"On time," I noted.

"—not late, as expected. So we got kinda rushed, and I didn't—"

"Tell your daughter about the woman you love?" Whitney interrupted shrilly, eyes snapping shut as she placed a hand against her chest. With a start, I realized she was near tears.

*Who is this drama queen?*

Kit started to protest, but Whitney's hand rose to cut him off as she gathered herself. Then, eyelids fluttering, she practically leaped forward, wrapping me in a bone-crushing hug. My eyes bugged as this complete stranger attempted to squeeze the life out of me.

"You poor, dear child!" Fingernails stroked the back of my head, and I couldn't suppress a shiver. Whitney pulled her head back to regard me. "Are you cold, darling? Sick? Kit, bring this girl inside before she catches her death!"

It was at least seventy degrees outside.

"We were just—" Kit began, but Whitney was already shepherding me toward the entrance to the townhouse, leaving him to hurry after us.

We climbed six steps to the door, then three more inside, entering a narrow living room with a giant recessed window overlooking the ocean. In the other direction was a dining area, then a small kitchen and keeping room in the rear. A staircase to my left led up to a third floor. On the opposite side, another set of steps led down to the lowest level.

"The layout is kind of funky," Kit explained from behind me. "Four floors, pretty much straight up. This whole block was built on the ruins of an old Civil War fort, so they had to follow the original foundation. But it's pretty spacious for two people. And there's a fabulous roof deck on the top level."

My eyes darted to the makeup-drenched woman with an arm still draped around my shoulders. "You don't live here?"

Her face flushed, then she tittered like a child. "Oh no, dear. Your father and I aren't engaged or anything like that." She released me, demurely hand-smoothing her sundress. "I live downtown, in the city proper."

*Phew.*

I wasn't sure about this goofy new dad of mine, but I'd made a snap decision about his ditzy girlfriend. That we weren't going to be roomies was the best news of the day.

"Your bedroom is upstairs." Kit nodded up the steps. "I'm giving you the one in front. It's bigger, and overlooks the ocean. Plus it's got the master bath."

My mouth opened, but he spoke right over me. "I *insist*. Honestly, I couldn't care less about bathroom size, and the closet in the second bedroom is really tight. You're a teenage girl," he explained to me needlessly. "You need way more space than me."

"Kit, I can't take your bedroom."

"You can and will." He made a chopping motion with one hand. "I've already moved my stuff anyway, and don't want to have to do it again."

I was touched. Kit Howard might be woefully unprepared to be a dad, but he seemed to have a good heart. *It's a start.* "Okay. If that's what you want."

"It's what *we* want," Whitney chimed in, flashing a set of perfect white teeth. For some reason, I imagined smashing a pie into her face. She'd probably faint at the mess.

"Would you like a tour?" Whitney offered brightly. "Or something to eat? You must be famished, with nothing but airplane food to eat."

The day had caught up to me. My head wasn't quite spinning, but close. I needed a break. A quick time-out to get my bearings. "Maybe just a few minutes in my room. Alone," I clarified, just in case she thought to join me.

"Of course!" Kit said quickly. "I'll get your bags."

"You poor dear," Whitney repeated with a sigh. "Yes. Rest is just the ticket."

"Thanks." I was halfway up the stairs before I remembered I'd never set foot inside this house before. "Which room is mine?"

"One flight up, sweetheart." Whitney wore an overly solicitous expression, as if I were an endangered species entrusted to her care. "End of the hall. Look for the bay window overlooking the sea."

It suddenly occurred to me that by evicting Kit, I'd banished Whitney to the guest room as well. Some manners were in order, no matter how much she made my skin crawl. "Thank you, Whitney. You've made this all a lot easier."

Her hands rose to cover her mouth as she nodded tightly. I feared I'd overdone it.

*What a bizarre woman.*

Taking the steps two at a time, I fled, in search of sanctuary.

# CHAPTER 3

The bedroom was small but well-appointed.

Bed. Dresser. Desk. Twin bookcases, aligned side-by-side. Everything in dark mahogany, the pieces matching and clearly brand-new. Kit must've crushed a Pottery Barn catalog.

No complaints, though. It all looked nice. A boy's effort at building a girl's room, yes, but he got an A for effort. Then I spotted a lilac duvet and lacy tangerine throw pillows, and knew Whitney's hand had been present as well.

I stuck my head into the closet. Not huge, but plenty big enough for the contents of my two suitcases. I wasn't a clotheshorse or anything, plus Mom and I never had the funds to bloat our wardrobes.

The bathroom, however, was a pleasant surprise. Two sinks, a stand-alone shower, and, yes, a soaking tub. I debated jumping into it right then, but held off. I didn't know what Kit and Whitney had planned, and the last thing this day needed was a bathroom-walk-in disaster.

There was a daybed beneath the bay window. I hopped onto it and gazed out at the smooth, glasslike ocean below. Kit had it right—the landscape was amazing. Soothing. I'd never had a view like that in

Massachusetts. As I watched, a pod of dolphins breached the surface, firing seawater high into the air. I said a silent thank-you for Kit's generosity.

Spotting an outlet, I plugged in my phone to charge. Then I leaned back against the wall, staring down at the deep blue sea.

*So. Here I am.*

The morning had been strange, no question. I thought about Kit and decided there was potential there. While essentially clueless, he didn't seem overbearing, or thickheaded, or mean. In fact, he seemed relieved at the idea of treating each other as equals. I could work with that.

*Whitney, though.*

She was going to be a problem.

Unbidden, comparisons to my mother paraded through my head. Mom had always been able to read my moods instinctively. Defused tension with ease. She'd had a gift for dialing down my type-A personality and getting me to relax. Basically the exact opposite of the bombastic blonde bombshell lurking downstairs.

Even when Mom skipped me up a grade level—something I'd complained bitterly about upon reaching high school; who wants to be youngest by a full year?—she'd been able to calmly explain her reasoning in a way I'd accepted.

But Whitney? She'd gotten everything wrong within seconds. It was almost impressive.

How often was she going to be there? Did she run Kit as completely as it seemed?

I saw my face in the windowpane. The curdled twist to my lips.

"Blargh," I whispered. My reflection nodded back grimly in response.

With a sigh, I rose and walked to the bathroom. Splashed cold water on my face. A glance at my iPhone told me it was only 10:15. Day One of my new life was dragging like a dredge.

*What now? Do I hide up here? Take a nap?*

*Can it last four years?*

I wished I had my suitcases. More specifically, the books crammed inside. I could read up here in safety, then maybe take a nap. But going down to ask for them might result in more unwanted bear hugs. Better not risk it.

My eyes drifted back to the window. The empty beach.

*How far does it go?*

A knock on the door made me jump.

"Tory?" Kit called, his voice slightly breathless.

"Yes?" Praying there wasn't a painful getting-to-know-you activity in the offing.

"I have your things." I heard him grunt, then the sound of shifting feet. "I don't want to disturb you, but these bags are pretty heavy. Not sure what you packed . . ." There was a *thump* as one of my suitcases hit the floor. "I can leave them out here for now, but I don't want you to have to lug them in there yourself."

Decision made.

I opened the door wide. "No problem. Come in."

Kit lurched forward and dropped both cases at the foot of the bed. Then he flexed his fingers, red-faced and sweaty. "Sorry," he mumbled. "Three flights of stairs. Should've made two trips."

I stifled a laugh. He was trying so hard.

"It's fine," I assured him. "Thanks for bringing my stuff up. I was actually thinking about going for a run on the beach, if that's okay?"

"What? Yes! Great!" Kit tripped over his own words in encouragement. "That's a wonderful idea. Morris Island is about four miles all the way around. Stick to the beach until you hit Cummings Point to the north, cut straight across the sandhills to Schooner Creek, then work your way back. You'll see Charleston Harbor, Fort Sumter, lots of stuff."

Cummings Point. Schooner Creek. Fort Sumter. The names meant nothing to me, but I nodded politely. "Will I get lost?"

Kit chuckled. "Doubtful. There's nothing else on the island. If you lose your bearings, just head south and look for the Morris Island Lighthouse. You can see our place from there."

"Lighthouse. Got it."

Kit smiled, lingering in the doorway, clearly pleased to have been useful.

"Thank you," I said, waiting patiently.

"You're very welcome." Still not moving.

Finally, "Could I have a minute alone? To change clothes?"

Kit jumped as if slapped. "Yes! Of course! So sorry." He banged into the doorframe in haste to escape, then growled curses while retreating down the hallway.

I closed the door behind him.

This time, I couldn't help but bark a laugh.

Apparently my father was one of the Three Stooges.

I dug out my running gear and changed quickly. I'd always enjoyed the activity, though not usually in November. Never liked freezing my butt off.

*Not here, though. Score one for the Lowcountry.*

I pulled my long red hair into a ponytail. Checked myself in a mirror. I'm not vain, but I don't like looking shabby, either. You never know who you might run into.

Green eyes stared back at me, unconsciously tallying my freckles with distaste. I was self-aware enough to know I wasn't bad-looking, but we all have things we'd change. My spots were a longstanding pet peeve.

*I look like Mom, though. I don't want that to change.*

Blindsided. Every time.

My lips trembled. I was racked by a sudden wave of sorrow. Angrily, I fought it back. Slammed a lid on the emotional cauldron still seething inside me, just below the surface.

*Not. Today.*

I stared at the floor until my breathing slowed and the pain retreated to its regular place in the corner of my mind. Finally, secure that my eyes were dry—and that my clothing covered all the necessary places—I nodded to my reflection like we were soldiers embarking on a dangerous mission. Which seemed about right.

Kit and Whitney were huddled in the living room, pretending to be doing other things. Both popped to their feet as I hit the bottom step.

"Have a good run," Kit said cheerfully. "Nice day for it."

"Are you *sure* you want to travel the island alone?" Whitney's eyes were tight with worry. "I could go with you, though I don't like to run. Or Kit could follow you on his bicycle."

Both prospects horrified me.

"I'll be okay." As politely as possible. "I run all the time, don't worry. And there's no one else out here anyway, right?"

Whitney nodded, but her pinched expression didn't change. "If you see a coyote, turn and run home as fast as you can. Yell out and we'll come quickly."

I nodded, though I was pretty sure she'd given me terrible wildlife advice. Then I slipped out the door and down the steps.

Outside, bracing salt air enveloped me like a glove. Sunlight bounced off the surface of the ocean, making my eyes water. Was it always so calm here? Up on the Cape, the sea tossed and turned like an insomniac, smashing anything within its grip. These placid waves made zero sense to me.

I was halfway across the lawn when the sprinklers activated, forcing me to scamper down to the beach below. Not the most dignified start to my run. But the idyllic setting soon wiped the irritation from my mind. Brushing fat drops from my sleeves, I did a slow 360, surveying the expanse of water, sand, and dunes surrounding me. The place really was beautiful. I could get used to all the fresh air. The acres of open space.

*Wish I had a dog.*

Nature's symphony was playing all around me. Singing insects. Crying gulls. The steady sigh of waves tumbling to shore, then running over wet sand. Not a single man-made noise disturbed the peace, something I wasn't used to.

*Like a dream.*

I headed north along the coast as Kit had suggested, falling into a comfortable rhythm. With my muscles working, my mind went pleasantly blank. A warm glow spread through me as I stuck close to the shoreline, jogging just above the high-water mark. The land rose and fell around me, often keeping the next stretch of beach out of sight. I was enjoying the surprise of not knowing what came next.

*I could do this every day.*

Then I heard voices. My spirits sank.

*I thought no one was out here.*

I slowed, then stopped, my view ahead blocked by a clump of jagged sand dunes. Though I couldn't make out any words, I could tell an argument was taking place. Frowning, I gazed inland, searching for a way around. But here the dunes reared high overhead and were covered in tough, thorny vines.

*That scrub grass is probably loaded with pricker balls. No thanks.*

I wasn't ready to turn back, but didn't want to see anyone else, either. Conflicted, I elected to sneak forward and peer around the dune. What I saw shocked me.

Three boys were huddled beside a tide pool, arguing about something at their feet. The closest was heavyset, wearing a red-and-blue Hawaiian shirt and clashing orange board shorts. As I watched—okay, *spied*—he began pawing his wavy brown hair, speaking animatedly to the other two. "We have to do something! I'm not letting Donatello die on my watch. I'm no karma scientist, but I know that'd be bad!"

The boy next to him—a short, skinny black kid with thick glasses—shook his head vigorously. He wore a white polo and pleated navy shorts. "Don't touch it!" he insisted, tugging an earlobe for some reason. "Those things might look cute, but they've got teeth."

Across from them, a third boy was glowering at the sand. Bigger than his companions, with shoulder-length black hair and a deep, dark tan. He had jeans on despite the heat, but he wasn't wearing a shirt.

*Hey now.*

I crept a few feet closer. They didn't notice. Weren't looking anywhere beyond the tide pool at their feet.

*What's going on?*

"It might be too dry." Long Hair frowned, tapping a fist against his chin. "Can they just lie in the open like this?"

"I have a bucket!" Hawaiian Shirt pointed to a trio of backpacks at the top of the beach. He took three running steps toward the pile. "We'll douse it with seawater!"

"Wait!" Glasses's hands flew up. "We don't know if that's a good idea. What if it can't breathe?"

"It lives in the freaking ocean!" Hawaiian Shirt shot back. "How could seawater hurt it?" But he froze, unsure what to do.

"Forget the bucket." Long Hair squatted beside something at the edge of the pool. "The tide's coming in anyway. Just help me lift. We'll push it back out to sea."

With Hawaiian Shirt out of the way, I caught a glimpse of what they were discussing.

My heart leapt into my throat.

"STOP!" I shouted.

All three jumped at once, their heads whipping toward me in surprise.

Without a second thought, I catapulted forward.

# CHAPTER 4

"**B**ack away from the turtle!" I yelled.

Hawaiian Shirt's eyes widened as I charged across the beach. "Whoa. Girl." His gaze darted to Glasses. "There's a girl here."

"I see that, Hiram." Glasses was now tugging *both* ears. Maybe he had an infection?

Long Hair rose, hand-shielding his eyes as I splashed into the tide pool. He didn't speak, but was tracking my movements closely. Then his face flushed scarlet. Spinning, he practically dove for a black T-shirt lying in the sand behind him.

*Shy. Huh.*

I noted these details, but my attention was focused on the animal in the tide pool.

"That's a loggerhead sea turtle," I said without preamble. "It's a protected species."

"We got that far," Hawaiian Shirt said dryly.

*Hiram. His friend called him Hiram.*

"What I mean is, you're not supposed to touch them." I knelt beside the animal, careful not to move too suddenly. The turtle watched me with ancient eyes, its head slightly withdrawn. "Mature sea turtles don't lounge on the beach unless there's a problem."

"So why not push it back out to sea?" Glasses said. "Isn't that where it belongs?"

Long Hair nodded but said nothing.

I shook my head, examining the creature's shell as I spoke. "If it's beached itself, this poor guy might be too injured to swim, and even sea turtles have to breathe every now and again. Pushing it underwater could drown it."

"Why'd it crawl up here?" the heavy one asked. "I'm Hi, by the way. That's Shelton in the glasses. Our talkative friend is Ben."

Long Hair nodded, fixing me with dark brown eyes.

A tingle ran my spine.

*Focus.*

"I don't know what's wrong." The rising tide splashed around my ankles, but I ignored it, trying to recall everything I'd ever read about sea turtles. On a hunch I knelt in the swirling salt water, trying to see beneath the giant animal. "It doesn't seem to be nesting."

My head was level with the turtle's. It shifted to regard me, but didn't make a sound.

*What's wrong, big guy? Help me help you.*

"You have a guess?" Hi said, genuine concern in his voice. "Is it sick or something?"

I sat back on my knees, brow furrowed. "In Massachusetts Bay, distressed sea turtles have usually been stunned by cold water. But I doubt that's the problem this far south."

I circled the animal and checked its opposite side. Nothing unusual jumped out at me.

Glancing up, I found the three boys watching me as much as the turtle. I wasn't sure which they thought was the stranger creature.

I had a strong feeling of being . . . assessed. Not in a creepy way. Something deeper.

For some reason, I didn't want to fail.

*But you're out of your depth. Do the right thing.*

"We need to call a marine wildlife expert." I stood, wiped wet, sandy hands on my running shorts. "Everything I've read says you're not supposed to touch or move an injured sea turtle unless the tide is about to cover it. Even then, you only move it above the waterline."

"Wait!" Hi pointed his index fingers at me, then fired them back toward the townhomes. "We know a turtle guy! A real one. He lives like a hundred yards away."

"Dr. Howard!" Ben and Shelton said at the same time.

"Kit! Of course!" My hands dove into my pockets. "My father's home right now!"

Then I winced. My iPhone was still charging in my room.

"Kit Howard is your *dad*?" Shelton glanced at his friends, who seemed equally surprised. "Look, the three of us have been living here awhile, and it's a pretty small group out here on Morris. Dr. Howard never mentioned having a daughter before. Never talked about you, I mean."

I shook my head. "Long story."

Sand rasped as the turtle shifted. Something shiny winked from beneath its leg.

"Wait." I squatted for a closer look, then a wave of anger swept over me. "I found the problem. Look."

A silver hook was digging into the turtle's right forelimb. "Some jerk was trolling with stainless steel hooks. And fishing line is still attached— see how it's wrapped around the flipper? No wonder this turtle can't swim. Every time that limb moves, the stupid hook digs in deeper."

Ben knelt beside me, staring at the metal barb. "What do we do?"

I tapped my bottom lip, considering. "We need Kit. Do any of you have your phone?"

"Was that a serious question?" Hi trotted up the beach, rummaged through a backpack, then hustled back. "I was already getting the shakes without it. You play Words With Friends?"

I ignored him. "Call my father. He needs to bring a medical kit and probably some wire cutters. Describe the injury and he'll know what to do."

*I hope.*

Hi gave me a level look. "Not that he isn't a super-cool dude, but I don't have my thirty-year-old neighbor's cell number programmed into my phone. Because that would be weird."

I looked to Shelton and Ben. Both shook their heads.

"I'll get him." Before I could respond, Ben spun and took off down the beach. Sand flew as he rounded the dunes in a blink.

"He's fast," I breathed.

"Like a puma," Hi confirmed. "I'd know, he's run me down more than once."

"True story." Shelton snagged Hi's phone, started snapping pictures of the turtle.

"So what do we do now?" Hi was eyeing the turtle, a queasy look on his face. "Can we at least get that hook out? Looks like it hurts."

I tore my eyes from where Ben had disappeared. Reexamined the wound. Though I knew I wasn't supposed to touch anything, like Hiram, I wanted to help the poor creature ASAP.

The hook was firmly embedded, but I could get my fingers around it.

*Are you really going to just sit there?*

"I'm gonna pull it out." My eyes never left the turtle. "We can't cut the line yet, or else this guy might crawl back into the water without Kit getting a look at the injury, but we can at least remove the barb from its side."

"Hold up, now." Shelton ran a hand over his scalp. "Ben'll get Kit, then he can handle it. What if it snaps at you? Or rolls over? That thing must weigh three hundred pounds."

"It won't roll over." Though the biting thing was a real issue—a full-grown sea turtle can snap off a finger if roused. But I just couldn't sit there doing nothing. "I'll be quick. Get in, remove the hook, get out."

Spoken with more confidence than I felt, but I was mentally committed at this point. I inched closer to the injured foreleg, rehearsing in my mind.

The turtle eyed me suspiciously. It tried to shift, but couldn't get turned around.

"This is a bad idea," Shelton whispered, eyes on the turtle's mouth.

"I'll, uh . . ." Hi edged back a few steps. "I'll make sure no other turtles show up."

I snorted despite myself. "Thanks."

Deep breath.

My fingers darted forward, wrapping around the hateful metal hook. I levered it from the turtle's leathery skin, then scrambled back as the massive creature wheeled to face me.

The creature gave me a hard look. A dribble of blood leaked from its wound. But the hook was out, dangling from the fishing line still wrapped around its flipper.

The tide swept in to soak me. I didn't care, was just happy to have done something constructive. Rising, I found Hi and Shelton regarding me with something akin to awe.

"Girl." Hi stretched the word in a singsong manner. "You are *hardcore*."

"Tory," I replied, smiling for the first time. "Tory Brennan."

Kit exploded from the dunes, puffing and blowing after a long sprint. He was still wearing khaki pants, but didn't seem to notice as he splashed into the tide pool, eyes glued to the injured turtle. A nylon bag bounced at his shoulder.

Ben was jogging along behind him, breathing easily. He flashed us a thumbs-up.

Kit dropped beside the turtle, unzipping his supplies. "Where's the hook?"

"I pulled it out," I said, pointing to the wound.

Kit gave me a sharp look as he examined the small gash in the turtle's leg. "That was a dangerous thing to do, Tory. Both for the animal and yourself. You should always call an expert in these situations."

I nodded, suddenly feeling guilty. "I just wanted to help."

His expression softened. "I know. And you did help—the hook is out cleanly and this cut appears to be superficial. Now let's get that line untangled."

Kit removed a pair of scissors from his bag. The turtle grunted, attempted to squirm away. "Easy, friend," Kit soothed, gently rubbing the turtle's shell. The animal seemed to calm at his touch. I could tell at a glance that my father was excellent with animals.

He carefully cut through the snarled fishing line, murmuring softly as he worked. Water poured into the tidal pool with the rising tide, soaking Kit's clothes, but he barely noticed, intent on freeing the turtle from its entanglement.

My respect for Kit grew by leaps and bounds. He wasn't just a book-ish marine biologist, he was a genuine healer. Kit cared more about this wayward turtle than his own comfort.

*I like this man.*

*Thank goodness.*

Finally, the line dropped away and the turtle's flipper came free. We all stepped back as the animal extended its forelimb. Then, slowly, it began shuffling toward the sea.

"Does that cut need treatment?" I worried the turtle would escape before we could help.

"That old man should be fine," Kit assured me, grinning as his patient waddled across the wet sand. "He's moving well right now, and it's a very small cut. Most sea turtles see far worse at some point in their lives. It was the fishing line that had him in distress."

Then he rubbed his chin. "But just in case . . ."

Kit dug into his bag a second time, then sprinted forward and stuck something to the turtle's shell. The beast turned its head irritably, but Kit had already retreated back to the group.

Then the massive turtle dragged into the waves and swam out to sea. In moments he'd vanished among the sandbars.

"Tagged him," Kit explained, seeming to notice his soaked clothing for the first time. "New LIRI prototype that stays on about a week. I'll monitor big boy's movements over the next few days, just to be safe. If he seems to be floundering—or ends up back on a beach—I'll scoop him up and take him to the aquarium for rehab. But I'm not worried."

I nodded, satisfied. "Thank you."

"Thank *you*. You guys did a good thing today. You should be proud." Kit nodded to the boys, who were standing a few feet away. Hi was gripping his friends' hands in turn, congratulating them on a job well done. "I see you've met the guys," Kit said. "I'll leave y'all to get more acquainted. And to get some dry underwear."

"Thanks, Dr. Howard," Shelton said. Ben nodded, while Hi held up a fist.

"Anytime, boys." Kit waved a hand at the rest of the island. "Make sure Tory sees all the cool stuff out here. You four will be seeing a lot of each other from now on." Then he strode back down the beach, whistling, a look of contentment on his face.

My dad. Not so bad.

I turned. Discovered three boys staring at me, unreadable expressions on their faces.

A memory of shouting at them bloomed in my mind. Storming up.

Taking over. Ordering them around. In my experience, boys generally don't like that stuff.

My nerves began to fray.

*We'll be seeing a lot of each other?*

No one spoke. The silent moment stretched.

*Blargh.*

# CHAPTER 5

"Um. Hello."

Best I could manage. I briefly considered fleeing into the ocean, like my turtle friend, but decided that wasn't very practical.

"How do you know so much about sea turtles?" Shelton was sweeping sand from his polo shirt with distaste. Hi looked curious, while Ben was still as a stone.

"I read a lot." Then I worried that sounded snotty. "About animals, I mean. For a while I wanted to be a vet."

Hi nodded sagely. "Cool. I want to be a talk show host. If Andy Cohen had washed up on this beach, I'd have handled it."

Ben said nothing, but watched me with those intense brown eyes. I fidgeted, pretending to search for something in my pockets. Uncomfortable under his scrutiny.

"Sorry about the yelling," I mumbled. "I got carried away when I saw the turtle."

"*Pssh.*" Hi flapped a hand in dismissal. "I like a woman who takes charge." Then his face reddened as he processed his own joke. "I mean, I'm not saying that—"

"It's nothing," Shelton interrupted smoothly. "I'm just glad we could help. A dead turtle would've ruined my weekend."

"You knew what to do," Ben said quietly. "We didn't." He shrugged as if that explained everything.

"So you're Kit's daughter, huh?" Hi yawned, stretching his arms. "How come we haven't met you before? I'm sure you've noticed it's a pretty small circle out here."

*Here it comes.* "I only met Kit this morning."

Three confused stares.

*No escape.* "My mother, she recently, um—" My pulse quickened, but this wasn't the first time I'd had to explain. "She died. In a car accident. I didn't even know about Kit until after it happened. So here I am," I finished, shoulders rising and falling.

Hi looked stricken, as if he'd committed a terrible error. Shelton was studying his shoes.

Surprisingly, Ben spoke. "Sorry. That sucks. Will you live here now?"

I was grateful for the change of subject. "Yes. I just moved in today, as a matter of fact. I've been a Morris Islander for roughly an hour."

"Well, nice to meet you," Shelton said, meeting my eyes again. "It's not so bad out here, once you get used to it."

"Consider us your welcoming committee," Hi added. He nodded toward the remaining backpacks, and we made our way up the beach. "Not that there are other options, since the four of us are the only kids living on this island."

"Really." I didn't know what to make of that. No girls at all?

"What grade are you?" Shelton asked. "Hi and I are freshmen. Ben's a sophomore."

"Freshman." I was hoping they wouldn't ask my age. I hated being the baby of every circle.

"Then you'll join us at Bolton," Hi said brightly. "We can spread the pain."

*The pain?*

"That's the school Kit mentioned on the phone," I said slowly. We reached the bags and the boys slung them on. "It's a good one?"

Ben snorted, kicking a pile of shells. Shelton just shook his head, removing his glasses to clean them on his shirt. "What's Kit told you?" Hi asked.

"Almost nothing. It's a private school, but that's all I know."

"Bolton Preparatory Academy is one of the finest academic institutions in the country." Hi spoke in an officious voice, fussily straightening his crumpled Hawaiian shirt. "A wellspring of leaders and great scholars throughout the history of Charleston. Admission is extremely difficult to attain, and a Bolton Prep diploma is worth its weight in gold. Truly, our school is a celebrated treasure of the Old South."

"Okay," I said, confused. "That sounds good."

"It's a nightmare," Shelton moaned.

"Horrible," Hi added with a wide grin.

"A jerk factory." Ben's lips had curled in a snarl. "Nothing but trust fund jackasses."

*Ah.* "That sounds . . . less good."

Hi smacked a fist into his palm. "First thing you gotta know is, everyone there hates us."

My eyes popped. "Oh, great!"

"These are some seriously rich kids," Shelton explained, looping his thumbs under the straps of his backpack. "Not sure if you know this, but LIRI pays for us to go there. Otherwise our parents couldn't possibly afford it."

*Kit's job sends me to private school?* "Your parents all work at LIRI, too?"

Ben nodded, but held his tongue. I could see it was a habit.

"My dad's a lab technician," Hi said. "Don't ask about my mom, she's crazy. Thinks she runs Morris Island. Ben's father runs the ferry that shuttles everyone there and back."

"*Both* my parents work for the institute," Shelton said. "Mom's a vet, Dad works in IT."

I nodded. "One big family." I glanced at Ben. Nobody mentioned his mother, so I didn't either. "And this place pays for us to attend some crazy prep school?"

"Yep." Hi and Shelton, in unison.

"But it sucks," Ben muttered. "Hard."

Hi shifted on the sand. "I mean, it's not *all* bad. The curriculum is really good, we just don't fit in with the other students. They call us 'boat kids' and 'island refugees.' I think some of them are legit mad that 'lesser' people have infiltrated their ivory tower."

"Bolton has killer science labs," Shelton chimed in, his voice warming to the topic. "Computer programming classes, too. And you should see the library. It's a freaking cathedral."

Ben chucked Shelton on the shoulder. "She doesn't want to hear about that stuff."

"No," I said quickly. "Honestly, that's what I care about most. I want to study forensics in college, which means I need a ton of bio and chem."

The boys fell silent for a moment, exchanging glances. I straightened, suddenly worried I'd said too much. I didn't want them to think I was some kind of science geek.

Even though, you know, I was.

Then, suddenly, Hi stuck out his hand. "Hiram Stolowitski, confirmed nerd. Same with these two. You're going to fit in just fine around here."

Amused, I shook. Then did the same with Shelton.

"Shelton Devers," he said formally. "What this doofus means is, we like learning new things, too. Don't feel weird around us."

I looked at Ben. He simply nodded. "Ben Blue."

"His dad's boat is named *Hugo*," Hi cut in. "It takes us to school every day. Don't be late to the dock on Monday. Mr. Blue sticks to his schedule."

My eyebrows quirked. "We take a boat to school?"

"To school, to town, pretty much everywhere." Shelton turned and pointed across the island. "Bolton Prep is all the way downtown, over there. It'd take forever to drive."

"I plan on buying a boat," Ben said suddenly. "Soon." Then he clammed up once more.

*Strange kid. But there's something about him . . .*

"Until that magical day, don't miss the ferry." Hi stroked his cheek, looking skyward in thought. "Hmm. What else don't you know?"

"Downtown Charleston is pretty cool," Shelton said. "Old. Historic."

"I've heard." Plus I'd studied a billion pictures online.

"We sometimes go into Folly Beach to hang out," Hi added. "You drove through it on the way here."

*That flyspeck town?* "I remember. Quaint."

Shelton aimed a finger north along the beach. "Some ruins up that way. Civil War stuff, pretty cool."

"Oh!" Hi exclaimed. "The lighthouse! Have you seen it?"

"Not yet." My head was spinning.

"Guys, slow down." Ben shook his head. "Tory's been here an hour."

"She needs survival skills, Benjamin." Hi flared an eyebrow my way. "We're on the edge of civilization, Brennan. Exiles. Nobody else within miles. To make it out here on Morris Island, you've got to know when to hold them *and* when to fold them. *Capisce?*"

My smirk was genuine. "Understood."

An air horn blasted behind me. I turned to see a cruise ship split the horizon, no doubt heading for the harbor. Dolphins were cavorting in its wake, leaping and diving as they followed the massive steel vessel into town.

"Island life does have its perks." Shelton grinned as we watched their fins cut the waves. "You won't see that in the Great White North."

"I'm from Massachusetts, not the North Pole. It's not *that* cold there."

Hi shook his head seriously. "North of Maryland, people live like animals. It's all igloos and coal mines. And sadness."

I shoved him lightly, rolled my eyes. Though I *was* enjoying the warm weather.

"Assault!" he howled, rubbing the offended limb.

Without looking, Ben reached out and slapped the back of his head. "Dope."

As we watched the cruise ship glide by, a feeling of peace settled over me. A sense of belonging took hold. Shelton and Hi were eyeing me surreptitiously—I could tell I still made them slightly uncomfortable —but they were sweet. Smart, too. It was obvious. Ben seemed more reserved, but no less pleasant company.

They'd spent their Saturday morning on the beach, trying to rescue an injured animal.

Exactly what I would've done.

*I have friends here. Good ones, I can tell.*

*This might be okay.*

# CHAPTER 6

"What were you guys doing out here?" I asked.

"Ben wanted to paddle into Schooner Creek," Shelton said, then hitched the bag on his shoulders. "There's an old canoe on the other side of the island we sometimes use. Morris is surrounded by sandbars, and we found one that just has crabs. They're even out during the day."

"They're hilarious." Hi made claw-hands and began scuttling sideways. "Killer dance moves, too. Popping fresh. We were going to toss them some scraps and watch the little buggers scamper in circles like drunks. That's what's in the bags. Plus the usual stuff."

"The usual stuff?" I asked.

"Oh, right." Ben spun and jogged twenty yards down the beach. He scooped something up, then turned and fired it toward us. I had a second's warning before a Frisbee sliced the air an inch above my head. I ducked as it skidded to a stop a few yards away.

"Sorry!" Ben shouted. He trotted back to us, face scarlet. "I was aiming for Hi. Got away from me."

"Because you have terrible form." Hi began digging in his bag. "I've got beef jerky in here if you want some, Tory. I found it in the back of my pantry."

*Yuck.* My palms rose. "No, thanks. I'm good."

"What were *you* doing out here?" Shelton asked me. "If you don't mind my asking."

"Running." I waved a hand at the natural beauty surrounding us. "I wanted to get a feel for the place."

"Running?" Hi halted the process of straw-stabbing a Capri Sun, fixed me with a blank stare. "Like, for fun? Seriously? Why would you do that?"

"Health. Exercise. Call me crazy."

"Thank you, I will." Hi punctured the juice pouch, shaking his head the whole time. "I only run if chased. Even then, I'm only going hard enough to outrun the next-slowest person."

"Who could you outrun?" Ben taunted. "No preschoolers out here."

"First off, don't sleep, some preschoolers are pretty damn fast." Hi took a moment to suck the tiny straw of his drink. "Second, I've never allowed you to witness my top speed. It's cheetah-like, I assure you."

Shelton snorted. "Didn't you finish dead last in the mile run this year?"

"I'd never let school officials see my true athletic ability," Hi scoffed, indignant. "They'd make me play quarterback, and the girls would never leave me alone."

"Right. Girls." Shelton jabbed a thumb at his friend. "Says the guy with a backpack full of toddler snacks."

"Which his mom packed," Ben added.

"Keep it up and I'll chug these all myself," Hi warned. "You can drink your sarcasm."

Ignoring the threat, Ben reached into Hi's bag and snagged a pouch. Shyly, he handed it to me. Surprised, I nearly fumbled it as Ben dug another out for himself.

A silent moment as we sucked down fruit juice meant for eight-year-olds. When we finished, I got the sense that no one knew what to do next. The turtle crisis had been resolved. Now it was just the four of us, standing on the beach, trying not to stare at each other.

*Should I ask to go with them? To the canoe? Or should I just go home?*

"Do you want to come with us?" Ben blurted awkwardly.

"Oh!" Pretending that wasn't exactly what I'd been thinking. "Sure. I mean, if there's room. And you want me to. As long as we have enough Capri Suns, of course."

"No. I mean yes. You should come. If you want." Red-faced again, Ben went to retrieve the Frisbee.

"Real nice, Benny." Hi shook his head with mock disgust. "You just ruined Manly Men Canoe Day. Now we'll have to talk about our feelings. Discuss body issues. Have a good cry."

My mouth dropped open to protest, but I could see the twinkle in Hiram's eye. He was joking, maybe even testing me. So I fired back. "Personally, I was hoping for an armpit-farting contest. Then we could wrestle for a while. See who can say 'bro' the most."

Hi clapped with delight. "Cool, bro."

Shelton shoved Hi sideways. "Can you not be an idiot for five minutes? We just met this girl! She's gonna hide from us in her room for the rest of high school."

"You don't understand the art of conversation," Hi responded primly, collecting our empties and zipping up his bag. "This is called 'breaking the ice.' But you're right. We should let Ben do the talking. The man is a wordsmith."

Ben scowled. Dropped his bag to the sand. The hand with the Frisbee rose.

"Don't even think about it!" Hi backpedaled, waggling a finger. "I've got a face-modeling appointment tomorrow!" But he clearly doubted his own powers of persuasion, for Hi whirled and fled down the beach.

Ben pivoted sideways, dropping into an easy crouch.

"There's a crosswind," Shelton noted, casually scratching above his temple. "Coming in off the water. And he really is faster than you'd think."

"Got it." Ben squinted into the dazzling sunlight. Exhaled. Then he fired the Frisbee hard and low. The disc dipped at first, skimming through the air mere inches above the ground before rising swiftly to strike Hi between the shoulder blades.

Hi dropped as if gun-shot. "My gallbladder!" he groaned, lying face-down in the sand.

Ben clicked his tongue. Straightened with the ghost of a smile.

Shelton golf-clapped. "Very nice. Much better than your first toss."

Ben flinched, shot me a guilty look.

I waved his unspoken apology away. "No harm, no foul."

We walked over to where Hi was still sprawled on his stomach. As we approached, he sprang to his feet, Frisbee in hand. "Now who's the one in charge!?!" he cried triumphantly.

"Hey, Hiram . . ." Shelton held up his palms, but it was too late.

Hi flicked his wrist, and the Frisbee zoomed straight for us. I ducked, but didn't need to. The disc took a sharp left turn, caught an updraft, rose, and sailed impossibly far inland.

"Oops," Hi said, shielding his eyes. We watched the plastic circle cross the face of the sun like an eclipse before disappearing beyond the dunes.

"Nice work," Ben said dryly. "That probably landed downtown."

"You chuck wagon!" Shelton snatched off his glasses to wipe them on his shirt. "That was an official Ultimate Frisbee disc. Now it's gone with the wind."

"Too much power, I guess." Hi shrugged an apology. "I *am* incredibly strong. We can all agree on that point."

I snorted. *This kid.* "I'm sure we can track it down, right?"

Ben frowned. "I think it landed near the sandhills. That's rocky ground, without a good path. We usually cut across this field from here, and avoid the cliffs altogether."

"You haven't explored that area yet?" Without knowing why, I phrased my next words as a challenge. "Too scary? Or do you not think we can find the disc?"

Ben didn't miss my tone, or back down. "Let's go." He strode into the line of dunes, headed for the island's grassy interior.

"Great," Shelton muttered. "Gonna get my shoes all dirty." But he followed Ben.

"Guys!" Hi cupped his hands to his mouth. "It's just a Frisbee. What if there's a bog monster? Or Sasquatch?" When neither boy stopped, he shook his head. Then he winked at me, firing another shooter. "Pro tip: If you challenge Ben to do something—*anything*—he's going to do it. We'll be looking for that damn Frisbee all day now."

"My bad."

Inwardly, I smiled. *I'm the same way.*

I followed Hi up a crumbling pile of sand. "Careful," he warned, skirting a stand of tall, reedy plants with cottony white balls on their tops. "Those cattails are federally protected. We're really not supposed to walk on these dunes at all, but . . ."

He shrugged, stepping carefully around the stalks, working his way down the dune's back side. Ben was standing a dozen yards ahead, gazing intently at the rolling grassland.

Hi was right. Ben looked determined to find the Frisbee. Beside him, Shelton began pointing northward, toward a clump of steep, thorny hills.

"What's that way?" I asked, as Hiram and I joined them.

"Cliffs." Ben was still scanning the high grass for a hint of blue. "The tip of Morris Island drops straight down to the water. We don't ever go there, because there's no beach."

"You can't even walk around." Hi nodded toward the beach we'd just left. "The sand gives way to rocks about two hundred yards farther up. To reach the creekside beaches, you have to cut across this meadow. That's all we usually do."

"Freaking chiggers." Shelton began aggressively scratching his shins. "We're not even in the scrub yet, and I'm already itchy."

"The disc must be over there." Ben was staring at a wild tangle of bushes beneath the sandhills.

"In the waist-high grass?" Shelton's lips twisted into a frown. "Why even look? Unless we step on the thing, that Frisbee is gone."

"Then let's step on it." Ben started into the field. With varying degrees of enthusiasm, we followed, fanning out in a loose line.

A part of me agreed with Shelton. The grass was impenetrable, and the four of us could only cover so much ground. But for some reason, I *really* wanted to be the one to find the Frisbee. The idea of not looking was unthinkable.

For the next five minutes we stumbled through the grasping plant life, searching for a needle in a haystack. I could hear Shelton griping. Hi wheezing as he wiped sweat from his brow. Only Ben remained quiet, never looking up as he stalked through the weeds, wholly intent on his mission.

The boys were so different from one another. One brash. One skittish. One quiet.

They looked nothing alike, and obviously came from different backgrounds.

A more unlikely trio I couldn't imagine meeting.

Yet despite these contrasts—and their constant ragging on each other—these guys were clearly best friends. They had an easy way. Relaxed. Trusting. Their equilibrium only disturbed by some random bossy girl who'd dropped from the sky into their Saturday.

I sensed that, at core, they were the same.

That they valued what was inside more than out.

*They remind me of . . . me.*

*At least, the me I want to be.*

We reached the far end, where the high grass dropped away. A cluster of hills rose sharply, musty and overgrown, vine-covered slopes baking in the morning sun. There wasn't a trail anywhere in sight.

"Welp," Hi said, scratching his chest.

"Told you," Shelton whined, but he looked disappointed.

Ben was twisting left and right, trying to decide where to search next, when Hi's whistle shattered the quiet. He aimed both index fingers straight forward. "How about that! I win."

Eyes narrowed, I peered in the indicated direction.

The Frisbee hung from a bush twenty yards ahead.

Shelton jogged over and freed the disc. "Hello, old friend."

"Where do I collect my reward?" Hi asked politely.

Ben smirked, made a rude gesture. "Here you go, sir."

I barked a laugh, but then something caught my eye. A slash of darkness in the otherwise lime-green hillside.

Curious, I strolled closer, dodging prickly vines for a better look.

Then I saw it. Goose bumps covered my arms.

"Um, you guys?"

Three sets of eyes found me.

I pointed to an inky black square in the weeds.

"What is *that*?"

# CHAPTER 7

There was a hole in the hill.

Low. Narrow. Trussed with wood. The gap was no wider than a pizza box, but I had a feeling that a larger space lay beyond.

Cold air seeped from the opening, like a refrigerator door left open.

The boys gathered at my side, staring down at the hole. "That some kind of animal's den?" Shelton whispered, one hand rising to tug on his earlobe. *Must be a nervous tic.*

I shook my head. "See how it's framed? Someone built this."

"So it's a tunnel?" Hi guessed. "Who'd dig one out here? Why?"

Ben straightened. Looked at Shelton, whose eyes widened.

"Battery Gregg," Shelton breathed. Hi's face lit up, but I didn't understand.

"I don't understand," I said, making it clear.

"Morris Island was part of Charleston's Civil War defenses," Shelton explained excitedly. "These hills overlook the harbor mouth. Back in the day, the Confederates put giant cannons up here so they could fire down on anything moving in or out."

Hi was nodding slowly. "Old maps say the rebels built bunkers on

Morris, but everyone assumes they collapsed a long time ago. No one's found one intact."

"Well, *we* just did." I grinned ear to ear. "Right?"

"Looks like it." Shelton motioned back toward the beach. "Let's go tell my dad."

I didn't move. *"Or . . ."*

"Or what?" Hi crouched before the opening, then chuckled. "You wanna crawl in there yourself?"

He looked back at me. I met his eye.

Hi blanched, eyes rounding. "You *do* want to go inside! *Hardcore*."

"Whoa!" Shelton backed up a few steps. "You crazy? That looks like a collapsing sand pit. Or a tunnel straight to hell."

Ben shifted but said nothing, staring at the hole.

"As much as it pains me," Hi said, straightening, "I have to agree with Shelton on this one. Who knows what's in there? Plus, I bet it smells bad."

Shelton shivered. "Bats. Snakes. Could be a bear in there for all we know."

"A bear?" Ben snorted. "On Morris Island?" But he made no move to get closer.

Shelton was not done. "We don't know what's in there. It could be a crypt. A mass grave. A ghost restaurant."

"Last one is my vote." Hi elbowed his skinny friend. "Probably a seafood joint. Maybe they serve haunted sushi?"

Despite Shelton's protests, I crept to the tunnel mouth and knelt beside it.

"Hello?" No echo. The sound died just beyond the opening.

"Be careful!" Shelton was on the balls of his feet. "You might wake something up!"

Seconds passed, and no disaster occurred. I gathered my courage and stuck my head into the gap, ignoring the sharp intakes of breath behind me. The entrance was narrow and dusty, rising so sharply I couldn't see more than a few feet ahead.

Frustrated, I wriggled deeper into the tunnel.

"Oh lord," Shelton hissed. "Can we talk about this first?"

I wiggled another foot inside, then raised up on my hands and knees, craning my neck until I could see over the hump. Beyond, the tunnel dipped back down. Light glimmered.

*What the heck?*

Snap decision. "I'm going in!"

Groans from outside.

"This girl might be crazy!" someone whispered. Pretty sure it was Hiram.

I wriggled over and down the bump, crawled a few feet, then popped into a chamber the size of a classroom. An inch of dust coated the floor. The walls consisted of squared timbers riveted together. The ceiling was higher than I expected, at least ten feet. A low door had been cut into the left-hand wall, leading deeper into the hill.

But I was drawn to the opposite side of the room, where a wide rectangular window had been carved though solid rock. A bench ran beneath it, splintered and covered in bird droppings. I stepped onto the thick wood, my hands resting in a deep groove in the stone windowsill.

My hand rose to cover my mouth. "Oh my."

Charleston Harbor spread out below me like a blanket. The window was halfway up a cliff that dropped to a rocky cove below. A wooden shelf overhung the window, faced with stone and shielding the chamber from sunlight.

*And from outside view, I bet. No wonder it's never been found.*

"Wow."

I jumped. Ben was standing right beside me, staring out at the ocean.

He held up a hand. "Sorry! I called your name, but you didn't answer. So I followed to make sure . . ." He trailed off.

*To make sure I'm safe? Is that why?*

"Amazing, right?" I looked around the room. "I wonder how long since the last person was inside here."

Ben ran a finger through a layer of dust. "Decades, at least. Maybe a century."

A muffled voice trickled through the entrance. "Are y'all dead? Please don't be!"

"We're fine, Shelton," Ben shouted back. "You and Hi get in here. It's cool."

An argument ensued outside. Finally, I heard scraping sounds as someone forced their way through the crawl space.

Shelton's head emerged from the gap. "This tunnel is *not* cool!" Covered in dust, he scrambled to his feet and began frantically smacking the front of his shirt. "Spiders! Are there spiders on me? I feel spiders!"

"Relax." Ben slapped the grime from Shelton's bony shoulders. "Nothing. Quit freaking out."

"I just crawled into a hill cave, Blue. Give me a sec, okay?"

"What's that about spiders?" Hi flopped from the entrance, breathing hard. "Not a fan!"

"No spiders," I assured him. "But the view is pretty outstanding."

Both forgot their complaints and charged forward.

"It's a cannon slit!" Shelton said excitedly. "You can see the grooves!"

"A rebel bunker." Hiram's eyes twinkled. "I bet this really is part of Battery Gregg."

"Told you!" Shelton chirped, then he patted his own back.

"I thought of it first," Ben grumbled.

"What's in there?" Hi pointed to the other opening.

"Haven't gotten that far." I turned back to the window. "Distracted by the awesome."

"Man, this is an *amazing* spot." Shelton began pointing out details below us. "We're at the northern point of Morris. That land across the water is Sullivan's Island, and the rock pile out in the channel is Fort Sumter, which used to guard the harbor entrance."

"This position makes sense." Ben tucked his long black hair behinds his ears. "With some big guns stationed here, no one could storm the harbor without getting blasted."

Hi wandered to the second opening and peered inside. "Dark." He squeezed through, then we heard a loud crash. A plume of dust billowed back through the door.

"Hi?" Ben dug into his backpack and removed a flashlight.

Hi's voice floated from the darkness. "I'm okay. I think. Ouch."

Ben shined the beam though the doorway. Hi was lying atop a pile of scrap wood. The second room was roughly proportional to the first, but without the open window slit.

"Nice move, slick." Ben spat dust from his mouth.

Hi remained on his back, wiping dirt from his eyes. "Next time let me know that you have a flashlight. Cool?"

"I always have one." Ben slipped through the gap to give Hi a hand. As Shelton and I watched, the mound shifted awkwardly. Something tumbled off, clattering for several seconds as it fell somewhere behind Hi.

And continued to fall. And fall.

"Stop!" I yelled, causing Ben to freeze in the act of hoisting Hiram to his feet.

"What was that noise?" Shelton asked. "All that rattling?"

My eyes zeroed in on a dark patch against the wall. "Ben, don't move, but shine your light over to the left."

The beam arced across the room, halting above an inky void.

"Yo!" Shelton hissed. "Don't move! There's another hole."

Ben instinctively shifted backward and the whole pile shifted. Hi slid closer to the gap.

"Oh crap!" Hi reached both hands toward Ben. "Help me help me help me!"

Ben didn't move, unsure what to do. Something rolled off and banged its way down the deeper shaft.

I fought for calm. "Okay. So. There's a hole in the back of the room. This woodpile hangs over it, so we need to get Hi off the pile without him falling down the shaft."

"Yes." Hi's jaw was clenched. "Without falling down the shaft. *Without*."

Ben was still frozen mid-crouch. "Do I go forward, or back?" He was sweating, but his voice was steady. I could tell he wouldn't panic.

I thought furiously. The woodpile was large, and didn't seem on the brink of collapse. "I think the stack will hold if you don't make any sudden moves. Ben. Very carefully, lean forward and reach for Hi."

Ben took a breath, then extended his hand.

For a moment, Hi just stared at it. Then he gripped it with all his might.

"Now pull him back slowly," I instructed. "Be careful, not too—"

The woodpile creaked. Hi panicked, dove toward Ben, who yanked him backward on top of him. There was a thunderous clatter as half the wood disappeared into the hole.

My pulse spiked, but when the dust cleared, I could see both boys near the entrance.

"Or do that." I laughed nervously. "Whatever works."

Hi was lying on Ben's chest, panting like he'd just run a marathon. "I love you, Benjamin Blue. I don't say it enough."

"Get off me!" Ben shoved him aside, then punched him in the gut.

"Don't be ashamed of your feelings," Hi gasped, rubbing his side as he stared up at the ceiling. "FYI, you guys, I found a giant hole in the back of this room. Watch your step."

"Not a hole." Shelton had snagged the flashlight from where Ben dropped it and was aiming its beam at the opening. "It's a square cut into the wall. And big."

"What is it?" I inched forward and stared down its maw.

"A mine shaft." Shelton scratched his chin, thinking out loud. "Maybe this bunker connects to others underground." Then his head whipped to me. "I'm *not* going down there, so don't even ask!"

Ben tossed a piece of wood down the shaft. "It's not steep, so quit worrying. You could climb down that thing if you really wanted to."

With his next toss, a section of the shaft's wall broke off. Dirt rained down the opening.

"Hmm." Hi gave me the side-eye. "Maybe we don't push our luck."

"Agreed," I said quickly. "I like exploring, but I don't have a death wish. That pit is out of bounds as far as I'm concerned."

The boys released matching sighs of relief. A quick survey found the rest of the chamber empty, so we returned to the front room. Again, my eyes were drawn to the postcard vista outside the window.

"I can't get over how incredible this is!" I drummed my thighs, excited. "What a secret to discover."

Shelton nodded, adjusting his glasses. "Who should we report it to?"

Surprisingly, Ben answered, "Why tell anyone?"

Shelton's head reared back, his mouth opening to protest. Then he shut it with a thoughtful expression. Hi was already nodding. "This *would* make a badass clubhouse. A place where we control the rules for a change. Super best friends need a sweet place to congregate. For book club. And snacks."

His lunatic rambling was oddly touching. "Is that what we are?"

Hi looked confused. "Huh?"

Now it was my turn to blush. "Super best friends."

Hi froze a beat, then barked a laugh. Embarrassed, Shelton began studiously cleaning his glasses.

I looked at Ben. He cracked the first smile I'd seen from him.

"Of course, Tory Brennan." Hi thrust out a hand, palm up. "Bring it in. Morris Islanders have to stick together."

Ben added his hand to Hi's. Then Shelton.

All three looked at me, grinning like monkeys. Waiting.

I damn near cried.

Stupid, but there it is.

I placed my hand on top of theirs. "Thanks, guys. I think I'm going to like it here."

"Oh, you will!" Hi slapped his other hand on top of the stack. "Secret-bunker-we-don't-tell-anyone-about-because-it's-the-bomb-and-belongs-to-us-now, on three!"

"What?" Shelton spat.

"Dope," Ben muttered.

"Got it," I said.

"One!" Hi called out. "Two . . . three!"

The cheer came out garbled, but our point was made.

A friendship, sealed.

I stepped back, filled with the warm glow of happiness for the first time in weeks.

"What could be cooler than this?" I asked, giddy with delight.

"Only one place I know," Shelton said. Ben quickly nodded in agreement.

I arched a brow in surprise. "Where?"

The guys looked at each other. Something passed between them.

"Should we go today?" Hi asked.

"Go?" I said. "Huh?"

"Definitely." Shelton rubbed his hands together.

"Go where?" I asked.

"My dad can take us," Ben said. "Next run's in forty minutes."

"Guys!" I shouted. Even stamped a foot, to their amusement. "Would one of you please tell me what you're talking about?" I continued in a calm, if exasperated, voice. "Where do you want to go?"

Three wide smiles.

"Tory, my dear," Hi intoned, "let us tell you about Loggerhead Island."

# SHIFT

# CHAPTER 1

That Sunday started like any other on Morris Island.

Moms.

Yelling up the stairs.

"Shelton Devers!" Her voice arrowed through my door like it wasn't even there. "Get out of bed, lazy bones! It's almost eight thirty."

"I'm up!" I lied, burrowing deeper into my blankets.

*Need my beauty rest.*

But I knew a personal visit came next. My mother does not tolerate slacking.

Groaning, I rolled from bed and stumbled to the bathroom, slapping my *Avatar* poster for luck along the way.

Toilet. Shower. Toothbrush. My brain slowly churned awake.

I was halfway through a second round of flossing—you've *got* to protect your gums—when One Direction blasted from my iMac's speakers.

New message.

"*That's what makes you beautiful.*" Mumbled, as I dropped into my desk chair.

Hey, I don't care. Haters gonna hate, but them dudes can *sing*.

I located my glasses—black, box-framed, with inch-thick lenses—and slid them onto my nose. Necessary evil. I've tried contacts a thousand times, but can't pop the little buggers into place. Something about touching my eyeball—I break into shivers just thinking about it.

The world snapped into focus.

An image of the Most Interesting Man in the World filled my screen. Hiram. Wanting to chat.

"What's *he* doing up?" I said aloud.

Mouse click. *My* new avatar—Donkey Kong preparing to Space Jump—appeared as I typed a response.

**Donkey Kong: Takeout or delivery?**

**TMIMITW: Hilarious.**

**TMIMITW: Searched level four, but can't find World Breaker mace. Near Coilfang? Need to increase my critical strike rating!!!**

"Rookie," I muttered, punching in a response.

**Donkey Kong: Defeat Fathom-Lord Karathress in the Serpentshrine Cavern. He'll drop it. Can you handle that? Or is this your first day?**

Two cursor blinks, followed by:

**TMIMITW: You're a first day.**

**TMIMITW: Thanks.**

"Any time, noob." I logged off and hurried downstairs. Drag your feet in *my* house, you end up cooking your *own* breakfast.

Luckily, Mom and Dad were just sitting down.

"Don't mind if I do." I snagged three silver dollar pancakes. My favorite.

"Big plans today, honey?" my mother asked between bites. Born in Japan, she had a round face and soft, delicate features. That morning, her long black hair was tied in a thick braid. "The weather's supposed to be gorgeous."

"None yet." Words I immediately regretted.

My mother abhorred idleness. A veterinary technician at the Logger-head Island Research Institute, she viewed work and fun as synonymous, and was frequently surprised when others didn't. She could strike quickly to fill a hole in my schedule.

And did.

"Well, there's a speaker on primordial lipoproteins at Charleston University this afternoon." She sipped orange juice straight from the bottle. Mom didn't stand on ceremony. "Or you could help me collect sea kelp down at Folly Beach. I'm running toxicity tests, hoping to figure out what's been causing the bird population—"

"Let the boy alone, Lorelei," Dad interrupted. Mildly. Nelson Devers was no fool. "It's the weekend. Shelton probably wants to spend time with his friends."

"That's right," I agreed hastily. "Tory asked me to help train Cooper."

Dad is ten years older than Mom, a former dockworker from the Bronx who'd joined the Navy and been stationed in Okinawa. They'd met at a Japanese community college where he'd been teaching computer science.

Nelson was the first black man Lorelei ever met. Crazy. When his enlistment was up, they'd married, then moved to Charleston for the weather. I'm the end result.

Dad also worked at LIRI and had just been named IT director. A position that made him Mom's superior at work. Not that he'd ever point *that* out.

"Fine." My mother aimed her fork at me. "But don't spend your Sunday playing Call of Warfare with Hi and Ben. You need fresh air."

"*Call of Duty*," I corrected. "And I won't. Promise."

At that moment, the phone rang. My father scooped up the handset. "Hello?"

As he listened, a frown creased his forehead.

"Who is it?" Mom mouthed.

Dad covered the receiver with his hand. "It's Kit Howard. There's been a break-in on Loggerhead—*huge* headache for him."

That caught my attention. LIRI was the only thing out there.

Dad listened a few more seconds before agreeing to something and hanging up. Then he rose and carried his plate to the kitchen.

"I have to meet with Kit for a minute." Rinsing his utensils. "A whole mess of computer equipment was stolen, which makes it *my* headache, too."

*Buzz buzz.*

My iPhone shimmied on the table.

Unlocking the home screen revealed a text from Kit's daughter, Tory Brennan. One of my closest friends. And my chief tormentor.

Don't get me wrong, Tory's cool. Straight-up brilliant, too. But she's impossibly headstrong, always getting me into trouble.

I stared at the message. Got that sinking feeling in my gut.

*This is how it starts. Always always always.*

Her "request" was short and sweet: Virals. Outside. Now.

I checked the recipient list, knowing what I'd find. Me. Hiram. Ben.

There are only four Virals in the world.

My pack. Three people with whom I share a special bond. Or a dark secret, depending on your take. Tory's wolfdog is one of us, too, but that part's just weird. I try not to think about it. Bad for my digestion.

"Something wrong?"

I glanced up to find my mother studying me.

"No." Thinking fast. "It's Tory. She wants to get started with Coop. Stay. Sit. All that stuff. I'd better get going."

I bused my dishes, then hurried out the door on my father's heels. Waste too much time and I'd be hauling sea kelp, no matter what Dad said.

Kit was standing on the grassy common that stretched from our town houses to the Atlantic. He's a bit on the short side, with a close-cut mop of curly brown hair and hazel eyes. That day he wore khaki pants, a blue button-down shirt, and worn loafers. And a grim expression.

Kit had been named director just a few weeks earlier.

LIRI was *his* responsibility.

A word about the neighborhood.

My friends and I live on Morris Island, a four-mile run of sand hills perched at the entrance to Charleston Harbor. We're light-years from downtown, with only a single strip of blacktop connecting us to Folly Island and the rest of the world.

No buildings. No people. Nothing but cattails, dunes, and rabbits.

As close to complete wilderness as you can get.

With one exception: our digs.

Built on the ruins of Fort Wagner, an old Civil War fort, our block consists of ten identical town houses owned by the Loggerhead Trust, which also owns LIRI and Loggerhead Island. The Morris units are leased exclusively to LIRI employees working out at the institute.

Ben, Hi, Tory, and I are the only teens living on Morris, making us perhaps the most isolated crew on earth. It's part of what connects us. That and our super-high, slap-you-silly intelligence. True story.

Here's the thing: We like books, learning, and—*gasp*—science, and aren't afraid to admit it. If other kids think we're uncool because of that, so what?

I don't need more friends. I got my pack.

Okay, our *main* bond is the designer supervirus that scrambled our DNA.

A nasty little pathogen that rewrote our genetic code. Opened evolution's doors.

Made us Viral, to the core.

The transformation welded us into a unit, but for me the connection started before that, when luck brought four kindred spirits together.

It all tied back to living out here, together, alone in the wild.

Morris Island, represent.

Kit was talking with a woman I didn't recognize. Definitely not his dingbat girlfriend, Whitney. That ditz traveled in a cloud of perfume you could smell a football field away.

Spotting my dad, Kit waved him over. The adults began speaking in hushed tones.

I snuck past them to greet Tory, who was hustling down her steps with Coop.

"What's the word, Brennan?"

She held up a hand. "Let's wait for the others."

*Don't like the sound of that.*

Tory is tall and thin, with red hair that hangs midway down her back. Pretty. Maybe more than pretty when she smiles. Piercing green eyes. Pale skin. A healthy dose of freckles. *Definitely* maybe, though she's like a sister to me.

Tory moved to Morris last year, after her mom was killed by a drunk driver. Must've been terrible. She doesn't talk about it, and I don't pry. I'm just glad she's here.

The whole thing was like something out of a movie—before Tory came to live with Kit, they'd never even met! Her biological dad, but a complete stranger. She still calls him by first name.

Those two make a strange pair. Neither seems to know what to do with the other, though they get along pretty well.

Nuts, huh? But that's life, I guess.

I squatted to scratch Coop's gray-brown ears.

He turned deep blue eyes on me, then nuzzled my hand, relishing the attention.

The love child of a gray wolf and stray German shepherd, Coop had grown to nearly seventy pounds. Not a beast you wanna mess with.

Everything Viral started with the wolfdog.

Patient Zero.

We were infected by the superbug while rescuing Coop, who was being used as a medical test subject. Unfortunately for us, the germ was contagious to humans. The newborn invader unzipped our human chromosomes and jammed canine genes inside.

We'd gotten sick. *Really* sick. Headaches. Sweats. Chills. Even blackouts.

And worse. Animal urges. Canine impulses.

A total nightmare, but the madness eventually passed.

That's when we discovered our powers. When we learned how to flare.

We developed abilities no one else on the planet possesses. Or can even fathom.

Physical strength. Sensory acuity. A host of other skills we're still figuring out.

So I guess I shouldn't complain. No virus? No flare power. No pack.

Our minds wouldn't have connected. Would never have melded.

I suppressed a shiver. I didn't understand the mental stuff, left that to Tory. But the four of us shared some weird telepathic bond. Coop, too. Maybe it sprang from the canine DNA. Maybe it's something all wolves possess.

I didn't know. Didn't like to dwell on it. We couldn't control it anyway.

Coop lived with Tory, but spent most of his days roaming Morris, terrorizing the local rodents. I'm just glad the mutt's on our side.

I rose, jabbed a thumb over my shoulder. "Who's the chick with Kit?"

"My aunt Tempe. She's visiting for the weekend."

"Oh my." I spun for a better look.

I'd heard all about Dr. Temperance Brennan, World-Famous Forensic Anthropologist.

She's Tory's idol. The girl never stops talking about her.

Dr. Brennan seemed in good shape for an older lady. Late forties. Dark blond hair, hazel eyes. She wore jeans and a Northwestern tee as she huddled with Kit and Dad.

"Here comes Hi." Tory was looking over my shoulder. "Finally."

I could feel her impatience. Tory with an idea surges forward like a tidal wave.

*And I get dragged by the undertow.*

Hiram closed his front door, yawned, and lumbered down the steps. He isn't the rushing type. Rosy-cheeked, portly, with a quick wit and razor-sharp tongue, Hi's the most sarcastic kid I know. It can be hard getting him to take something seriously.

Hi scratched his wavy brown hair, then stretched. "A little early for booty calls, Tory." He wore yellow pajama pants paired with a brown FOMO T-shirt.

"Funny."

Tory crossed her arms. Glanced at her watch. She practically oozed impatience.

Hi reached down and patted Coop's back. "Hey, killer. Eat any squirrels today?"

Finally, Ben Blue strolled up in his usual black tee and shorts.

At sixteen, Ben was the oldest member of our pack. He's five foot ten and rock solid, with dark eyes and shoulder-length black hair, a by-product of Native American roots. Ben sported a deep tan, earned by countless hours spent aboard *Sewee*, his prized Boston Whaler runabout.

Ben lived in the end unit with his father, Tom Blue, who operated LIRI's shuttle service between Morris, Loggerhead, and downtown Charleston. Ben's mother, Myra, lived in a Mount Pleasant condo just across the bay.

Ben cocked his head toward the adults. "That about the break-in?"

Tory nodded. "Kit's pretty worked up. Last night, somebody stole a bunch of equipment from Lab Three. Kit needs to figure out exactly what's missing."

As Tory spoke, my dad turned and headed back toward our unit. Kit and Tempe walked over to join us.

Tory ordered Coop to sit. Stay. She really *was* training him, with mixed results. That wolfdog could be as obstinate as his owner.

"Nothing to worry about," Kit said brightly, though his expression suggested otherwise. "Just some funny business out at LIRI. Nelson is going to check our inventory and we'll get it sorted."

"What was taken?" Tory's scowl mirrored Ben's.

"More like what *wasn't*." Kit shook his head. "Lab Three was ransacked. Laptops, three blade servers, the moisture/solid analyzer, a centrifuge, the nanoparticle tracking system, a pair of microscopes, some other items." He nearly sighed. "Pricey things, all of them. Whoever broke in knew what he was doing."

"Or she," Tempe corrected. "Or they."

"What about the security tapes?" Tory was laser-focused. "Or the live video feed? Where was security?"

"Electronic surveillance was down last night." Kit waved a hand in frustration. "Maintenance. At midnight, the whole system went offline for program upgrades. Like I said, this—" a glance at Tempe, "—*person* or *persons* knew the score. They broke into Lab Three, cleaned house, and then slipped out with the equipment undetected. What I've got to figure out is *how*."

"The service elevator," Tory said without hesitation. "With the cameras off, the guards would be blind to its movement. And what about the dock? They must've gotten the stuff out by boat."

Kit half smiled. "My thoughts as well. But don't *you* worry about this, kiddo. Hudson has his security crew investigating, and we'll file a police report. Plus, LIRI has insurance for this very reason."

"I know a few detectives at CPD," Tempe said. "They're good. And CSU will turn that lab upside down and inside out. If there's a speck of evidence, they'll find it. Take that to the bank."

Tempe's effect on Tory was comic.

She straightened like a soldier under inspection. "Of course, Aunt Tempe."

But I knew *that* look. Recognized wheels turning behind Tory's eyes.

Butterflies took wing in my stomach. It didn't take a mind reader to see that Tory wanted to impress her aunt.

"I'm heading out there to assess the damage." Kit cast a hopeful look at Tempe. "I wouldn't mind if you came along. A forensics expert might come in handy this morning."

"At your service."

With that, the pair excused themselves and headed inside.

Tory watched them go.

She got that stubborn set to her jaw, as if a challenge had been made.

The butterflies became hummingbirds.

*She'll jump in. And drag us all along, like always.*

Hi sensed it, too. "Should I go change clothes?" The fool sounded eager.

"Meet by the dock in five." Tory was already moving. "*We* need to get to Loggerhead first."

Ben smirked but shrugged his agreement. Hi gave an enthusiastic thumbs-up.

I sighed. There was no point arguing.

"Fine. But let's at least *try* not to get into trouble?"

I'm not sure Tory heard me. She was halfway up her stairs, Coop at her side.

I pushed my glasses back up the bridge of my nose.

*Gonna be one of those days.*

# CHAPTER 2

I hustled inside and grabbed the keys to *Sewee*.

The old man was out in *Hugo*, shuttling people as usual. Not that he'd have bothered me. Tom Blue wasn't that type of dad.

Keys in hand, I hurried back outside and down to the Morris Island dock. I was quickest, as usual, so I prepped my boat while the others took their sweet time.

Checking the outboard motor, I couldn't help but laugh at Dr. Howard. Once again, he had no idea what Tory was planning. She'd slip right under his nose, as usual.

For a smart guy, Kit was clueless. He never saw what was coming next.

Not with Tory.

Not like me.

*Tory's aunt might be wise, though. She's no dummy.*

I shook my head. In the end, Tory would get her way. Always did. Her insisting the Virals investigate the break-in had been the least shocking thing in the world. She *lived* for mysteries like this. It's what I liked most about her.

Not that there was much I *didn't* like.

A sigh escaped my lips. I glanced around quickly, making sure no one heard.

*Just get the boat ready, Ben.*

Footsteps thumped on the wooden planks. I looked up to see the doofus twins. Hi now wore red plaid shorts, a sky-blue pocket tee, and slip-on, black-and-white checkerboard-print sneakers. Shelton sported a white polo and green basketball shorts. Neither of those guys could dress worth spit.

I hadn't changed clothes. Didn't feel the need.

I spotted movement on the hill—Tory, jogging down from the townhomes.

*No wolfdog?*

She'd stuck with her gray Outward Bound tee and tan shorts, but had pulled her hair back in a ponytail. Even dressed down, she was beautiful.

Not *model* gorgeous, or anything fake like that, but . . . striking. I can't really explain it.

And what's the point in trying? We're just friends.

*And even if you weren't, she's out of your league.*

Irritated, I brushed the thought away. But knew it was true.

Tory was destined for Big Things. Renown. Honors. Any dope could see that.

Me? I just hoped to land a gig like Dad's shuttle route. Work outdoors.

"We should design matching outfits." Hi stepped aboard and bounded into the passenger chair. "Crime fighters usually wear sweet gear. And helmets."

"We're *not* crime fighters." Shelton flopped onto the aft bench. "And I'm putting this whole trip under protest. Messing with a real-deal crime? At LIRI? We're headed for *disaster*. You heard it here first."

I caught Hiram's eye, then pointed to the bench beside Shelton.

"Boo." But he complied. We went through this almost every time.

The copilot seat was for Tory.

"You had better plans today?" Not a boating enthusiast, Hi was already snapping on a life jacket. "We're investigating *actual* criminal activity. How cool is that?"

Shelton snorted. "We might get busted for obstructing justice. How's that gonna play at your house?"

Hi tightened the final strap. "Lots of extra time at temple. I'll survive."

"Stow those lines." I pointed to a pair of ropes securing the stern. "And hustle up, you know she'll want a quick getaway."

Though I kept it to myself, I actually agreed with Hi. The day was looking way more interesting than when I got up.

"Take it easy on the way out, Blue." Hi grimaced while coiling a length of thick nylon. "I haven't puked in days, so I've got some catching up to do."

"Not on *my* deck," I warned, well aware of Hi's weak stomach. "Aim overboard."

I unhooked the bowline, double-checked the buoys, then slipped into the captain's chair. My favorite spot on earth.

Tory bounced aboard. "Let's go, let's go!"

"Since you asked so nicely." But I fired the ignition.

"No Bow Wow?" Hi said.

Tory shook her head. "Unfortunately, Coop's not well suited for this type of trip."

"See!" Shelton slapped his forehead. "We *are* gonna buzz the crime scene!"

Tory simply winked.

Maneuvering *Sewee* from the dock, I spun her clockwise and hit the throttle. Spray kicked up on both sides as we knifed across the breakers.

I almost grinned with pleasure. But I'm not the smiley type.

"Once more, it begins." Hi's face was green. "We need a helicopter."

"Take the shortcut," Tory instructed. "Please," she added, as if suddenly aware she'd been barking orders.

In truth, I didn't mind. Despite being youngest, Tory was our unac-
knowledged leader. She had the knack. I was okay with her making
most of the decisions.

Not that I'd ever let that on.

I nosed *Sewee* toward a warren of sandbars a hundred yards off-
shore. Only shallow-draft vessels like my runabout can negotiate them,
and even then you need to know the proper route.

Not many did besides me. A point of pride.

After a few twists and turns, accompanied by Hi's groans, we cleared
the maze and hit open water. Morris receded behind us. Moments later
a tiny landmass took shape on the horizon. Gradually, the green-brown
blur sharpened into an island.

As we motored close, details emerged. A bone-white beach fronting
high-canopied trees. Thick, tangled undergrowth. Gentle waves, spinning eddies in the wet sand. Not a building in sight.

I cut the engine and let *Sewee* drift. A habit of mine. You never know
what you might see, if you're quiet.

A hawk shrieked from the gloom of the island's interior. Crickets
hummed. Palmetto palms swished and rattled in the breeze.

And everywhere, the hooting of monkeys.

No matter how often I visited, Loggerhead Island always gave me a
thrill.

A wild, untamed place, forgotten by time. Shrouded in mystery.

"We're in a bit of a hurry." Tory. Gently.

My expression soured, but I restarted the engine. We cruised down
the shoreline, headed for Loggerhead's southernmost point. Minutes
later I pulled *Sewee* alongside the island's single dock.

A glance spurred Hi and Shelton into position. As I eased close they
tossed the ropes, then scrambled up to tie us off. I killed the motor.

"Permission to disembark, sir?" Tory had one foot on the quay. She knew I liked being captain, and was half apologizing for bossing me around.

"Granted." I tapped my watch. "Shore leave, two hours."

"Then we'd better dash."

One final boat-check, then I followed the others down the pier. They waited where the paving stones gave way to a packed-earth trail, as close to a permanent road as you'll find on the island.

Barely half a square mile, Loggerhead is even smaller than Morris. No permanent structures exist anywhere outside the LIRI compound.

We climbed a steep path and hiked into the woods.

The hooting gave way to howling.

"Monkey Town seems riled today." Hi was scanning the canopy. "Banana crisis?"

The central forest is home to Loggerhead's boisterous rhesus monkey colony. Dozens of free-ranging troops, squabbling in the trees or at feeder stations scattered about the woods.

No cages or corrals. The crafty little buggers go where they please. It's not like they can escape—there's nowhere to go.

The LIRI compound is fenced to keep them *out*, not in.

But yammering primates aren't the only game in town. Cooper's wolfpack family still patrols the woods. Every year, loggerhead sea turtles breed on the island's protected beaches. Endangered seabirds nest in the tidal marshes. Deer, boar, duck, fox, raccoon, and dozens of other woodland critters inhabit the ponds, dunes, glades, and meadows.

Pure, undisturbed nature. Peace and quiet. Well, except for the monkeys.

I love the place. It's one of a kind.

Cresting the final rise, we headed down a gentle slope toward LIRI's front gate.

Which stood open. Weird.

I looked around. None of the dopey rent-a-cops were in sight.

"Where to now?" Hi asked as we reached the chain-link barrier.

"Lab Three," Tory answered. "Scene of the crime."

"Inside Building One," Shelton pointed out needlessly. "Which means dealing with security."

"Which means Hudson," Hi finished. "Gonna be a problem."

Terrific.

If anyone could ruin my day, it was that guy.

# CHAPTER 3

B en was already scowling.

*Never a good sign.*

Tory turned and gave me her Serious Face.

"Hiram." She forced eye contact. "We need to get by security without a fuss. So keep the jokes in check, um-kay?"

"*Scusi?*" I raised both palms in shocked affront. "Those dudes freaking *love* me. We're talking about forming a boy band. Techno-pop stuff."

Her eyes rolled. "We need access to Lab Three. That's not gonna happen if they call Kit to confirm we're allowed upstairs. Which is what they'll do if you piss them off. So don't. *Capisce?*"

"Totes." I flashed my patented thumbs-up. "I'll be a perfect gentleman."

Tory's expression remained skeptical.

I doubled the thumbs-up. Smiled wide.

"God help us."

With that, she strode toward Building One, the rest of us a step behind.

The LIRI complex is bombtastic. Totally baller. It consists of a dozen modern glass-and-steel structures surrounded by an eight-foot chain-link fence.

Only two ways in: the main gate we'd just invaded, and a smaller one around back. Security is tight: motion-sensing cameras, keypad entries, auto-locks, you name it.

Hidden in the woods, the place felt like a Bond villain's secret hideout.

Translation: I heart LIRI.

The larger buildings consist mainly of offices, conference rooms, and research labs. The smaller ones are mostly sheds, workshops, and garages that store the institute's heavy equipment and supplies.

Building One houses LIRI's executive suite, administration hubs, the most primo offices, and the three largest labs.

And security headquarters, unfortunately.

My dad, Linus, worked in there, too. Kit had just promoted him to the exalted position of chief lab tech, which completely rocked. The Stolowitski clan's rise to power cannot be stopped.

I knew Pops would be crapping his shorts about the stolen equipment. The theft was as much in his domain as Shelton's dad's.

*So let's solve this bad boy. It's Big Shot time.*

Tory paused outside the building's hermetically sealed entrance.

Her shoulders rose. Fell. Then she marched straight through the sliding glass doors.

Shelton and I followed. Ben brought up the rear, as usual.

Tory had the coolest head. In tight spots, we usually let her do the talking.

Sometimes, of course, I couldn't help myself. I'm not made of stone, and these clowns were such *easy* targets.

Our luck was bad.

Security Chief David Hudson was manning the kiosk.

He stood as we approached, hands robotically smoothing a meticulously pressed uniform. Hudson was somewhere north of forty, with close-cropped gray hair.

His mouth formed a hard line, eyes suspicious.

Polished shoes gleaming, Hudson stepped from the kiosk to block our entrance. Hips squared, he stuck out one hand. "State your business."

Ermahgerd. *What a toolbox.*

"Good morning, Chief Hudson." Tory flashed her dimples at Robocop. "We're headed to Lab One. My father asked me to check something for him."

"I have no order to that effect."

"Kit will be here in a few minutes. He'll fill you in."

"You'll have to wait until Director Howard arrives." His expression soured, like he'd just caught whiff of a horrific fart. "A *crime* has been committed on these premises. *My* premises. Perpetrators unknown. Therefore, I've sealed the building until further notice."

Hudson's eyes narrowed, as if suddenly considering a new group of suspects.

"I'm afraid we can't wait." Tory fumbled for words. "You see, thing is, um . . ."

I stepped forward, ignoring her warning glance.

I couldn't help it. This guy was a big pile of stupid.

"This is an emergency, Chief." I waggled an index finger. "The midi-chlorians have already been isolated by centrifuge. If we don't take a blood count now, the samples will be useless."

Hudson blinked. "Midi-what?"

I nodded companionably. "Midi-chlorians. Our flux capacitor has isolated their Force-rendering properties in the organelles of a rare species of Arctic tauntaun. Professor Vader at, uh . . . Dagobah University is extremely excited."

More confident nodding.

Hudson's rigid façade cracked, ever so slightly.

He grabbed a folder from his booth and began flipping pages. "Is Vader a visiting researcher? I assume *De-go-ba* is a foreign institution."

"Correct." I spoke fast, knowing confusion was key. "Just outside of

Hoth. Dr. Vader asked Director Howard to monitor his Jeffries tubes, so that the . . . uh, the proper gigawatts, weren't too, um . . ."

Inspiration fled. I floundered.

Luckily, Shelton stepped into the breach.

"So the Sith Foundation doesn't have to repeat the chemical displacement process." Shelton yanked his earlobe, a nervous habit. "That'd be a logistical nightmare."

"You're telling me!" Recovered, I flashed wide eyes at Hudson. "This experiment has been running for months."

I could sense Chief Jackass wavering.

*Time for the stick.*

My voice dropped to a serious tone. "Kit would be here himself, right now, if he didn't have this awful security breach to deal with."

Hudson winced. His department, and he knew it.

I was preparing my finishing move, but Tory beat me to the punch.

"We can wait down here if you'd like." Innocent. Then she twisted the knife. "But if those samples expire, my dad will freak. I'm not sure his temper can handle another disappointment this morning."

Hudson stiffened. Then he jabbed a finger at a clipboard on the counter. "Sign."

I heard Ben snort, then cover it with a cough.

Shelton's foot tapped mile a minute.

Tory carefully printed and signed her name, trying not to appear hurried.

I struggled to keep a neutral face.

Tory laid down the pen. "We'll be in Lab One."

Hudson hesitated. Seemed on the verge of changing his mind.

*And now, the carrot.*

"Good work today, Chief." I extended my hand. "We heard Kit bragging that you're the only reason the thieves didn't swipe everything not nailed down. The thin blue line, he called you. Don't quote me on this, but you might be in line for a commendation. Like, an accomplishment medal. Super, great stuff."

"Yes. Well." Hudson accepted the handshake distractedly. "That was nice of him to say."

I caught Tory's eye. Tipped my head toward the stairs.

"We won't be long." Tory strode past Hudson without glancing back. Shelton was practically in her back pocket. Ben sauntered in their wake, a wry look on his face.

Hudson watched them go, eye uncertain. His lips parted as if to call them back.

I leaned in conspiratorially. "I also overheard Director Howard say he planned to review your findings first thing."

Hudson started, as if he'd forgotten I was there.

"He was awfully upset." Left-eye wink. "I'd have that report buttoned up, if I were you. Word to the wise." Right-eye wink.

"Yes. Yes of course."

"Okay, then." I clapped Hudson's shoulder, then hurried down the hallway, trying not to laugh. *What a maroon.*

"Oh, Mr. Stolowitski?"

I froze. Worried the shoulder tap had pushed it too far.

"Yes?" Swiveling to face him.

"Thieves may be hiding somewhere on this island." Hudson gave me a hard look. "I'll inform *your* father you're here. Just to be safe."

"Excellent." *Crap crap crap.* "Saves me the trouble."

I hustled to join the others by the elevator.

Problem: Dad didn't know I was coming out to Loggerhead that morning. And if he called home, Mom would find out I'd lied about my plans.

That meant trouble.

Ruth Stolowitski was not to be trifled with, especially by her own son.

She'd *swim* out here if she thought I'd played her.

I caught up with the gang just as the elevator arrived. Tory entered and pressed three. Waited until the doors closed.

"Midi-chlorians?" She grabbed the bridge of her nose. "*Dagobah University?*"

I shrugged. "Hey, it worked."

Her hands flew up. "Why couldn't you keep it simple? Or believable?"

"Because *unlikely* and *complicated* are easier to sell. That's a fact. Besides, what are the odds Lieutenant Fake Cop has ever watched a *Star Wars* movie? Is there a number less than zero?"

"Negative one," Shelton said. "And I can't believe you said 'a species of tauntaun.'"

"*Arctic* tauntaun," I corrected. "Personally, I thought 'Dr. Vader' was the low point. But we got away with it, that's all that matters. Almost, anyway."

Ben laid a hand my shoulder. "Almost, Thick Burger?"

He squeezed. I swear my collarbones creaked.

"Unhand me! You're tearing my rotator cuff!"

Ben released his grip. I rubbed my aching limb. "If you ruined my baseball career, you'll hear from my lawyer."

"Hi!" Tory clapped her hands in agitation. "Explain."

"No biggie." I flexed my shoulder, casting accusatory glances at Ben. "But Hudson's gonna tell my father we're here. And he *could* come looking for me, since I gave my mom a different explanation of our whereabouts."

"I don't want to know." Shelton's palms covered his glasses. "Wait. Yes, I do. Where are we supposed to be right now?"

"I told her we were going to a shark festival." Offhand. "In Walterboro."

Ben chuckled. Tory's eyes found the ceiling.

"That doesn't even make sense!" Shelton's hands shot outward. "And nobody goes to Walterboro. Why do you *do* that?"

"Conceptually, it's hard to visualize," I agreed. "Maybe it's more of a film society than a traditional festival. Or a *Jaws* fan-fiction conference."

Mercifully, the elevator doors opened.

"Enough." Tory stepped into the hall. Lights off. No one in sight. "Let's hurry, we don't have much time."

The third level consisted of offices, the smaller Lab Two, and the sprawling Lab Three. A cubicle village filled the center of the floor. From where we stood, narrow hallways ran left and right.

Though usually packed with lab-coated techs and scientists, that day the corridors were deserted.

"Coast's clear." Tory hurried down the left-hand passage to a well-lit chamber spanning the building's eastern end. A floor-to-ceiling Plexiglas wall separated the room from the corridor, which turned ninety degrees and continued to the building's rear.

"Whoa boy." Shelton's eyes bugged behind his lenses.

Lab Three was a showroom-sized rectangle, interspaced by half-a-dozen workstations in the room's middle. Industrial-sized storage cabinets lined the windowless outer walls, with a bolted stainless-steel countertop running just beneath.

"Jeeeeeez." I understood Shelton's astonishment.

When I'd last visited with my dad, Lab Three had been jammed with all kinds of dope equipment. Like a scene from an outbreak movie.

Now it looked like a war zone.

Workstations were stripped. Cut wires hung from tabletops. A computer bank was completely missing, its security cables severed. Servers, modems, routers, you name it. All gone.

Files lay scattered everywhere. Broken glass covered the floor. Several cabinet doors stood ajar, their contents smashed, scattered, or missing.

"This place was freaking trashed," Shelton squawked. "It's like a tornado passed through here."

I knelt beside pile of empty drawers. "Whoever did this didn't make *any* attempt to conceal their crime. It was a smash and grab, pure and simple."

Tory's eyes were roving the room. "We need a plan."

"Looks like ninja work," I quipped. "We should check for throwing stars."

Ben shot me a look, but my excitement grew unchecked.

Honestly? I was thrilled.

Not that LIRI had been jacked. Or that Lab Three had been totaled. That was all uncool.

I was stoked because we were standing at the scene of a legitimate crime. A true heist. A bona fide whodunit.

And the Virals had a chance to solve it.

*Finally, some action.*

I was about to crack a joke, but the look on Tory's face made me reconsider.

She was horrified. As though her own home had been robbed.

Horrified and very, very angry.

Then Tory's expression morphed to another I knew well.

Eyes narrowed. Teeth gritted. I'd seen it before.

Her hands found her hips.

Tory Brennan was thinking. Planning. Weighing options. Making choices.

Tory's the only person in the world smarter than me. She could cut to the heart of any problem. I'd follow her lead anywhere.

*And she's kinda crazy, too, which makes her fun.*

I shelved the urge to spout one-liners. Put on my game face. Got ready to rumble.

It was time to make someone regret messing with our turf.

# CHAPTER 4

Unclenching my fists, I tried to quell my anger.

Hi was looking at me strangely. Was that eagerness on his face?

"Tory?" Shelton was nervously eyeing the empty hallway. "What's our play?"

"We search this lab," I replied. "Top to bottom. Let's divide the room into sections and each take one."

"What are we looking for?" Ben asked.

"Trace evidence. Hairs, fibers, paint chips, anything that looks out of place. Watch for strange marks, too. Scratches or scrapes. If we can determine *how* the robbers operated, we'll know more of what to look for."

"Careful what you touch," Shelton warned. "The police haven't been here yet. We don't want to implicate *ourselves*."

"Good thinking." I scanned the open cabinets, spotted a package of latex gloves. Stepping carefully, I walked over and snagged the box. "Everyone grab a pair."

Properly gloved, we each moved to our assigned sector.

*Needle in a haystack.*

I shoved the thought aside. *All* forensics was a needle hunt.

My thoughts flew to Aunt Tempe. How impressed she'd be if we helped crack the case. That weekend, my hero worship was full-blown.

Being honest with myself, wowing Tempe was the reason I wanted to investigate.

*Then pay attention. A wandering mind misses clues.*

I combed my zone systematically, front to back.

I'd chosen the far-left quadrant, which ran along the wall. Bringing my face close, I inspected the countertop, nose inches from the gleaming steel. Then I moved to the first of two workstations in my area. Shattered glass covered its surface. A scuffed area marked the former position of an electron microscope. The second station had once held a computer terminal. Now only stripped wires remained.

Minutes ticked by. Five. Ten. Twenty.

I didn't need Shelton's grumbles to know we were running out of time.

"Nothing," Ben called from the other side of the room.

"Same," Shelton echoed.

Hi was back where he'd started, a frown crimping his features. "I got squadoosh. Anyone know a good psychic?"

I felt discouraged. Smothered it. "We do it again."

The boys watched me, saying nothing.

"We've only done one pass!" I gestured to the chaos covering the floor. "You're *sure* you didn't miss anything, in all that?"

Shelton tugged his ear. "The cops are on the way, Tor."

"And your dad," Ben added. "I'm surprised no one's here yet."

"Then we shouldn't waste time chatting." I made shooing gestures with my hands. "Get to work."

A few looks, but the boys did as I asked. I knew they would. In moments we were all on hands and knees, combing the floor for anything useful.

I was starting to despair, when I spotted something.

There. By the base of the wall.

A tiny brown sliver.

I dropped to my belly and shimmied under the counter.

"Tory?" Hi had completed his second sweep. "Find a cookie?"

"I *think* . . . there's something . . ." Moving cautiously, I plucked the tiny splinter between my thumb and index finger, then gingerly scootched backward and stood.

"Whadayagot?" Shelton was shirt-wiping his glasses. "Because my section is Zero Town, population nothing. Unless you like broken beakers."

I peered intently at my find. "It's wood. A chip."

"The case breaker!" Ben said sarcastically. "Call the feds!"

My head shook in annoyance. "It doesn't match anything, though. At least, nothing that I've seen over here." My eyes scoured the rest of Lab Three for anything that might explain the tiny wedge.

The boys looked, too. Spotted nothing likely.

"The only wooden items are the cabinets," I said.

"And several were crowbarred. Look." Ben lifted a cabinet door that had been ripped from its hinges.

"But the cabinet wood is totally different." I held the sliver close to one. "These doors are made of processed boards. Some kind of composite material, held together by adhesive."

"They're also lighter in color," Hi added. "And layered, to be more pliable. That chip came from something else."

Hi turned to Ben. "Check the lab for anything else made of wood. And make sure the other cabinets are identical to this one."

Ben's hands found his pockets. "I don't think so."

"Got it." Hi swiveled back to me. "I'll check the lab for anything else made of wood and make sure the other cabinets are identical to this one."

"Good plan," Ben said.

"I'll help," Shelton said. "We *should* be hustling."

The two boys hurried to make another sweep.

I rotated the splinter in the palm of my hand. Triangular shape. Two sides rougher than the third, which was darker, smooth, and worn.

Holding the fragment up to the light, I noticed the grain was barely detectable.

And something else.

"There's *goop* on this." I tilted my hand back and forth, watching the light play over the chip's surface. "A coating. Or residue. Sticky."

Impulsively, I held it under my nose. "It smells like . . . nuts."

"Nuts?" Ben scoffed. "Sure you're not just hungry?"

"Zip it." I sniffed again. "Maybe . . . more like grass. Or tree sap. I know I'm not making sense."

Hi and Shelton rejoined us.

"No other wood," Hi confirmed. "That specimen appears to be a for-eign particle."

"Which doesn't necessarily mean it's related to the break-in," Shelton countered. "It could've hitched a ride in here on someone's shoe. For all we know, it's been there for weeks."

"It's a place to start." I dropped the chip into a plastic glove, tied off the opening, and slipped the makeshift specimen bag into my pocket.

Hi rubbed his hands together. "What next? Should we start some interrogations?"

"Let me think." Unnecessarily waving for quiet.

The boys waited. They trusted my instincts, and my ability to discern patterns. Skills that had served us well before.

*Except now you've got nothing.*

Just a slice of wood that doesn't match the local wood.

An idea took root.

I moved to the closest shattered cabinet. "This was hacked open, right?"

"More like pried." Ben pointed to deep gouges where the door met its frame. "See how the wood split, right at the edge? Someone jammed an object into the gap, then wedged it open."

The idea congealed into a theory.

"A tool." My mind was fitting pieces even as I spoke. "The robber must've used an implement to crack them. Some sort of lever."

Three blank looks.

I tapped my pocket. "This splinter isn't from the doors. It's from the *tool*."

Ben's brows formed a V. "The instrument had to be metal, Tory. These doors fractured under some pretty serious force. I don't think something wooden could've done the job without leaving a *lot* more splinters. My guess is they used a crowbar. Pure steel."

"Okay." Thinking furiously. "Damn."

Shelton spoke up. "What if the wedging part was metal but the *handle* was made of wood?"

"Like an ax?" Hi rubbed his chin. "You think Jason Voorhees might be our man?"

"I'm just saying. Lots of tools have wooden grips."

"Wait." I squinted at nothing. "Hold up a sec."

Hi's mouth opened, but Ben snagged his arm. "Let her think."

I barely noticed. Blocked them out. Tried to pin down what was bothering me.

Loggerhead. LIRI security. A shattered lab. All that missing equipment.

*Something doesn't track.*

I considered the evidence, one point at a time.

"This crime. It's odd." I began to pace. "No alarms, no video, no record of any kind."

"Happened during the software upgrade," Shelton reminded. "They got lucky."

"Not a chance." Back and forth. "The thieves *knew*."

The issue nagging at me came into sharper focus. "This heist was too neat *and* too dirty. Outside of this room, there are no kicked-in doors, smashed locks, or downed gates. Nothing to indicate a break-in occurred at all."

I swept an arm around the room. "Until you get in here. Inside *this* lab."

I froze, the answer on the tip of my tongue.

Muffled steps sounded in the hall.

"Move!" Ben hissed.

In a panic we bolted from Lab Three, Hi closing the door behind us. We booked down the corridor to the back of the building, around the corner, and up another dark hallway, putting the maze of cubicles between the noise and us.

We stopped. Listened hard.

Someone coughed. More footfalls.

I heard Kit's voice, followed by a gruff tenor I didn't recognize.

"Police?" Hi mouthed.

I shrugged.

I peeked over a cubicle wall. The elevators were directly across from where we were crouched. One set of doors was closing, the new arrivals already moving toward Lab Three.

Waving the others to follow, I continued to the west end of the building, turned another corner, and bolted for a stairwell dead ahead.

Thirty adrenaline-pumped seconds later, we were back on the ground floor.

"That was fun." Hi was red-faced and puffing. "Hope no one left anything behind."

"This way," I whispered, stripping off the latex gloves and stuffing them in my back pocket. The others quickly followed suit.

Our next move had occurred to me in mid-flight.

"Where?" Shelton hissed, but I was already marching to the security desk.

As I'd suspected, Hudson was nowhere in sight. He'd undoubtedly gone upstairs with Kit and the others.

Another guard was sitting in the kiosk.

"Carl!" I called brightly. "How are you today?"

Carl Szuberla looked up from his magazine, expression guarded.

He'd probably been chewed out at least once today already. Hudson seemed the type to blame his subordinates if something went wrong.

"Hello, Miss Brennan." Built like a lumpy bowling ball, Carl's immense girth was jammed into a sky-blue uniform barely able to contain it. "Director Howard just went upstairs."

His expression abruptly clouded. It must've occurred to him we'd come from inside the building, not out.

Though reliable, Carl was not the sharpest knife in the drawer.

He was perfect.

"Right. Kit sent me down with a question." Assertively. "He wants to know whether the gates were opened at any point last night."

Carl's piggish face bunched into a knot. "Why didn't he ask the chief? Hudson worked the graveyard shift, not me."

"Kit wants the log checked. No stone unturned. That kind of thing."

Sighing, Carl rose and waddled into the communications room. A few moments later he returned. "Neither gate was opened last night."

"But wasn't the electronic system down?" Shelton asked. "How can you be sure?"

"Both gates are zip-tied during any system maintenance." Carl tapped his logbook. "Chief Hudson noted that both ties were in place this morning."

"Excellent." I headed for the exit. "Thanks so much."

"Wait." Carl gestured toward the elevator. "Aren't you going to inform Dr. Howard?"

"I'll text him. Thanks again!"

We hurried through the doors, down the steps, and into the courtyard.

LIRI is arranged in two lines of six buildings each, facing one another across a large central green. Flower-lined paths crisscross the courtyard, with stone benches set at intervals for those seeking fresh air.

I beelined to a grouping in the center of the quad.

"Ready to explain?" Hi dropped onto one of the benches. "Because I just exceeded a walking pace, and that's *not* my thing."

I did a quick 360 to see if anyone was within earshot, then motioned for the others to huddle close. With varying degrees of enthusiasm, they obeyed.

"I've got it."

"Got what?" Ben asked. "Dementia?"

"The answer." Hitching my thumbs into my armpits. "I've solved the case."

"Inconceivable," Shelton said. "Because I'm more lost than ever."

I bounced on my tiptoes. Popped an eyebrow a few times for effect.

"You're annoying me," Hi stated. "Stop it, please."

"Why was Lab Three the only room smashed?" I asked. "How come the rest of Building One didn't suffer the same treatment?"

"Access," Hi said. "The thief, or thieves, had a way into the building, but not the laboratory."

"Very good. And how is *that* possible?"

No response. I was enjoying this.

"*Because*—" I drew out the word, "—the raid was an inside job."

"*Pssh.*" Hi slumped back on the bench. "I've thought that from the beginning. The police will, too. How else would the crooks know exactly when the security system was down?"

"Okay, hotshot," I challenged. "Then who did it?"

"I don't know." Hi crossed his arms. "*You* don't either."

"Who has access to the buildings, but not the labs?" I asked. "Yet would also know when the security system was down for maintenance?"

"A LIRI regular." Shelton's face lit up. "But someone *not* on the scientific staff! Otherwise, the robbers would've known the proper codes, or had keys, and wouldn't have needed to tear up the room!"

Ben nodded. "Makes sense."

"Okay." Hi began gnawing his thumbnail. "So we've narrowed the profile to a LIRI employee without lab access. But that's still, what, fifty people?"

"Roughly." Then I smiled ear to ear. "But we can trim the field even more."

Dramatic pause.

They glared. I ate it up.

"The gates, silly boys." I tapped my temple. "They never opened, even after the equipment was swiped. Which *means*—" smacking my palm, "—whoever took the gear *couldn't get it out of the compound*."

Both arms, raised in triumph.

Met by puzzled looks.

"The equipment must still be on the grounds!" I spun, finger outstretched. "In one of these buildings. Find the loot, we find the crook."

"Crap balls!" Hi breathed. "That's freaking genius."

"You did it!" Shelton took a hop-step toward Building One. "Let's tell Kit!"

"Or . . ." I flashed a wicked smile.

*What would Tempe do?*

"*We* find it ourselves."

Shelton's eyebrows shot to his hairline. "But how? There are a dozen buildings."

I pulled the glove from my pocket and held it aloft. "We've got a few tricks up our sleeves, don't we?"

"Oh." All three at once.

They understood.

I reached for my sunglasses.

Squeezed my eyes shut.

**SNAP.**

# CHAPTER 5

I hate it, every time.

The shift is terrible, like being shoved into a washing machine filled with molten lava. Then electrocuted. Then beaten by a sock filled with doorknobs.

*Quit whining, Shelton. Light the torch.*

Slipping off my glasses, I closed my eyes and mumbled a prayer.

I focused on darkness. Tight spaces. Drowning. Hairy, crawling spiders.

Anything that gives me the creeps.

I still have to scare myself. Fear is my only trigger. I don't know why, but if I'm not spooked, the power just won't come. But I'm getting pretty good at it, and that day I had no problem. Guess I was nervous already.

*Contact.*

**SNAP.**

The power jolted through me.

As the flare unfolded, fire exploded in my chest. Icy needles danced on my skin. Bolts of electricity shot through my veins.

Gasping, I gripped my knees. Sweat coated my body.

I tried to catch my breath as every sense blasted into hyperdrive.

The world sharpened to laser clarity.

My eyes cut like diamonds, could make out the tiniest crack in the sidewalk.

A hidden symphony flooded my ears, abruptly divisible into hundreds of individual components. Burrowing insects. Flapping wings. Leaves, sighing far overhead. I heard them all.

Subtle aromas crammed my nose—honeysuckle, from a garden fifty yards away. A dozen varieties of grass. Tory's mango shampoo. Even Hi's armpit sweat. *Blech.* I tried to keep my stomach from emptying.

I could detect the slightest vibration against my arm hairs.

Could taste different sands and salts on the breeze.

I *flared.* Tapped my canine DNA.

I never enjoy how the wolf came out to play. But the pain is worth it. The results are *ridonkulous.*

"Everybody ready?" Tory slipped on sunglasses to hide her glowing, golden eyes.

We all had them, now that we'd switched on—wolf irises shining with inner fire. The only outward sign that our powers were active. The reason Virals carried shades 24/7.

Tory's whisper was plenty loud for me. Flaring, I could hear her heartbeat.

Here's the thing—somehow, the supervirus affected each of us differently. We can't explain it. Maybe the little bugger enhanced strengths we already had. Maybe it exploited individual weaknesses.

Who knows? We don't have the answers.

But we do have the skills.

For me, I could hear like an owl. Better, probably. More acutely than the other Virals, though they had crazy sharp ears, too. But mine left theirs in the auditory dust.

Hi backhanded his nose, then wiped his shorts.

"Good to go," he wheezed, cheeks crimson, dark lenses in place.

He spun a quick circle, scanning to make sure we hadn't been seen.

Hiram had the best eyes, hands down. Flaring, he could count a bird's feathers at a hundred yards.

Ben flexed his fingers, then rolled his shoulders. When it came to pure physical power, he got more pop than the rest of us. He became superstrong, and lightning quick, like a ninja grizzly bear.

"Take the lead, Tor." I slapped on my shades—no need for a prescription with the wolf unleashed. My eyes were telescopic.

I'd grasped her plan right away.

When flaring, Tory had the best nose, by far. Her sniffer was so sensitive, she could smell people's *emotions*. Crazy. Seriously. Crazy.

Her talent had to do with sweat and identifying hormones and pheromones, or something like that. But damn! It even freaked *me* out.

Whatever the explanation, the ability was real. I'd seen her operate.

"Stick close to the fence." Tory pointed to the chain-link barrier enclosing the compound. Then she ripped the plastic glove and removed the splinter. "We'll start at the front gate and move clockwise, toward Building One. We'll circle behind each building and I'll try to catch the scent."

Hi nodded. "Circle their behinds."

Ben cuffed the back of Hi's head.

"Let's do it." Tory clapped her hands, which sounded like thunder in my brain.

Hi fired two hand-shooters, unfazed by Ben's cranial assault. "This loser's going *down*, Charlie Brown."

One by one, we arrowed toward the fence.

As we moved, *it* happened.

That strange, familiar feeling blossomed inside my mind.

The sense of connection. Oneness. A hidden link between me and my pack.

Don't ask me how, but I could almost *feel* where the others were. How fast they moved. What they intended to do next. Sometimes, if I concentrated hard enough, I could even catch a whiff of their thoughts.

The sensation made me nervous as hell.

*Leave that stuff to Tory.*

At that moment, Tory glanced over her shoulder. At me. She flashed a wry smile.

Shivers ran my spine.

Tory believed we had a spiritual connection. Some kind of shared consciousness, springing from our canine DNA. I get the willies just thinking about it.

Sometimes, when flaring, Tory could send us messages mind to mind.

At times, I'd been able to send back.

Telepathy? A pack mind? Is this what wolves experience every day?

I didn't know, but the whole business scared me to death. Fact: The idea of someone reading my thoughts gives me heart palpitations. Even Tory. Some things are just too personal to get comfortable with.

Tory is always the nucleus. The rest of us can't kick-start a mind link. We wouldn't know where to start. But even *she* doesn't understand how the link works. She can't control it either—the ability comes and goes without warning. Go figure.

One more puzzle to unravel.

Being Viral can be scary business.

Reaching the fence, Tory paused and placed the sliver under her nose. A moment passed, then she nodded.

"The residue has a funky mix of odors," she said. "It's mainly earthy, like grass or wheat. But there are traces of . . . sweetness. For some reason, I keep thinking of raisins."

"Get after it, hound dog!" Hi crouched, slapped his leg twice, then jabbed a finger down the fence line. "Track!"

Ben delivered a second head smack. "Dope."

Hi rubbed his dome. "That's assault, bro. Times two. And flare slaps hurt more."

"Sue me." Ben turned to Tory. "Ready?"

She nodded. "Circle the compound. Sweep each building. Catch the scent."

"Works for me." I fell into line.

"There'll be repercussions, Blue," Hi warned, taking up the rear. "Shock and awe. Punitive damages."

"Looking forward to it," Ben replied without turning.

We moved slowly along the perimeter. Building One. Shed Three. Vehicle Depot A. Building Four. Tory shook her head each time.

A hundred yards, and we reached the back of the complex. Turning right, we hustled past the rear gate to the opposite side of the courtyard and the second row of buildings.

To anyone watching, it would've been a bizarre scene. Four teens in sunglasses, creeping around LIRI's perimeter, following a redheaded girl who sniffed the air like a Labrador. Thankfully, there was no one in sight.

Tory was methodical. At each structure she'd probe the back door, or any other opening, breathing deeply. Then she'd move on, disappointed. In no time we'd returned the front gate.

Tory stopped, jaw clenched in frustration. "This isn't working."

I won't lie—I was relieved. "Let's tell Kit what we know."

"We didn't go in the buildings," Ben pointed out.

Unconsciously, my fingers rose to my earlobe. "We can't sneak inside every one. We don't have that kind of access. And I'm not taking a third chance with security. Too many lies."

"So let's buzz the front doors," Hi suggested. "Maybe we get lucky."

Tory nodded. "If that fails, we'll try something else."

I suppressed a sigh. "Something else" didn't sound like my suggestion.

We moved along the inner courtyard path, until we drew level with Building One.

"Let's skip it," Tory said. "Security will be a pain. We can always come back."

That's when my ears perked.

Without flaring, I'd never have heard it. I was sure the others didn't.

*Swish. Hum. Swish.*

*The doors!*

"Building One!" I hissed. "Somebody's coming out!"

# CHAPTER 6

Running is *not* my thing.

Tory might exercise for fun, but not me. That's what video games are for.

"Move it, Hi!" Ben hissed, then bolted after Shelton and Tory.

"Why?" I whisper-shouted. "We didn't *do* anything! I'm comfortable giving up!" But the others were barreling for the hedge on the opposite side of Building One.

*You're flaring, you idiot! Haul ass!*

"Not cool!" Fortunately, I can be quick when necessary.

Flaring, I could practically fly.

Head down, I booked past the front doors just as two figures emerged from inside. Kit. Hudson. Their heads turned as I zoomed by and out of sight.

My faster buddies were already hunkered behind the greenery.

"Keep going!" I didn't slow, kept hauling full speed. "I think Hudson saw me!"

Shelton winced. "The *last* thing we need."

Now in the lead, I sped past Shed Three, then zagged behind a row of dogwoods. The others piled in beside me.

"There's no cover here," Ben warned. "But the vehicle depot has a retaining wall. We can duck behind that."

He and Tory sped forward in a blink. Wolf powers unleashed, they moved like smoke. Shelton followed on their heels. I watched the trail behind us. Somebody had to.

I heard sneakers on concrete. Knew they'd reached the hiding place.

"Moves like Jagger," I whispered, then pounded after the others.

Behind me, my enhanced ears detected footfalls.

*Frick!*

Twenty yards. My objective lay dead ahead.

My shades flew as I vaulted the chest-high wall.

And landed on Ben.

"Ack." He toppled backward with a thud. "Get off me, Double Stack!"

"Serves you right," I panted. "Vengeance is mine."

Ben's knee connected with my gut.

"Ooof!" I rolled to my back, crawled for cover, and collapsed.

Ben crouched beside me, rubbing his face. "You almost broke my nose."

"You punctured my lungs. And my spleen. And my ovaries." Not true. But flaring, I could feel bruises forming in my midsection. "You'll pay for these crimes, Blue."

"Any time, chunk." Ben slapped my back. Which hurt, too.

"Shh!" Shelton sat, back pressed to the wall, ear cocked toward Building One. Seconds ticked by. Finally, "No one's coming."

Then he rounded on Ben and Tory. "Why are we all runnin' and hidin' in the first place? Why not just snuff our flares? News flash: They already *know* we're out here! And we haven't done anything bad. Not yet, anyway."

"I'm not ready to quit." Tory pulled a twig from her hair. Her eyes were still hidden behind black Ray-Bans, but I recognized the stubborn set to her chin. "I want to finish *our* inspection, without interruption."

*Classic Tory.*

"God, I respect you," I deadpanned, flat on my back.

"Shut it, Hi. We'll check this garage first, then the other buildings on this side of the courtyard, one by one, like before. Any objections?"

Hearing none, Tory popped to her feet.

I rolled to my side, fully intending to stand.

Didn't happen. My lungs weren't ready for duty just yet.

So I lay on the concrete, panting, plotting my revenge on Ben.

Vehicle Depot A resembles a small fire station. Three garage-like doors provide access to a single mechanic's bay. To the right of the doors, a separate entrance leads to a few small offices, workrooms, and an employee break room.

The wall sheltering us was barely five feet high, and separated the depot's rectangular driveway from LIRI's main courtyard. Inside the wall, to the building's left, a grassy area stretched to the hedge line bordering Shed Three.

I lay in the wall's shadow, directly facing the last garage door.

From my unique vantage point—face to the concrete—I noticed something.

Wet specks. On the pavement.

Curious, I lifted my head slightly. Zeroed my flare vision.

Details snapped into HD. The specks became fragmented streaks.

Parallel lines, a foot apart. Nearly invisible.

*Tracks. Wheels?*

LIRI had a fleet of ATVs, but they used wide tires, suitable for off-road terrain.

But these treads were thin, more like those of a bicycle. Extremely light, too. Without my flare vision, I'd never have noticed them. The tracks couldn't have been there more than a few hours. In another, they would fade completely.

"Something that rolls," I murmured. "But not a motor vehicle."

Shelton looked up. "You say something?"

I didn't answer. My eyes traced the lines across the driveway.

Another surprise. Instead of joining the path, they swerved into the grass.

"Huh."

I rose to my hands and knees and crawled to where the concrete ended and the grass began. Then, pressing my cheek flat on the pavement again, I examined the yard.

There. Twin ranks of broken blades, running directly toward the hedge.

"Hey, now."

I sat back on my heels and squinted hard at the bushes. Spotted a gap right where the tracks ended. The damage was plain to see. Snapped branches. Crushed leaves. As if something heavy had been forced through them recently.

But what?

Then I had it. "A hand truck."

"Hiram?" Shelton was eyeing me closely. "You okay, man? 'Cause I'm *not* getting a hand truck to lift your sorry butt. Suck it up."

"No." I bounced to my feet. "Look at these wet streaks. The grass. That hedge. Something heavy was rolled through here. I'm guessing a hand truck."

Tory was beside me in flash. "Where? Show me."

I explained my observations, step by step.

Shelton whistled. "You see like a damn eagle."

"Great work, Hi." Tory beamed.

I drank in the praise. "Also, whatever the load was, it came through here in the last few hours."

Shelton frowned. "How can you tell?"

"Wet wheels." Tory looked to me for confirmation.

"Correctamundo. It hasn't rained for days. Whatever made these tracks must've rolled through last night's dew. These tread marks will evaporate soon. They're almost gone now."

Ben chucked my shoulder. "Nice work, Thick Burger."

"Thank yourself. If you hadn't viciously assaulted me, I'd never have noticed."

Ben nodded stoically. "So in a way, *I'm* the hero."

I snorted. "Benjamin, you've done it again."

"These tracks lead . . . there." Tory walked to the last garage door in the row.

Though dirty, it looked serviceable. But a trio of rusty barrels blocked it.

Ben walked over and tugged the handle. It wouldn't budge.

"Aha." He kicked the base of the door. "There's a spiffy new padlock."

"Look at the pavement near the wall." Shelton pointed to a spot a dozen yards away, in the corner of the driveway. Red-brown accretions tarnished the concrete. "Those are rust stains, from *these* barrels. They used to be over there. Somebody's hiding something!"

I puffed out my chest. "I'd like to take a moment to thank all the little people who contributed to my success. Shelton, you've always been a stand-up guy, and—"

"Can it, Hi." Ben shoved one of the barrels. "Water, I think. Half empty."

Tory was all business. "We have to get inside."

"On it." Ben tossed Shelton his shades, wrapped his arms around a barrel, lifted, and hauled it to the side. Golden eyes gleaming, he repeated the process three more times until the doorway was clear.

Tory looked at Shelton. Pointed to the padlock.

"Why not get Kit?" Shelton whined. "Why break in?"

"Because we don't know if we're right," Tory said calmly. "What if these tracks have nothing to do with the theft? You feel like looking ridiculous?"

"Always bullying me into felonies," Shelton mumbled.

He pulled out his key chain and selected from his trusty lockpick set. In moments Shelton was on one knee, jimmying the padlock.

"Wish I'd never bought these stupid picks," Shelton grumbled. "Now I'm a damn universal entry card."

"Poor baby." Tory squeezed Shelton's shoulder. "Victim of your own talent."

"Ain't *that* the truth."

Ben moved to the wall to keep watch. He needn't have bothered.

In less than a minute I heard a click.

Shelton stood, handed Tory the padlock. "There." Shaking his head. "One more B and E for my juvie record. I'll never be president."

"*Pssh.*" I flapped a hand. "The Oval Office is perfect for a criminal like you."

Tory reached for the handle and pulled. This time, the door rose easily.

Single file, we snuck inside.

# CHAPTER 7

L ast to enter, I lowered the door behind us.

Little daylight cut through the dirt-crusted windows high overhead, leaving the room draped in shadows. Safely alone in the dark, we all pocketed our shades.

"Ben?" Tory's irises blazed in the gloom. "Find a switch, please."

*Why? We can see just fine.*

But I searched the wall and flipped on the halogens. Light flooded the depot.

My eyes quickly adjusted.

When flaring, *everything* I did was quick.

Tory, Hi, and Shelton had clustered in the center of the room.

I looked around. We were in a typical mechanics' garage.

The room was a large square, with three vehicle bays stationed against the far wall, each housing a pair of four-wheel ATVs. Between the bays, large windows looked in on several small offices accessed by a door in the corner.

Heavy equipment lined the left-hand wall, along with metal shelves and three bulky storage bins. The right-hand wall held a row of workstations, each with a tool chest, stool, and large table. A second door led to the other section of the building.

I recognized a few items. Others left me baffled.

LIRI is remote and needs full-service maintenance capability. Short of actually making spare parts, this facility could handle just about any breakdown.

"Check this bad boy out!" Hi was admiring one of the four-wheelers. "Vroom vroom! What I wouldn't give to take this puppy for a spin."

"Break your fool neck." Shelton rapped an odd metal grillwork welded to its rear. "What's this thing? Looks like a giant bicycle basket."

"It is." Tory said. "These ATVs are used to stock the monkey feeders scattered across the island. The feed bags are too heavy to carry, especially if you're heading to the swamp, or up to Tern Point."

"Nonsense." Hi slipped into the driver's seat. "These are terrorist first-response vehicles. We keep them to repel pirate attacks. Or to fight the monkeys, when they finally evolve and try to take our planet."

"Doofus." I barked a laugh.

Tory suddenly stiffened. "I smell it!"

Three heads swung her way.

"My bad." Hi's face flushed scarlet. "It's a big room, and I didn't think anyone would notice if—"

"No." Tory waved off the comment. "And, *ew*, by the way."

Tory stuck her nose to the grillwork. Inhaled. "Here! Same scent as on the wood chip." Her eyes widened as something clicked. "It's the monkey chow! Wheat. Soybean. Raisins. Why didn't I put it together before?"

Shelton raised the roof. "Which means we're on the money!"

Tory's eyes cut to me. "Does the other depot service feeder ATVs?"

I knew the answer. "Nope. It houses two more four-wheelers, but they're lighter models used mostly for vet emergencies."

I slapped the vehicle beside me. "These babies do all the feeder runs."

"So where do they store the grub?" Hi hopped down. "That's the question, right?"

*You know that, too, Benny boy.*

I pointed to the hulking bins in the left corner. "Right. There."

We raced over. Three minivan-sized storage containers were lined up in a row. Each had a single yard-square metal door, set five feet off the ground. A pair of steel steps had been welded to the base of each bin for easier access.

"They're big enough," Shelton said. "You could hide a horse inside one of these."

Hi flourished a hand toward the grimy bins. "A trio of boxes, but only one prize." He wrapped an arm around Tory's shoulder, pretending to hold a microphone in his other hand. "Young lady, you're our next contestant!"

I felt a pang of jealously, but stomped it to death.

*Dumb. Dumb dumb dumb.*

Tory played along, wide-eyed and enthusiastic. "What can I win? A new Prius?"

Hi arched a single brow. "Choose correctly, and you'll receive the undying respect and admiration of your peers! Plus a Twinkie."

Then his yellow eyes narrowed, his tone dropping to an ominous growl. "Choose wrong, and we'll lock you inside the bin, then feed you to the monkeys."

"Sounds wonderful!" Tory stepped forward and inspected her options. Then she pointed to the filthiest of three. "This one."

"May I ask why?" Hi extended his fake mike.

Her reply was non-nonsense. "Because it's the only one locked."

She climbed the steps and lifted a glossy black padlock securing the bin's door.

"Oh man." Shelton kicked the base of the container, then winced and grabbed his foot. "Ouch! That was stupid. Don't anybody else do that."

"Check the other two first?" I suggested.

"Obviously." Hi stepped up, swung a bin door, and peered inside. "Filled to the brim with monkey feed. And I'm not gonna lie, this stuff looks mighty tasty. Like a giant box of trail mix. When *are* we eating lunch, anyway?"

"I hope the gear isn't buried in there," Shelton said. "Could get messy."

"Not a good place for storing laptops." Hi hopped back down to the floor. "Might void the warranty."

I opened the next bin with an echoing clang.

"Nothing." Sticking my head inside. "Empty."

Hi reached up and grabbed Tory's hand. "Looking good for that Twinkie!"

Another jealous twinge. Ruthlessly extinguished.

*What's wrong with me lately?*

"Door number three." Tory tapped the lock. "Shelton. Work your magic, please."

"At least I got a 'please' this time."

They switched places. But Shelton had barely lifted a finger before stepping back and shaking his head. "Sorry, folks. No can do. This is a Granit closed-shackle padlock, not some BS school-locker model. High security design, too. This sucker uses an ABUS Plus disc cylinder with two hundred and fifty thousand key variations. It *can* be picked, but I need different tools. I only carry the basics on my key chain."

Tory chewed her lower lip. I could practically see her mind racing.

I stepped up to examine the locked bin. It was old and battered, its color morphed from pewter to a dingy reddish brown.

My flaring eyes traced the rusty metal door. Noted the decaying hinges.

"Okay." Tory spoke aloud as she worked through ideas. "We need some kind of cutters. The padlock looks solid, but maybe if—"

"Relax."

Planting my feet against the side of the bin, I gripped the door handle with both hands and jerked backward.

Nothing. The metal held.

Digging deeper, I closed my eyes. Tugged again.

The steel whined, but refused to give.

"So it's like that." I slid my feet up until I was practically hanging sideways.

"Take it easy, slugger." Hi drew a hand across his neck. "Know when to say when."

"I'm just getting warmed up."

Deep breath.

A growl escaped my lips as I wrenched with every ounce of strength in my body, willing the door to move.

*Creeeeeeak.*

*CRACK!*

I flew backward, skidded across the concrete floor, and crashed into Hi's legs.

Hi went down like a bowling pin, knocking over a bucket beside the closest ATV. Something brown and sticky oozed onto his checkerboard shoes.

"I'm cursed!" he moaned. "These are limited-edition Vans."

**SNUP.**

My flare vanished.

Losing the power was always a drag. Normal human senses seemed almost a punishment. Like some part of me died. I hated the feeling.

It took a moment to realize I still gripped the bin door in my hands.

Flipping it aside, I tried to clear the cobwebs.

"Whoa!" Shelton offered me a hand, golden light fading from his eyes. "Nice job, Hulkster."

I shrugged, still woozy. "Simplest solution."

A glance at Tory. She was beaming at me with normal emerald-green irises.

I felt my cheeks flush. "Help me up, Devers. I nearly broke my neck."

"What *is* this gunk?" Hi was wiping his shoes with a dirty rag. "Not cool."

His flare was gone, too. *Why do they go out as one?*

"Hey, guys?" Shelton slipped on his prescription specs and pointed to the now-open bin. "Moment of truth."

"Wait!" Hi scrambled to his feet, oily sneakers squeaking on the concrete. "This is *my* game show!"

Hi charged up the steps. His upper body disappeared inside the container. I heard rustling noises, then he reappeared with a MacBook in one hand and modem in the other. "Anyone wanna play some *Halo*?"

"Oh, snap!" Shelton started dancing Gangnam style. "Somebody get that girl a Twinkie! Hell, give her a whole box!"

We ran to Hi, who started handing down hardware. Laptop. Server. Microscope. Centrifuge. The dollar value rapidly climbed into the tens of thousands.

We formed a chain, stacking the stolen equipment on the concrete floor. As the pile grew, I couldn't help smiling like an idiot.

We'd actually foiled the robbery. *Amazing.*

So why the look of annoyance on Tory's face?

"What is it?" I asked.

She waved at the expanding pile of gear. "We still don't know who took it."

"Hey, we did the hard part." Hi handed a router to Ben and climbed down. "That's the last of it. Let the cops figure out who's guilty. What *we* need to focus on is this footwear disaster. Somebody owes me a new pair of kicks."

He stamped his feet, trying shed liquid from his dirty soles.

"Whoever did this is no genius." Shelton adjusted his glasses. "What was the plan here? Keep the gear in this bin, forever? Sneak it out one piece at a time? Child, please. Once security is back online, there's zero chance of getting this stuff through the gates, much less off the island."

True. As heists go, I thought this was a particularly dumb one.

But, as usual, Tory had a better take. "No. It would've worked."

We all stopped to listen.

"It's clever, actually." Tory rapped the storage bin with her knuckles. "This was probably just for the night."

Shelton crossed his arms. "How can you know that?"

"Think about it. The crook planned this break-in for a night security was down. But the gates are always monitored, even then, and the last regular shuttle leaves at eight. So he stashed the equipment here, *knowing* he couldn't possibly get it off the island aboard *Hugo.*"

"*Very* true," I said. "My father's no dope. He'd prevent anyone from transporting a horde of high-tech equipment off Loggerhead."

Tory began to pace. A good sign.

"Even with no cameras, it's practically impossible to get something bulky past LIRI's fence unnoticed." She pointed to the closest ATV. "But *these* go out every Monday morning, to restock the feeders. And they always carry a massive load."

Suddenly, the answer jumped out at me.

*Of course.*

"So the thief dumps the stuff in here until morning," I said slowly, marveling at the plan's elegant simplicity, "then wraps everything in feed bags, loads an ATV, and drives it all right through the gate."

"Wow." Shelton's eyes rounded. "Hiding in plain sight."

Hi nodded appreciatively. "And once *outside* the fence, our devious felon could stash the gear anywhere. Pick it up later by boat. Just like a pirate, really."

"By this time tomorrow," Tory finished, "the whole thing would've been over."

"Hold up." Shelton's palms rose. "If the crook couldn't get the hardware out, then how'd *he* get out?" Eyes widening, he dropped into a battle-crouch. "Is the *thief* still in here, too!?"

Tory shook her head. "With security down, a motivated criminal could slip over the perimeter fence easy enough. It's not razor-wired or anything, to protect the monkeys from injury. I bet the jerk either secretly stayed behind after the last ferry, then went to work and climbed out, or came back by private boat after midnight, scaling the fence twice."

I kept my face blank, but inside, I marveled. Tory puts things together so fast!

"Real talk," Hi said, "we're the only reason the scheme didn't work. No chance Chief Tight Pants or those cops figure it out fast enough. I'd say we rock pretty freaking hard."

"But we still don't know *who*!" Tory threw both hands above her head.

"True, but we've narrowed the pool of suspects." Hi began ticking points on his fingers. "LIRI employee. Has access to the depot. Makes feeder runs. Probably works on Monday. That can't be more than a half-dozen people. Have Kit check the time sheets. Easy."

I ignored Hiram. Watched Tory instead.

And knew she'd rather explode than hand off this investigation.

That's when I got my idea.

# CHAPTER 8

"What about the tool, Tory?"

"Huh?" Ben's question snapped me from a funk.

*We're going to solve this. We ARE.*

I couldn't imagine quitting. What kind of detective leaves a job half done?

"The cabinets in Lab Three." Ben spoke slowly, but with uncharacteristic eagerness. "They were pried open, remember?"

He pointed to the row of workstations against the opposite wall. "Wouldn't the criminal use something he could trust?"

*Of course.*

I felt a jolt of excitement. "Something he worked with every day!"

"Brilliant deduction, my Native American friend!" Hi nodded sagely. "No, really, I'm being serious. Good thinking, Blue."

"Makes sense," Shelton agreed. "If I'm about to risk a felony, I'd use a tool I was familiar with. One I could count on."

"You're a genius." I reached out and squeezed Ben's shoulder.

He stiffened. Then reddened.

I snatched my hand back. *Touchy.*

Hi was already crossing the garage. "Let's check for anything strong enough to force a cabinet. Maybe we'll get lucky."

"The doors were made of pressed wood that splintered," I reminded everyone. "There might be shavings stuck to the implement. Or maybe broken glass. Even *dust* could be significant. Go slowly, and be careful."

Six workstations lined the wall. Each had a massive, freestanding toolbox labeled by name in black marker on dirty masking tape.

Hi took the first station and began opening and closing drawers. "Hello, Lionel Alonso. Are you a dirty, stinking thief?"

"Simon Rome." Ben began rifling the second workstation. "Let's check *you* out."

Shelton looked a question at me.

"You take . . . Kenny Hall." I gestured to the next station in line. "I'll check out . . . Frank Glasnapp."

I searched the tool chest systematically, inspecting the top drawers first, even though they seemed too small. My hypothesis was correct. Screws. Hinges. Bolts. Nails. Nothing suitable for B and E.

I switched to the lower section. These drawers were wider and deeper, and held more promising items. Hammers. Screwdrivers. A socket wrench set.

But my careful inspection came up empty.

If Glasnapp was our guy, he didn't keep his instrument of choice in here.

The boys also struck out. We double-checked an ax Ben discovered, and two crowbars owned by Mr. Hall. None showed signs of recent use.

"Though we can't be a hundred percent sure," I grumbled. "If the crook wiped the tool down, we'd never know."

"Two more to go," Shelton said. "Double up?"

Hi nodded. "Shelton and I will take . . . John Johnson? Hey, great name, guy."

I moved to the last workstation. "Ben and I will check this one. Trey Terry."

Terry's tool chest had larger compartments than the first I'd checked. We found a pair of hedge clippers, a rotating circular saw, a portable air compressor, and a collection of hatchets.

"This guy must work in the woods," Ben guessed. "These things are probably used to clear brush from around the feeders."

"But everything's clean," I muttered. "No shavings, no embedded plastic, *nada*."

"We got nothing, too." Shelton closed the last of Johnson's drawers. "Weak sauce."

"So we struck out on this one." Ben casually spun a hatchet in one hand. "But we found the loot, and Kit can follow Hi's plan to ID the crook. Still a win in my book."

Ben attempted a second twirl, but missed the catch. The hatchet crashed to the floor.

"Easy, circus freak!" Hi hopped backward. "I like my toes where they are."

"Sorry." Ben chuckled. "In my defense, the handle is slick."

Two neurons fired in my brain. Synapse.

"The handle," I murmured. Then, "The handle!"

Ben reached for the hatchet, but Shelton scooped it first. "Not a chance, you. No more blade juggling on my watch."

My hand shot out. "Gimme that." I knew my voice sounded odd.

"Okeydokey." Shelton passed it over with a quizzical look.

"Don't *you* get all choppy-stabby on us, Tor," Hi warned. "That's no way to deal with frustration."

"If I do, you're getting hacked first." But I focused on the object in my hands.

I flipped the hatchet upside down and held it by the blade. The handle was made of wood, stained dark brown. Its surface scratched and pitted by a lifetime of hard use.

And there was a lovely little chip at the base of the handle.

I felt a charge of adrenaline.

I snatched the splinter from my pocket and pressed it into the gap on the handle. All three boys straightened.

But my hopes were immediately dashed.

The splinter didn't match. Not in size, color, or grain.

Ben dove for the tool chest. "There are *five* more of those in here."

He grabbed two of the hatchets and handed them to Shelton and Hi.

"Not this one," Hi said. "No gash on the handle."

"Same story here," Shelton said.

Three more came out in quick succession.

*There.*

I seized the last implement from Ben's fingers. This one was larger, more a small ax than a true hatchet. Its handle was a foot long, worn, and stained dark brown.

With a one-inch, triangular notch at the bottom of the haft.

Heart pounding, I inspected the notch closely. The damage seemed fresh, with pale yellow wood still visible in the center of the breach. Inhaling deeply, I detected the faintest whiff of monkey chow.

My hands trembled with excitement.

Willing myself calm, I placed the splinter from Lab Three into the fissure.

Perfect fit.

Color. Shape. Grain. All a flawless match.

"Gotcha."

"Trey Terry." Shelton triple-jabbed his index finger. "You. Are. Busted."

"We're gonna be *studs*," Hi crowed. "Maybe there's a cash reward? How should we tell everybody?" He stroked his chin. "Should we be all like, 'Hey Kit, come check out this awesome garden hose we found,' and then *BAM*, we're holding microscopes over our heads? Or should we play it ultra-cool, like cracking this case is no biggie. I'm torn."

I looked at him strangely. "Hi, we're not taking credit for this."

"Do what now?" Hi's forehead creased. "I don't think I heard you right."

"Are you taking stupid pills?" Shelton snapped. "We can't draw that kind of attention to ourselves. *Any* attention. You should know that by now, Stolowitski."

"We're still Viral," Ben said quietly. "We're only one mistake away from being caged like lab rats. Always. The best thing we can do is go unnoticed. Period."

I nodded. "For us, there's no such thing as good publicity."

"Oh, come on!" Hi actually stamped his foot. "We can *explain* this one! Step by step! The world won't suddenly suspect we've got super-powers, they'll just think we're awesome and brilliant. And I, for one, like that idea!"

Hi searched faces, hunting for an ally. Found none.

*Go easy. You're the one who wanted to impress Aunt Tempe.*

"Hey, *I* know you're awesomely brilliant." I offered a high five. "What more do you need?"

"Fame. Glory. A book deal."

"I'll buy you a Twix."

Hi buried his face in his hands. A beat, then, "I do love those."

He sighed. "Fine. Deal." Slapping my palm with his. "But I want the full candy bar. None of that mini, Halloween-sized crap."

Shelton was tugging his earlobe again. "But how do we put it together for a dope like Hudson *without* tipping our involvement?"

I grinned.

"That's the fun part."

# CHAPTER 9

*F*ire hazard?
  I read the email a third time.

**To:** LIRI Director Christopher Howard.
**Re:** Fire Suppression Alert, Vehicle Depot A.
**Subject:** WARNING

The automated sprinkler system at LOGGERHEAD ISLAND,
LIRI COMPOUND, VEHICLE DEPOT A has been disengaged.
This constitutes a preventable fire hazard under the
terms of LIRI's property insurance agreement. Immediate
remedial action is required.

Note: This message is part of the automated warning
system. Do not reply.

I rubbed my eyes with both palms. Pinched the bridge of my nose.
What a day.
I'd been director for weeks, but this was a first.

Frankly, I wasn't sure what to do.

*This job is going to kill me.*

But I knew I had to investigate. We'd already been robbed. I didn't need a fire.

Frustrated, I stood and strode from my office. Being Sunday, the rest of the director's suite was empty. The rooms still made me uncomfortable —I still thought of this area as belonging to my predecessor. Probably always would.

"One thing after another," I said aloud.

I took the elevator to the ground floor and crossed to the security desk.

Carl was on duty, not Chief Hudson.

*Why am I relieved? I hired the guy.*

"Any word on my daughter, Carl?"

The portly guard shot to his feet. "No sir, Dr. Howard. *Director* Howard."

He snatched off his cap and began spinning it in his hands.

I suppressed a sigh. Carl and I used to swap jokes.

"Relax, Carl. And, please, call me Kit. It's no big deal, I was just curious. The kids show up without warning, then they drop off the grid."

This only made Carl fidget more. "Should I look for them, sir? I mean, Director. Er, Kit."

"Forget I asked." I waved the guard back to his seat. "If anyone needs me, I'm heading over to Depot A for a sec."

"Yes, sir, Director Howard." Carl winced. "Doctor. Kit."

I slipped through the glass doors, shaking my head. Things would never be the same. The price you pay for being in charge, I guess.

A part of me missed how things used to be.

Sometimes, I felt like a fraud. A little boy, sneaking around in Karsten's impossibly large shoes. I worried the other LIRI veterans thought the same about me.

At times like this, I missed being plain old Dr. Howard, the nerdy marine biologist who obsessed over loggerhead turtles. People liked that guy. They didn't stammer, or grow quiet when he approached the water cooler.

Those days were gone. But if the cost of saving LIRI was being forced to manage it, I was willing to pay.

Plus, let's be honest. Being the boss *does* have its perks.

Once outside, I followed the path to Vehicle Depot A. I tried my key, but a shrill beeping erupted the moment I touched the knob.

*Hudson has the system back online. Thanks for the heads-up.*

Moving to the keypad, I punched in a seven-digit code and swiped my card. There was a hum, then a flash as the sensor took my photograph. The door swung open.

I entered a narrow corridor. To my left was a door leading to the garage. To my right was a row of employee lockers, a pair of offices, and a storage closet. My objective was straight ahead: a maintenance room housing the sprinkler controls.

I didn't bother with the lights, and soon regretted it. Halfway down the hallway something snagged my pants.

*Rip.*

"What the heck?" I retreated a step and fumbled for a switch.

The halogens sputtered to life, revealing a long black cable jutting from one of the lockers. The casing had been cut, exposing the copper wire within.

The cable had snared me.

*Dang it. I just bought these Dockers.*

Extricating myself, I shoved the cord back inside the locker.

Unsafe. I'd need to have a word with . . . Glasnapp? Johnson?

*Mental note: Find out who runs this department.*

I proceeded to the maintenance room and opened a sleek black panel.

*At least I know where the sprinkler controls are, right?*

A message was blinking in red: Water supply manually disengaged.

I frowned. The shutoff valve was in the main garage.

I closed the panel, retraced my steps, and entered the mechanics' bay. The water pipes were in the corner, beside several large bins that stored monkey feed.

The problem was immediately apparent—the emergency handle had been turned perpendicular to the pipe. Which meant the valve was closed, shutting off the system's water supply. A tiny red sensor was flashing like a railroad signal.

Why had the flow been disengaged? When? By whom?

*This makes no sense.*

Was someone goofing around in there?

My mind leapt to Tory and her friends. I wouldn't put anything past those four.

Don't get me wrong, they're great kids. Bright, energetic, polite. Tory especially—with my daughter, every day was a learning experience. I no longer doubted her IQ was higher than mine, and I hold two PhDs.

But honestly, I couldn't *believe* the things they got into.

After a moment's reflection, I dismissed my suspicion.

Even with security down, they'd have had no way of getting in here.

Baffled, I stretched to my tiptoes, grabbed the handle, and repositioned it parallel to the pipe. The sensor blinked twice, then stopped altogether.

*One issue solved.*

I'd taken two steps toward the door when I saw it.

Black cable. Hanging from the corner feed bin.

*Like that cable in the locker.*

Curious, I climbed to the bin's opening and tugged the handle. And nearly toppled off the steps as the entire door came free in my hand. It dropped to the floor with a reverberating clatter.

Irritated now, I peered inside.

My head nearly exploded.

Stolen lab equipment nearly filled the space.

*What are the odds . . .*

Then a second thunderbolt struck home.

I hurried out to the lockers and found the one that attacked me.

My hand froze an inch from the handle. Could I legally open it?

Did I need a warrant? Probable cause? A witness?

*Screw it. I'm responsible for this facility.*

I engaged the latch, was surprised when the locker opened easily.

Inside were three lengths of cable, a LIRI laptop, and a router.

"You are *so* busted!" I shouted at no one, angrier than I'd realized.

Slamming the door, I scanned the locker's face.

Found a name.

Trey Terry.

# CHAPTER 10

I was sorting email when Kit burst into the guest office I was using.

"Can you help me with something, Tempe?" Brusque. "Outside?"

"Sure, Kit." Intrigued. "Should I bring a weapon?"

"No, nothing like that." Kit's jaw tightened. I could tell he was barely keeping his agitation in check. "I think I solved our break-in. Looks like an inside job, but I need to be certain."

"Really?" My interest piqued. "That was quick work."

"Dumb luck, mostly. But I put the pieces together on my way up here."

"Let's talk while we walk." Logging off Gmail. "I'm all ears."

"I need you to compare some wires down at the vehicle depot." Kit shook his head in exasperation. "My prime suspect appears to be both deviously clever and a complete idiot."

"Wouldn't be the first criminal to fit that mold."

We descended to the ground floor, exited Building One, and turned left.

The September sun felt warm on my face. It would be cold in Montreal by now, maybe even frost at night. Even Charlotte could get chilly this time of year. But not Charleston—summer still lingered down here by the coast. I had no complaints.

Kit gestured vaguely up the flower-lined path. "The garage is two buildings down."

"You said something about dumb luck?"

In clipped tones my nephew explained what he'd discovered and outlined his theory. "Terry must've planned to sneak the stuff out during a feeder run." Kit's frown deepened. "Scary thing is, I think it would've worked."

"Makes sense. A crafty scheme, actually. Except for jamming incriminating evidence inside his locker. And leaving more hanging from the hidey-hole."

Kit's brows shot up. "That's the part I don't get. How can you be that cunning and then botch the whole thing with such foolish mistakes? If he'd kept everything tucked inside the bin, I'd never have found it."

"These dolts get sloppy all the time." *Don't I know it.* "Wipe down a steering wheel, but forget the turn signal. Buy quicklime to dissolve a body, but pay with a credit card. It's the little details that sink them."

Still, what Kit was describing *was* odd.

Such basic mistakes. The skeptical part of my brain rose and stretched.

We reached the depot and made our way to the vehicle bay. A spectacularly round security guard was stacking equipment in the center of the room. Chief Hudson hovered behind him, cataloging and photographing each item.

Two piles of short black cables sat on opposite sides of the gear.

I didn't need instruction.

I knelt beside the first pile. "These came from the locker?"

Kit nodded.

Scanning the garage, I spotted a circular magnifying lamp attached to a workbench. I lifted a single cable from the first pile, then snagged another from the second. I carried both pieces to the workbench.

Thumbing on the light, I brought the cables into focus under the lens. It took only seconds. "We have a match."

"You're positive?" Kit asked, crossing to me.

"See how the plastic casing is scored in the exact same fashion?" I moved so Kit could see. "And there was an irregularity in the cutting edge—the encased wired is frayed identically. That's practically a signature. I can check the other samples, but I have no doubt. These two cables were clipped by the same blade."

"Thank you, Aunt Tempe." Kit jammed a hand into his pocket. "If you'll excuse me, I have some calls to make."

Kit hurried off, already punching his cell. "Detective Hansen, please. It's Kit Howard from LIRI . . ."

When Kit had gone, out of habit, I let my eyes rove the "scene."

Something caught my attention in the feed bin corner.

The floor. An unnatural reflection of light off the concrete.

"Chief Hudson?" I called out.

He glanced up from his clipboard. "Yes, Dr. Brennan?"

"The missing equipment was discovered over there? In one of those bins?"

Hudson paused before answering. "Yes. In the farthest container."

"Thank you." I walked to the corner and knelt before the bin in question.

Hudson watched, but didn't interfere.

I was right. There was something on the floor.

A pattern, pressed to the concrete.

*Like a waffle iron.*

I pulled out my iPhone and snapped a picture.

"Anything amiss, Dr. Brennan?" Hudson's tone was frosty. "Please don't touch anything."

*This freaking guy.*

"Of course not."

The impression could be nothing. But I had that itch.

I moved my eyes slowly across the floor, foot by foot, expanding the radius outward. A similar waffle mark lay by the mechanics' workstations.

"Hmm."

Hudson appeared at my elbow, a stony expression on his face. "We've already searched Mr. Terry's workspace. Please don't disturb it."

Ignoring him, I glanced toward the interior door. "Can I access the employee lockers through there?"

"Yes, but the door is locked." Hudson didn't move.

I waited.

With a grunt Hudson produced a key ring and opened the door.

"Knock for reentry." Lips so tight they blanched at the edges, Hudson resumed cataloging evidence.

Locating the lockers, I squatted for a closer look at the floor. Saw immediately.

Two more waffle prints. I snapped another iPhone shot.

These marks were fainter than those in the garage. More recent?

A bit puzzled, I returned to the door and knocked as instructed.

Waited. Knocked again.

Finally, the heavy guard opened the door. "Chief Hudson headed back to his office."

"Of course he did." I read his name tag. "Thank you, Mr. Szuberla."

*Time to find Kit.*

On the driveway, another gleam caught my eye. I dropped down once more to inspect it. Waffle print. Barely perceptible.

As I snapped my third pic, the answer struck me.

"A sneaker."

*The police should check for a matching shoe.*

I did a thorough 360, but found no more shoe prints.

"These suckers *always* leave a trace."

I slipped back into the depot. One more pass wouldn't hurt.

◇  ◇  ◇

Thirty minutes later, I found Kit in his office, still on the phone.

He twirled a wrist, indicating I should sit. A minute later he hung up with a grunt. "We got him. Trey Terry, one of our environmental techs."

"That was quick. You're certain?"

Kit rolled his eyes. "Terry folded as soon as the cops appeared on his doorstep. Confessed to everything. Not that it matters, since a LIRI laptop was sitting on his table."

"Not a bad day's work."

"The guy's been with us seven years." Kit sighed. "We paid him well. I'll never understand why people do things like this."

I shrugged. "Greed. Opportunity. Some perceived slight."

Kit's expression grew thoughtful. "I checked Terry's file. He was passed over for a supervisor's gig last spring. The job went to Glasnapp, who has more experience. Maybe that pissed him off."

Kit leaned back in his chair. "I just can't believe how sloppy he was."

I debated how much to share. Decided to go full out. "About that. I found some distinct—"

The phone rang. Kit answered, then covered the mouthpiece. "Police," he mouthed.

I nodded, rose, and slipped from the office. My discovery could wait.

Exiting the director's suite, I walked to the elevators, admiring the modern offices populating the floor. Despite the morning's excitement, I couldn't help being impressed with LIRI. What a wonderful place to work. Nicer digs than mine in Charlotte or Montreal, that's for sure.

On a whim, I snuck into a corner office for a bird's-eye view of the grounds. Gazing through the glass, I saw the entire complex laid out below.

And spotted my grandniece and her pals, lounging on benches in courtyard.

Watching Tory, feelings of love and pride surged through me. Such a terrific young lady. So smart! There was a fire in her eyes that reminded me of . . . *me.*

Kit was doing a great parenting job, though I wasn't sure who actually ran their household.

*The kid's a pistol.*

Impulsively, I decided to join Tory and her friends.

I swung back into Kit's office just as he was finishing his call.

"Tory's in the courtyard. Thought I'd go say hi."

"I'll come, too." Kit popped from his chair. "I have no idea why she's out here. Not a novel state of affairs."

I smiled sympathetically. "She's headstrong. Ambitious. Those are good things."

"She's a rampaging rhino and I'm a parked car." Kit laughed. "Life is certainly more interesting since she came to live with me. You know she wants to become a forensic anthropologist? Must have good taste in role models."

When they spotted us coming, whispers flew.

Teenagers. Always changing. Never changing.

"Why, hello there, guys!" Kit spoke with exaggerated animation. "Fancy meeting you here!"

"Hi, Dr. Howard." The skinny black kid was fidgeting with his earlobe. I struggled to remember his name. *Sheldon? Elton?*

"Hey," the chunky one said. *Hiram?* He seemed bummed. Slouching back, he muttered something about a mountain-sized Twix.

The muscular kid simply nodded.

Tory was the only one who seemed glad to see us. "Hey, Kit. Didn't you know we were coming?"

"No, I did not," Kit said patiently. "You neglected to mention it at breakfast, outside on the lawn, or as you bolted out the door."

"Oh, sorry. My bad." She smiled sweetly.

Kit shrugged.

Hiram suddenly sat up. "Any news on the break-in?"

The other kids shot glances his direction. For some reason, they glared.

*Huh?*

Kit missed the exchange. "You're not going to believe this. The robbery was an inside job. One of LIRI's own techs."

"Get out!" Hi exclaimed.

"Oh." Sheldon/Elton studied his shoes. "Neat."

Muscle Boy didn't even blink.

*Huh?*

"Wow." Tory cocked her head. "Tell us what happened."

"The suspect made several crucial mistakes." Kit summarized what he'd pieced together in the last few hours. "Though I still don't get why Terry shut down the sprinkler system," he finished. "Maybe he worried the equipment would get wet."

"Sounds like you saved the day." Tory, face neutral. "Great job, Kit."

Hiram groaned and slumped back again, staring up at the sky.

Their reactions surprised me. No curiosity? No barrage of questions? Earlier this morning, Tory had seemed fascinated.

Now? She simply smiled. Listened. Nodded in the appropriate places. Only one word described her expression. *Smug.*

Something wasn't right. I looked each of them over, top to toe.

Hiram lay flat on his back, legs outstretched, sneakers propped on the bench's stone armrest. He wore an older style of tennis shoe—a black-and-white checkerboard pattern popular two decades back. Hideous.

I recognized the brand. In middle school, my daughter, Katy, had been obsessed with Vans.

But more importantly, with his feet up I could see the tread on his soles. Waffle print.

Identical to the marks I'd found inside the garage and by Terry's locker.

The marks I hadn't described to Kit. Given Terry's confession, my finding had no longer seemed important.

Casually, I pulled out my cell phone and examined the three photos I'd taken.

Then I stepped closer to Hiram and scanned the bottom of his shoe.

*I'll be damned.*

Hiram noticed me eyeballing his footwear. Eyes narrowing, he tried to swing his feet away, but overbalanced and rolled off the bench.

"Nice one," Sheldon/Elton said. Muscle Boy smirked.

I caught Hiram's eye. "Cool shoes. Classic tread. Very distinctive."

"Thanks?" He sounded a touch nervous.

Hi lurched back onto the bench, but kept his soles firmly planted on the ground.

In my periphery, I noticed Tory watching me intently. The smugness was gone.

*My my my.*

My eyes dropped to the images on my iPhone.

These four were hiding something. What?

I was sure they wouldn't have done anything *really* wrong. But I was equally certain of something else: They'd been inside that garage.

I looked at Tory. Our eyes locked. She knew I was suspicious. Which confirmed my suspicion.

I held her gaze. Saw what I needed to see.

*Keep your secret.*

Pocketing my phone, I snagged Kit's elbow. "Come on, Monsieur L'Directeur. These guys didn't come out here to hang with us."

"Right." Kit ruffled Tory's hair. "Stay out of trouble."

Walking back toward Building One, I felt eyes on my back. Knew Tory was tracking our retreat.

And I had a devilish thought.

"Give me a sec, Kit. I'll meet you inside."

"Sure thing."

I snagged my phone and selected the best footprint photo of the series.

Attached it to a text message.

Selected the recipient.

Hit send.

Paused. Waited.

Out in the courtyard, I saw Tory reach into her pocket. She glanced down, then stiffened.

Her eyes whipped my way.

With a five-finger-waggle, I slipped inside.

*Gotcha.*

# SWIPE

# CHAPTER 1

It's safe to say I'd never seen anything like it.

Comic-Con.

Nerd Nirvana. Geek Paradise.

The entertainment event of the year, every year.

And the boys and I were at ground zero, strolling the packed exhibit hall floor.

"Check out *that* guy." Ben nudged my arm, nodded toward a gawky teenager dressed in a puzzling assemblage of red-and-blue-cardboard boxes. The pimple-faced boy was leaning against one of the room's massive pillars, scarfing a slice of pizza. "I didn't know Optimus Prime was a fan of pepperoni."

My nose crinkled at the sight. "Robots need fuel, too, I guess."

Ben shook his head, a smirk framing his dark brown eyes. "No. Just, no."

I was forced to jump aside as a gaggle of black-robed ninjas stormed past us, intent on a free T-shirt line forming at the video-gaming station just ahead. My fourth near-trampling of the morning.

"This place is crazy!" Edging farther from the cavernous chamber's main thoroughfare, I ran fingers through my tangled red hair. "I might buy one of those *Hunger Games* bows for personal protection."

"Crazy *awesome,* you mean." Hi's voice. Somewhere behind me. "I'm never leaving this convention. Ever. Tell my mother. I live here now. How come no one ever mentioned Comic-Con before? This is the sum total of everything cool in the universe."

I sighed, turned. Abandoned my effort to make it look like we weren't together.

Hi's chubby face beamed as he took in the fanboy glory surrounding us. He wore an unlicensed Iron Man costume purchased online. The full-body red-and-yellow spandex left little to the imagination. A dozen people had asked for his picture already.

Shelton stood beside Hi, in a daze, dressed like Obi-Wan Kenobi: tan robes, black leather utility belt, flowing brown cloak. And his boxy black specs, of course. We'd just passed the Lucasfilm floor display—complete with Han Solo frozen in carbonite—and he'd yet to recover the ability to speak.

Ben rubbed his face with both hands. "I told you guys not to talk to me in those . . . outfits." He was wearing his standard jeans and plain black tee. Shocker.

Hi snorted. "This is Comic-Con, bro. *You're* the one that looks out of place."

Frankly, he was right.

The exhibit hall was packed, with more visitors rocking cosplay than not. The giant room had been divided into sections, then rows, then booths, each packed with the weirdest stuff imaginable. I'd never seen so many bizarre things crammed into one place. "Geek Paradise" was putting it lightly.

I'd made a token effort in the wardrobe department: Wonder Woman tank, blue shorts.

I'll fly my freak flag, but only a smidgen.

After all, the whole reason we were there was to see Tempe.

Can't look the fool in front of Dr. Temperance Brennan. No, ma'am.

We'd stopped beside a wooden pirate ship rising twenty feet from the floor, complete with swashbuckling actors brandishing cutlasses and handing out promotional hats. Across the aisle, zombies in prison uniforms were locked inside a chain-link fence, mumbling about the new season of their show, returning Sundays at ten.

We'd been there an hour and barely crossed a third of the convention floor. The room stretched on and on, jammed by endless rows of comic-book vendors, TV and film promotions, memorabilia displays, novelties sales, and every other oddity under the sun.

More madness per square foot than any other place on earth.

And 100,000 people to go crazy over it, of course.

I was about to forge back into the herd of wide-eyed weekend superheroes when noise exploded around me. Lights began flashing at one of the towering movie studio booths just ahead. Ominous piano music boomed from its massive speakers as celebrity faces appeared on a bank of giant TV screens: the cast of some vampire show on cable.

"Nobody move!" I warned, my danger sense tingling.

Sure enough, a herd of teenage girls thundered down the walkway, fangs exposed, black leather jackets flapping, their white-painted faces contorted by screams of ecstasy.

"Let's get out of here," Ben shouted through cupped hands to be heard over the thumping music. "Where are we meeting your aunt Tempe?"

"Her panel ended ten minutes ago." I pointed beyond the crush of jabbering supernatural creatures to a less congested area of the exhibit hall. "She's signing books at her publisher's booth, somewhere over there."

Tempe had spoken in one of the conference rooms upstairs, where the lunacy was slightly more contained. The second floor of the convention center hosts earnest discussions on topics of all kinds: YA fiction. The legal rights of zombies. LARPing. How to master Dungeons & Dragons. You name it. And that's not even *mentioning* the bigger ball-rooms, which present the major TV show panels, movie launches, and celebrity appearances. But those events are next to impossible to get into, so we didn't bother. No way I'd stand in line all day. Not when there was so much else to see.

"I'm making a break for it." Tucking his black hair behind his ears, Ben shouldered his way into the crowd. "See you on the other side."

I waved at Hi and Shelton, who'd stumbled into a group of costumed superheroes.

"Let's go." I pointed beyond the bloodsucker traffic jam.

"I just photo-bombed the Avengers!" Hi cried, red-faced and glowing.

Thumbs up. I try not to be a hater.

Tempe's presence at the convention explained ours. A year earlier, she'd written a section of a nonfiction book examining the exploding popularity of forensic science in pop culture. To everyone's surprise, the work had become a national bestseller.

Attempting to maintain sales momentum, the publisher had booked Tempe for a Comic-Con panel entitled "Forensic Science in Entertainment: The Effects of New Scientific Principles on Old-School Mystery Writing."

A free trip to San Diego isn't something my great-aunt will turn down.

After some googling, Hi had *insisted* we tag along.

Surprisingly, Kit had agreed. Or perhaps not so surprisingly—a few days without the daughter around must've appealed to Dad. His girl-friend, Whitney, had seemed positively delighted at the prospect.

Hi's mother took some convincing, and Shelton's parents made him promise to call twice a day, but both eventually granted permission. Ben had no trouble at all. So Tempe secured the badges, and here we were. Sunny San Diego in mid-July. The epicenter of media rollouts.

We wormed into the slow-moving press of bodies, pausing occasionally to whisper and point. I swear, some girls will use *any* event as a chance to show too much skin—if I never see another slave Princess Leia costume again, it'll be too soon. Though I doubt my male companions would agree.

Eventually, we reached the book section, a slightly quieter neighborhood.

"Look!" Hi elbowed Shelton's ribs. "Those chicks are dressed like Khaleesi! The Mother of Dragons! *We. Need. That. Pic.*"

"Those are Night's Watch dudes with them." Shelton raised both arms, smiling ear to ear. "That crew might be our best friends!" The two took off without a backward glance.

I glanced at Ben, who shrugged. "I'm a Sansa man."

My eyes rolled. "Let's just find Tempe. You can hunt cosplay fantasies later."

Ben's eyebrows quirked into an "innocent-man" look. "*I* didn't just run off to Westeros. Lead the way. Maybe Tempe's in that Ewok village up ahead."

Weaving through a throng of steampunkers, I finally spotted Tempe, sitting at a folding table, chatting with fans and signing books. The line stretched around the corner and out of sight. Behind her stood an officious-looking man in a charcoal-gray suit. He was grinning broadly, no doubt tabulating the number of books sold. Tempe's appearance was clearly a success.

Angling toward the booth, Ben and I were halted by a burly-armed woman in a yellow "Event Staff" polo. "Sorry," she huffed, pointing in the opposite direction, "but the line ends two rows over, near those Batman stuffed animals."

I smiled politely. "Thank you, but we're actually with the author."

"Of course you are, dear." Skeptical. "You have special passes . . . or some such thing?"

I shuffled my feet, somehow feeling awkward even though I was right. "No, ma'am. I don't think there *are* passes for that." I edged sideways to see around the woman's shoulder. "If I could just . . ."

I waved for Tempe's attention. Failed to snag it.

Ben stepped in. "Dr. Brennan is family. She's expecting us."

"Yes. Yes, of course." But the woman didn't move. "You're her . . . ?"

"Niece and nephew," Ben said firmly, easing the two of us past the still-hesitant line monitor. "We just need to grab her attention."

We hurried forward. The yellow shirt spun to watch us.

"Nephew?" I whispered.

"What, you don't see the family resemblance?"

"Uncanny."

Just then Aunt Tempe glanced up, spied us, and signaled for us to join her. The guard returned her attention to the queue, eyes hunting for new line-jumping transgressors.

"Hey, kiddos!" Tempe's face was flushed, from exertion or all the attention, I wasn't sure. "See anything cool?"

"There's a life-sized Superman made of Legos." I slid around to Tempe's side of the table. Several impatient autograph seekers watched with jealous eyes. I guess the book really *was* a hit.

"I never had enough patience for Legos." Then Tempe nodded to a mountain of gray drawstring pouches stacked near the end of her table. "Be sure to take a swag bag."

I scooped one and tugged it open. "Oh, neat idea!"

Inside was a rudimentary CSI kit: an LED penlight, two rubber gloves, a tiny magnifying glass, and a pocket-sized booklet on proper crime scene investigative techniques.

Ben mumbled a quiet hello, eyes glued to his sneakers. For some reason Tempe made him uncomfortable. Although, to be fair, almost all adult interactions had the same effect on Ben.

Tempe greeted the next person in line, answered a question, then signed her name on the title page. "Where are Hi and Shelton?" she asked, without looking up.

"Not sure." Then I spotted them, being held up by the same insufferable guard lady.

"On it." Ben scooted off to the rescue.

"How long are you going to sign here?" I asked Tempe.

"As long as books keep selling, right, Dr. Brennan?" Hovering at Tempe's elbow, the gray-suited man flashed an obsequious smile.

"Yes, Miles," Tempe replied pleasantly. "I'll sign them all. No need to fret."

"No worries at all," the man said smoothly, raking his comb-over with long, spindly fingers. "This is simply *wonderful,* Dr. Brennan. Things are going even better than I'd hoped."

"So glad I could help," Tempe quipped, but I noticed a twinkle in her eyes.

She was enjoying herself. Everyone loves a taste of fame.

The man extended a manicured hand. "Miles Stanwick, publicist, nonfiction."

"Tory Brennan. Grandniece. High school."

Stanwick's grip was like a dead fish, clammy and limp.

I resisted an urge to wipe my palm.

The boys arrived, Hi chattering nonstop. "We posed on the bridge of a replica Starship *Enterprise.* That's a genre cross-up, but who cares? I'm gonna Facebook the crap out of these pics!" Then he noticed Tempe was paying attention. "Oh. Err. Please excuse me, Dr. Brennan. I didn't know that you . . . like . . . listened when we talk."

"Not a problem." Tempe smiled as a nervous college girl approached with a hardback. "And for the last time, call me Tempe. I plan on Facebooking some shots myself."

As the boys pocketed gift bags, I rose to my tiptoes and peered down the aisle. At least a hundred people were waiting, with varying degrees of patience.

Tempe followed my sight line. "You guys should go. I'll meet you when I'm done."

"You sure?" I checked my watch. "The *Bones* panel begins in thirty. I was hoping to check it out."

"You didn't see the line," Shelton groused, shaking his hooded head. "Imagine Space Mountain, but times a billion. Ain't happening."

"Wait." Stanwick raised a well-manicured finger. "I was given a few VIP passes. I won't be using them, so . . ."

Shelton and Hi closed in like jackals.

"You have passes?" Hi's fingers dug into the sides of his costume. "That we can have?"

"For Ballroom Twenty?" Shelton. All business. "For *realsies*?"

"Yes." Stanwick produced four tickets from his jacket pocket. "Enjoy."

I knew he was trying to get rid of us, but didn't care. Stanwick was offering the most coveted thing at Comic-Con: access. We were all for that.

Hi literally yanked the passes from Stanwick's hand. Then he winced. "Sorry. I just . . . this is big-time."

"Understood. Now go have fun." The man actually shooed us a little.

We spun, searching for the closest exit. The panel was upstairs, in the convention center's second-largest venue.

Passing the overzealous guard, Hi stopped and waved the tickets. "Got those passes you were wondering about," he announced in an overly loud voice. "Heading up to Ballroom Twenty."

The lady nodded irritably. Others in the crowd cast envious glances. Hi ate it up.

I was about to scold him for showboating when a piercing scream rose above the exhibit hall's usual din. Shouts erupted, followed by a hundred voices whispering at once.

Ben's head swung left, then right. "What in the—"

A second bloodcurdling cry cut across the room. I finally located the source: Two rows over, a mob was ballooning in front of a large stage.

Something about the excited whispers. The craning necks. The flurry of camera flashes.

Whatever was happening didn't feel scripted.

I glanced back at Tempe. She'd stopped signing, was studying me, a curious look on her face. "Something's up," I mouthed, pointing toward the hubbub.

Tempe rose and, despite startled protestations from Stanwick, slipped around the table to join me. A third howl split the air just as she arrived.

"Trouble?" Tempe asked.

"Think so," I replied. "But who knows, here? Could be we're all getting punked."

One of her eyebrows rose. "Want to check it out?"

"Um, *yeah.*"

# CHAPTER 2

The man was dressed as RoboCop, armored head to foot by interlocking metal panels.

Impressive, had he not been the one screaming hysterically like an eight-year-old girl with a spider in her hair.

The throng behind him swelled, pointing and murmuring in hushed tones. Tempe and I cut through the gawkers, the boys on our heels, jockeying for a clear look.

RoboCop, visibly shaken, was staring up at the stage with both hands on his helmet. A younger man in a Joker costume stood dumbstruck at his side, mouth open and breathing hard.

"The T-800 is gone." RoboCop's voice cracked as he grabbed the Joker by his purple suit lapels. "Missing! *Taken!* How is that possible!?"

"I don't know." His companion backpedaled, palms flying up. "*I* didn't touch it!"

Edging closer, I could see broken glass glinting onstage.

Tempe spoke at my ear. "Something was stolen."

"And it wasn't small." Shimmying sideways so the boys could see, I pointed to the center of the platform. "Whatever got swiped was the focal point of that huge glass house."

We were bunched before a towering display that occupied space enough for five regular booths. It was styled to resemble a 1950s movie theater, with plush red carpet covering the floor and a neon "Movie Magic" sign hanging overhead. The stage itself was large and elevated—the type used for outdoor concerts—and set with famous memorabilia from films throughout history. Metal side staircases served as entrance and exit.

Parked on the platform's near side was Ecto-1, the iconic red-and-white 1959 Cadillac ambulance-hearse combo driven by the Ghostbusters. On the opposite end was the A-Team van, black and gray with its vintage red stripe and eighties spoiler.

Between the vehicles rose chest-high pillars topped by Lucite boxes. One held Luke Skywalker's original lightsaber from *Return of the Jedi*. Another contained the ruby-red slippers Dorothy wore while off to see the Wizard. A third box sported a scale model of the first Starship *Enterprise*. There were a dozen more dotting the stage.

But everyone was staring at the platform's centerpiece: a giant, house-sized glass case backed by a bloodred wall. Inside the enclosure, on the left, was a puffy, foam-rubber replica of Shrek, standing at least ten feet tall. On the right side loomed an equally gargantuan King Kong.

The two figures loomed menacingly, frowning down at the convention, their hulking forms flanking a raised central dais.

Which was empty.

Except for broken glass.

Hence RoboCop's panicked shrieks.

Yellow-shirted event staff were gathering at the foot of the stage. Their leader appeared to be a hefty blond man with a curly beard. He yelled into a walkie-talkie, his finger jabbing up toward the shattered case. Then, holstering his radio, he gestured for three staffers to follow as he stomped toward the metal steps.

"Oh no." Tempe shot forward to intercept Curly Beard.

Ben poked between my shoulder blades. "What's she doing?"

"Telling that guy to leave the crime scene alone," I answered. "He probably doesn't have any forensic training. Tempe does."

Then I was knifing through the crowd, headed for my aunt's side.

"Tory!" Shelton barked. "Hold up!"

*Not a chance.*

If Tempe managed to wiggle her way into this investigation, I was coming along for the ride.

"Wait for me!" Hi shouted, attempting to muscle through the crush of onlookers.

"Hang back a sec," I yelled over my shoulder. "This may not work."

Ben placed a restraining hand on Hi. "Let's leave this one to the geniuses."

"I'm pretty freaking smart, too," Hi grumbled.

"Just be cool." Shelton tugged his ear. "For all we know, they'll both get arrested."

Tempe had Curly Beard cornered, was ticking fingers as she spoke.

RoboCop spotted Tempe and stomped over, arriving just as I did.

"Who are you and why are you interfering?" Red-faced, the man seemed on the verge of passing out. The Joker hung back, eyes wide behind his garish face paint.

"My name is Dr. Temperance Brennan," she replied patiently, "and I was telling this gentleman that he shouldn't contaminate the crime scene. I'm assuming something was stolen?"

"Yes!" RoboCop shrilled, removing his helmet to reveal a mass of stringy black hair. He was younger than I'd thought, somewhere in his mid-twenties. "They took the T-800! It's gone!"

Tempe frowned. "The T-what?"

"The *Terminator*!" RoboCop squeezed his eyes shut, as if gathering his strength. After several deep breaths he continued in a slightly calmer tone. "Not the one Arnold played, obviously, but the robot from the sequel's opening sequence. It's the *only* full-sized Terminator machine ever wholly constructed of metal. It's *priceless*."

"Priceless?" I instantly regretted speaking.

RoboCop fixed me with a baleful glare. "Yes, little girl. Well, no actually—I suppose it *has* a price. This T-800 was purchased at auction for *five hundred thousand dollars*."

Curly Beard whistled. Then he unclipped his walkie-talkie and shouted into it.

RoboCop began peeling off his costume, layer by layer. "Who are you anyway? Why am I discussing this with convention guests?" The Joker moved to assist with the dismantling, but was angrily waved away.

"Dr. Brennan is one of the foremost forensic scientists in the world." I couldn't keep the edge from my voice. "She can help process your crime scene. You're lucky to have her."

"Yes. Well." He seemed to regain a sliver of composure. "Thank you, then. I'm Lawrence Skipper. I'm responsible for this display. Until they fire me, anyway."

I noticed a ripple in the crowd. "Aunt Tempe. Police."

Two uniformed officers broke through the ring of onlookers and joined us by the stairs. "Who's in charge here?" asked the older of the two. He had thick gray hair and a handlebar mustache. The younger cop was tall and painfully thin, with a long, narrow nose and tiny mouth.

"I am." Skipper had shed the last vestiges of his costume, looked slightly ridiculous in a tight black turtleneck and wrinkled athletic shorts. "Lawrence Skipper, Multi-Media Magic Properties. We've been robbed. Although for the life of me I can't figure out how."

Young Cop flipped open a notepad. Old Cop turned to Tempe. "And you are?"

"Dr. Temperance Brennan." She produced an official-looking ID from her pocket. "I'm a board-certified forensic anthropologist, and consult for the medical examiner's offices of both North Carolina and

Quebec. I'm here promoting a book on forensic investigation techniques in film, and noticed the commotion. I'd be happy to assist with the crime scene."

Old Cop gave Tempe an appraising look, then spoke softly to his partner, who was scribbling furiously. Young Cop nodded, took Tempe's ID, then moved off and began speaking into his shoulder radio.

"Name's Flanagan." Old Cop extended his hand, which Tempe shook. "If you've got CSI experience, I'm glad for the help. We don't have a team stationed at the convention, and won't be able to secure this area very long. Too many people. But I'll need your daughter to step aside while we work."

"I'm her assistant," I blurted before my aunt could speak. "We're a package deal."

*You will* not *shut me out of this, copper.*

"That's correct," Tempe agreed. "Things will go a lot smoother if you allow Tory to assist me."

"Very well." But I could see the disapproval in Flanagan's eyes. "Please wait a moment while I get this sorted. I need an okay from my sergeant before you touch anything."

The boys snuck to my side while Tempe and the officers conferred.

"You getting arrested?" Hi asked, sweaty beneath his Iron Man leotard.

"Not yet," I replied. "They might even let Aunt Tempe and me work the scene."

Hi dropped his voice an octave. "What's the story?"

I quickly relayed what we'd learned.

"A real T-800?" Shelton's eyes widened behind his lenses. "Oh man, I'd *kill* to see that."

Ben's face grew pensive. "A thing like that would be big, right? Heavy?"

Shelton and Hi nodded in unison.

"So how'd the crook get it out of here?" Ben waved a hand at the cavernous chamber surrounding us. "There must be a hundred thousand people at Comic-Con."

I shrugged. Then a wheedling voice caught my attention.

"I *can't* explain it." Skipper was pacing behind me, a cell phone to his ear. "Jenkins and I did a final check at six this morning. *Everything* was accounted for and show ready. I left Jenkins to drape the stage for the big reveal at ten." Pause. "No, Connors didn't show up. I'm sure he was off playing war games, or whatever he does. Jenkins and I did it without him."

*Jenkins? Connors?* My gaze slid to the Joker, leaning dejectedly against a stanchion.

*He must be one or the other.*

Skipper massaged his forehead as he spoke into the phone. "I didn't even know the T-800 was gone until I pulled the curtains. It makes no sense. How could anyone haul a six-foot Terminator machine out of the exhibit hall undetected? It weighs two hundred pounds. And at least a dozen other vendors were setting up close by."

Skipper winced at whatever was said in response. "Understood, sir. I'll do my best."

He clicked off. Covered his eyes. Then, exhaling deeply, Skipper hurried over to Tempe and the officers.

"So people were around all morning." Hi shaded his eyes to peer up at the stage. "Yet someone busted open that glass house and carted away a life-sized robot. Ballsy."

"Crazy, more like." Shelton wiped his glasses on his Jedi robe. "And stupid. If the thing really is one of a kind, how you gonna sell it? Sounds like a surefire way to get busted."

I heard my name called. Glanced at Tempe, who waved me toward the stairs.

"I'll keep you posted," I told them, hurrying to join her.

"Get what you can," Officer Flanagan instructed as Tempe and I climbed to the platform. "You've only got a few minutes before that glass will have to be cleaned up. It's a clear safety hazard. There's too much commotion in here to effectively seal the area, anyway. We've had two assaults and an attempted arson since breakfast, and the day is still young. I don't have personnel to spare."

Skipper's face purpled. "But we have to find the T-800! My boss—"

"Has been contacted," Flanagan interrupted. "He's not happy, but that's not my problem." The grizzled cop turned to us. "Five minutes, then maintenance."

"Understood." Tempe nodded for me to follow her across the stage.

We weaved through the display pillars, alert for anything overtly suspicious, then reached the enclosure at center stage. I felt eyes upon me—dozens of people on the convention floor had stopped to watch, chattering excitedly.

I blocked them out. Focused on the task at hand.

*I'm assisting Tempe. My wildest dream come true. Don't screw it up!*

The display case was a fifteen-by-ten glass rectangle backed by a red wall. Three large panes faced forward, with the left and right sections still intact. The center pane, however, was completely shattered. Shards of glass littered the enclosure floor.

I glanced at Shrek and started. "Aunt Tempe, look."

The giant troll had been hacked to pieces, leaving a carpet of green foam-rubber chunks inside the display case. My head whipped left— King Kong, at least, seemed to have been spared the same indignity. The hulking gorilla glowered down at me, appearing fully intact. A placard indicated it was a theatrical prop from an old Broadway musical.

Between the two was a massive, obvious void. The dais was empty.

My eyes darted to the rear wall.

Specifically, to a hand-scrawled message taped there.

"Well, well." Tempe ran a hand over her mouth. "Someone's talking."

Together we stepped inside the case, carefully avoiding the pools of glass fragments.

The note was short and to the point:

*We have the T-800.*

*Transfer $50,000 to the Paypal address below, BY NOON TODAY, or the machine will be destroyed. Shrek was only the beginning.*

Tempe and I shared a glance.

"You have one of those grab bags from my signing?" she asked.

I tapped my pocket. "Right here." Then I snapped a pic with my iPhone.

Tempe checked her watch. "The deadline is less than two hours from now."

"Guess they're in a hurry." But something nagged at me. I stepped closer to the ransom demand. "How much did RoboCop say this thing was worth?"

"Half a million." Tempe tapped her lip, considering. "The low demand is shrewd. Small enough for the owner to obtain quickly, and not too much to risk to save the investment. But still a hefty chunk of change."

I nodded, but my uneasiness persisted. "But why not at least *try* to sell the Terminator on the black market? Even at half its value, they'd net five times as much money. If you're capable of getting that thing out of here undetected, why not take a shot at a bigger score?"

"Got me." Tempe did a slow 360, surveying the rest of the enclosure.

"See anything of use?" I asked, duplicating her move.

"Nothing obvious, and we don't have time to do this properly." Tempe pointed to the note. "One sheet of blank copy paper, affixed to the wall with blue-green duct tape. The tape is sloppily cut, as though done in a hurry, or maybe even ripped by teeth."

"Could it be tested for DNA?" I suggested.

"For a smash-and-grab robbery?" Tempe shook her head. "Probably not in the budget. But the tape itself might tell us something. Tape can usually be identified by manufacturer, and fibers within a roll can be matched microscopically."

"But we'd need to find the specific roll used." I looked out at the sea of vendors and booths. "How many rolls are floating around this exhibit hall? Hundreds? Thousands? I doubt we have that kind of time."

"Agreed." Tempe frowned, eyes still surveying the stage. "Other than the note, there's almost zilch to work with here. I wouldn't bet on finding fingerprints. Seems too professional."

I nodded, feeling deflated. "Other than the glass."

"True."

Tempe removed a swag bag from her pocket and pulled on rubber gloves. Then she squatted and selected a shard the size of her fingernail. "This is tempered glass. Very strong, and safety-designed to fragment upon impact. Similar to what's used in car windshields. Expensive. It takes a lot of force to break this stuff. Almost like . . ."

She rose. Scrutinized the red backstop of the case.

"What are you looking for?" I asked, spinning to follow her gaze.

"Bullet holes. A gunshot seems the most likely way to shatter one of these panes. I could whack at this glass all day with a golf club, and still get nowhere."

We examined the enclosure's rear wall top to bottom. No bullets. No holes. Then we scanned the floor for shells or casings. *Nada.*

"I guess that's out." Tempe's brow crinkled. "So how in the hell did the perp break in?"

I removed the gloves from my gift bag, snapped one on, then reached down and snagged a block of lime-green foam rubber. "Shrek sure took a beating."

Tempe nodded, hands on her hips. "It's weird. One figure slashed, one stolen, and one untouched."

"Maybe they're making a movie critique," I joked lamely. "No more CGI."

"Dr. Brennan?" Flanagan was outside the enclosure, looking impatient. "That's all the time I can spare. This debris is a public safety hazard, and the scene is drawing eyeballs like flies. Officer Palmer and I can't secure the area alone regardless. I have to let the staff clean up."

Tempe gave him a level look. "At least have your partner snap some photos."

"Will do." Flanagan barked new orders into his radio. A staticky voice responded.

Tempe carefully removed the ransom note, then began digging in her swag bag. "Who knew these suckers would be so handy?"

"You're always thinking ahead," I quipped.

Tempe snorted. "Thank my publicist, who'll likely kill me for abandoning my post. Can you fill your other glove with glass fragments, and then find a plastic bag in your kit? It's empty. Please gather a few sponge-rubber samples in there."

I did as instructed. Then, when Tempe wasn't looking, I slipped a few of each into my pocket. You never know.

Tempe placed the ransom note inside her own plastic bag, then handed it to me. "Tie off that glove, then seal and date the two baggies, please."

Which I did. But not before tearing a scrap of tape off the note.

I can't help myself.

"Okay, ladies." Flanagan shifted unhappily. The lanky officer appeared at his back, digital camera in hand. "Let's go. Palmer will shoot the scene, as you requested."

Tempe shrugged. "Best we can do, I guess. Come on, Tory."

With a last look at Shrek and Kong, I followed her from the case.

# CHAPTER 3

Three Yellow Shirts fired across the stage, toting brooms, dustpans, a vacuum cleaner.

Below, the Joker and a rail-thin woman in a navy pants suit were roping off the stage area. The looky-loos began to dissipate, drawn by more exciting action springing up elsewhere on the convention floor.

As Tempe and I descended, I spotted the boys waiting impatiently behind the cordon.

Skipper closed in like a falcon. "Find anything?"

Tempe handed Officer Flanagan the ransom note. His mustache actually bristled as he read the message.

Skipper, reading over his shoulder, paled, then yanked out his iPhone.

"Is there another way onto that stage?" Tempe asked.

Skipper answered in a strangled voice, offhandedly tugging at his turtleneck. "There's a trapdoor at stage center, but it's kept locked, and is barely large enough for someone to crawl through anyway. No one could steal the T-800 that way. Jenkins has the only key." He gestured toward the Joker.

*Interesting.*

Tempe must've had the same thought. "Mr. Jenkins?" she called.

The Joker turned and raised a shaky hand. Tempe waved for him to join us. He complied, though his every step oozed reluctance.

"Do you have the key to the trapdoor?" Tempe asked.

Jenkins nodded, not meeting her eye. "Locked it last night, after we sealed the display case. Did it alone, because my partner bailed early. It's still secure. Just checked."

*Only key, and alone. Veeeery interesting. But where was the other guy?*

Tempe opened her mouth to say more, but Flanagan interrupted. "Can you give me your report, Dr. Brennan?"

Seizing on the diversion, Jenkins slunk away to the front of the stage.

Tempe watched his retreat thoughtfully. Then she began to relay our findings, which were essentially nothing. Whoever snatched the Terminator had covered their tracks.

The pants-suited lady joined Tempe's circle, along with a white-bearded senior in a Hawaiian shirt. I slipped away to my friends behind the rope. Hi and Shelton were fidgeting impatiently, like dogs waiting to be unleashed.

Hi waved the VIP tickets at me. "Fifteen minutes until the *Bones* panel starts."

"They don't let you in late," Shelton warned.

Ben yawned, covering his mouth. "Anything interesting?"

"There's a ransom note." That got their attention. "If the owner doesn't fork over fifty K by noon, the robot gets it. Zero clues. No sign how or where it was taken."

Ben tucked his hair behind his ears. "How'd they break the glass?"

"Couldn't tell." I glanced at my aunt, now holding court to a rather large audience. "Tempe said it'd take a tremendous amount of force. We even looked for evidence of gunshots, but struck out."

Ben crossed his arms. "Something's bothering you." A statement, not a question.

I grunted, half lost in thought. "Whatever shattered that glass must've been loud. Yet no one seemed to hear it."

Hi pursed his lips, curious despite himself. "The note was handwritten?"

"Short and scribbled." I recited the exact wording of the message. "I think the author intentionally disguised his or her penmanship. The paper was secured by ragged pieces of blue-green duct tape."

"That won't help," Shelton mused. "Half these booths are held together by that stuff."

"True." Hi spoke slowly. "But the T-800 *had* to leave this room somehow. Which means a door. And if there were people around, even just a few—"

"The exit point would have to be nearby." I rose to my tiptoes. "How many do you see?"

Shelton pointed across the room. "Two on the far wall, but you'd have to pass the Marvel Comics area. Too risky. Plus those doors lead to the lobby. Aren't people usually lined up outside by six o'clock?"

Hi nodded. "Way earlier than that."

I jabbed a finger at the opposite wall. "They must've gone *that* way, into the bowels of the convention center. Otherwise they'd have wheeled the thing by hundreds of witnesses."

"Two doors," Ben noted. "Both off-limits to visitors."

I clapped my hands, energized. "That's where we start."

Hi looked stricken. "But . . . but . . . *Bones* . . ."

"We've got passes, Tory." Shelton, almost pleading. "*Passes.*"

Ben glanced at Tempe's knot of listeners. "Why not just tell those cops?"

I tilted my head, brow furrowed. "I don't even know how to answer that question."

"Here we go." Shelton buried his face in his hands. "Even on vacation we're gonna break the law. I might as well *burn* this costume. This isn't how a Jedi Master acts."

"How do we get through the gatekeeper?" Ben pointed to a yellow-clad female staffer monitoring the doors. "I don't think Hi's magic tickets will get it done."

"Wasted tickets," Hi muttered.

I chewed my lower lip. "We improvise. But first I have to throw Tempe off our scent."

That part was blessedly easy.

Tempe was surrounded by the two police officers, a gaggle of Yellow Shirts, and the iron-faced woman in the navy pants suit. Skipper was nearby, his RoboCop helmet tucked under an armpit as he whispered to the grandpa in the Hawaiian shirt. Both were scowling at Jenkins, who was removing his Joker makeup over by the steps.

Spotting me, Tempe extricated herself from the dour-faced company. "Sorry, but I'm stuck here awhile. That note has everyone riled up." She leaned close, pointed to the woman. "That lady runs the exhibition hall. She's furious about the incident, but doesn't have a clue what to do. The guy in the tacky bongo-drum shirt is the T-800's owner. I think he's been phoning his bank."

That surprised me. "He's going to pay?"

Tempe drummed her fingers on her leg. "I'd call it a coin flip. Officer Flanagan wants to trace the money, but I doubt they get set up in time—the deadline is in less than ninety minutes. I think he'd rather pay than lose his property. The short timetable has everyone jumpy."

My hands found my head. "This is so crazy."

Tempe nodded. "But you guys shouldn't waste your whole day with this. Go have fun. I'll text you when I can shake loose of this fiasco."

*Perfect.* "Okay. We'll watch that panel, then wander a bit, maybe check out . . ."

I trailed off. Had spotted the solution to my next problem.

Two event-staff badges were sitting on the stage steps. Unattended.

Tempe missed my distraction. "Let's grab lunch downtown after I'm done. I hear the Zombie Walk is an absolute riot. We could eat outside and watch."

"Yes." Eyeing the badges. "Good idea."

"Dr. Brennan?" Pants Suit was pointedly looking at her watch.

Tempe squeezed my hand. "See you later."

"Bye."

*Go time.*

Feigning nonchalance, I drifted toward the stage. Breezy. Natural. Nothing to see.

I leaned against the steps. Casually placed both hands behind my back.

The boys watched in total consternation. Ben squinted at me, then raised both palms.

*Hold on a minute, doofuses.*

Groping blindly, I snagged the badges and shoved them into my shorts. Fake yawn. Shirt tug. Then I strolled away, face blank, desperately hoping I hadn't been spotted, and that the badges wouldn't fall out along the way.

Thankfully, neither happened. I walked stiffly over to the boys.

"Let's go," I whispered needlessly, then attempted to melt into the crowd.

"Tory?" Hi's voice called from behind. "Did you get hit in the head?"

Ignoring him, I hurried ahead, crossing three aisles before ducking into a relatively quiet corner. When the boys caught up, I was practically dancing with impatience.

"Why the stealth sprint?" Shelton whined, pushing his glasses back up his nose.

Hi adjusted the waistband of his garish tights. "Not gonna lie, Brennan. You get weird sometimes."

"Zip it." I flashed the staff badges. "Lookie."

"Oooh." Hiram's eyes widened. "Very nice, but only two?"

"Best I could manage." I gave Hi and Shelton an appraising look. "I doubt your costumes would fly anyway. I'm planning to impersonate event staff."

"I look fabulous and you know it." Hi cocked his chin toward Ben. "You think taking *him* is a good idea? He's not exactly smooth with the cover stories, if you know what I mean. Meanwhile, that's kinda my wheelhouse."

Ben glared at Hiram, but I spoke first. "He's right, actually. Like it or not, this is Hi's specialty. And you *do* get that guilty look."

Ben snorted. "You think they're letting this—" he waved a hand at Hi's outfit, "—disaster back there? No chance."

Ben wheeled on Shelton. "What about you?"

"About me not sneaking around the bowels of this building?" Shelton lifted both palms. "I'm *fine* with that, believe me." Then he dodged Ben's eye. "Hi should be the one."

Ben looked from face to face, incredulous. "How is that going to work? Hi didn't pack a change of clothes, did he?"

Hi smiled. "No. I didn't."

Shelton's gaze remained glued to the floor.

I shuffled sideways. "You see, the thing is . . ."

Ben's eyes widened. He took a step back. "Oh no. Not in this lifetime."

"Ben, be reasonable," I said. "Hi can't wear what—"

"I'm not putting on those tights." Ben looked ready to bolt. "They're ridiculous. And he's been wearing them all damn morning. That's disgusting!"

"I resent that," Hi said primly. "I took a long shower at the hotel, plus I Gold-Bonded up to reduce chafing. The AC's been pretty strong in here, so everything's nice and dry—"

"I'll wear the Jedi stuff!" Ben's voice edged toward panic. "Hi can have my clothes, I take Shelton's, and *he* wears the tights."

Shelton scoffed. "My gear won't fit you, man. You're, like, twice my size. But you and Hiram aren't too far off, though he won't be needing your belt."

"Then let's just forget it," Ben pleaded. "Who cares about this stupid robot anyway?"

"Ben," I said sternly. "We have to help Tempe investigate. Stop being so sensitive."

I crossed my arms. "Now, are you a team player or not?"

○     ○     ○

Hi emerged from the men's room, cuffing Ben's jeans and straightening the black tee. "The fit's not too bad," he reported. "Baggy, but kinda gangster."

"Where is he?" I asked.

"Oh, Ben's not coming out." Hi chuckled. "Not until you're gone."

Then Hi whipped out his iPhone. "Don't worry, I snapped a shot when he wasn't looking and ran. Related note: Ben legitimately might kill me later. I'll need your help with that."

I giggled at the pic. Ben was squeezed into Hi's absurd red-and-yellow leotard, a horrified expression on his face. He looked a thousand shades of miserable.

He also looked . . . good. *Very* good, to be honest.

The spandex stretched tightly over his muscular frame. Ben might feel like a clown, but he'd turn a few heads in that getup. If he ever left the bathroom, that is.

I pushed the thought from my mind.

"You ready?"

Hi smiled broadly. "Just follow my lead."

I felt a spike of anxiety, but choked it down. "Okay, Hiram. But remember, we're investigating a crime, not demonstrating how clever you are."

"Why can't we do both?"

Hi slipped a badge around his neck and walked briskly toward the door.

# CHAPTER 4

The Yellow Shirt held up a hand as we approached.

She was no older than twenty—a short, squat woman squeezed into crumpled tan slacks and the ubiquitous event-staff polo. Square-cut bangs framed beady eyes that blinked behind a pair of banged-up wire-rim glasses. The rest of her lank brown hair was pulled back into a severe ponytail.

"Restricted area." She had a surprisingly high-pitched voice. "Staff only."

Hi smiled, held up the lanyard hanging from his neck. "Staff we are, thanks."

The bangs rose. "Where's your polo? Comic-Con staff are required to wear the official shirts. At *all* times."

The upraised hand dropped to a radio at her hip.

I did not want her to unclip it.

Hi's smile never wavered. "I hear you . . . Pam?"

The woman crossed meaty arms. "Stacey. Nobody named Pam works in the section."

Hi wheeled on me, voice scolding. "Because we're at the wrong door, no doubt!"

Startled, I actually stepped backward. "Sorry?"

I had no idea. Instinctually, I dropped my gaze to my sneakers.

"*Sorry* doesn't ice the caviar in Mr. Cruise's green room." Hi used air quotes to drive home the point. "I know you're new, Brittany, but this isn't going to cut it. At all."

Stacey edged a step closer. "Mr. Cruise? You mean, the movie star?"

Hi slapped a hand to his face, hiding an exaggerated grimace. "See what you did?" he hissed at me. Then suddenly, he was all smiles at Stacey. "Let's keep that last bit between the three of us, what do you say?"

"Oh, yes sir." Stacey nodded seriously, straightening her back. For a moment, I thought she actually might salute. "We're trained to be very discreet." Then her shoulders bounced as she broke out in giggles. "I'm a *big* fan!"

"Aren't we all." Hi winked. "We're his advance team. He's due to arrive any minute." He turned, fixed me with a second glare. "And he'll expect his cranberry lemonade when he does. And the rib platter!"

Stacey's face grew troubled. "Aren't you a little young to be working for . . . that particular gentleman?"

"Thanks. Get that all the time." Hi tapped his temple. "Scientology."

There was an awkward pause while he didn't elaborate.

"Oh." Stacey nodded slowly, confused but attempting to hide it. "Of course."

"Welp, no more time to waste." Hi took a step toward the door.

"The thing is—" Stacey squeaked, shifting her bulk to block him. "I *really* can't let you back there with just your badges. It's *restricted*. You're supposed to have a wristband, too, or be on some kinda list, I guess, although they never gave me one for this door. You see, *lots* of regular people try to sneak back there, so we have to be sticklers for procedure. My boss, Dave, said no exceptions."

Hi's mouth hardened. "Fine. Contact your supervisor. We'll need to be directed to the proper door."

As Stacey reached for her walkie-talkie, I flashed him a panicked look.

*What are you doing, Hiram?*

Fortunately, my anxiety played right into Hi's game.

Hands clasped before him, he gave me the evil eye.

"Stacey?" He didn't glance her direction as he spoke. "When you get ahold of Dave, let him know that someone needs to be escorted from the premises." To me: "This was strike *three,* Brittany. You're out. Curtains. Game over. The end. *Fin.* I need assistants I can count on."

Sensing Hi's play, I finally spoke. "I'm so sorry, Mr. Sto—house."

Wince.

But I kept going.

"I thought this *was* the way back to the green room." In my saddest-sack voice possible. "I didn't think we needed those wristbands until we got to the stage. Honest! I *can't* get fired, I need this internship for school. My dad will *freak . . .*"

Head dropping, I faked a few sniffles.

That's when I saw them.

Glass fragments. Dotting the floor mat on which we stood.

*Bingo!*

"Mr. Stohouse?" Stacey looked genuinely pained. "I think she made an honest mistake. No need for anyone to lose their job or nothing."

"This *mistake* is costing me time!" Hi thundered, hands flying up theatrically. "We need to be set up in *ten minutes,* but now we have to find another way back inside. And she forgot the wristbands."

Hi's performance was epic, but I was focused on the glass.

Shoulders heaving with a few fake sobs, I let my swag bag drop to the floor. Squatting to retrieve it, I scooped two tiny shards and shoved them in my back pocket. Then I curled my arms around my knees and blubbered like a baby.

Stacey broke. Wiping her hands on her slacks, she stepped aside and nodded toward the door. "How 'bout you hustle inside and we forget this ever happened?" Her wire rims glittered as she nervously scanned for observers, like a dealer watching for the cops. "Just this once. You can snag those wristbands and get 'em on. No one will be the wiser."

Hi sighed. "Very well. I'll excuse Brittany's debacle, but only because we're in a hurry." Then he leaned close to Stacey and whispered conspiratorially, "Mr. Cruise could be coming through *this* door at any minute. Keep your eyes peeled."

"*This* door? But they never . . . this really isn't the way . . ." Stacey visibly gathered herself, practically quivering with excitement. "You got it, Mr. Stohouse."

"No," Hi answered solemnly, stepping around the guard and hurrying me toward the forbidden door. "*You* have got it, Stacey. In spades. I daresay you're the best event-staff-security door watcher in this entire outfit. Bravo."

Reaching the exit, I noticed a "No Trespassing" sign taped to its face.

Felt a jolt of electricity.

Stacey watched in surprise as I tore down the sign on our way through.

"This way, no one can follow us," Hi said mysteriously. Nonsensically. "We were never here."

Stacey nodded grimly. Flashed a hidden thumbs-up.

When the door closed behind us, I blew out a sigh of relief.

"That only worked because she's a low-watt bulb," I pointed out.

"I factored that in," Hi insisted, hazel eyes twinkling. "But we'd better hustle. Wanna explain why you're stealing paper signs?"

I tapped the blue-green duct tape hanging from its edges. "Looks exactly like the type on the ransom note."

"Aha!" Hi nodded appreciatively. "What do you think it means?"

"At the very least, we know our crook used the same brand of duct tape as the event staff." I reached into my back pocket. "But when you factor in *these* beauties, I think we're on to something. These fragments were lying on the mat at Stacey's feet."

"Tape *and* glass." Hi rubbed his chin thoughtfully. "Still pretty circumstantial. Even if the Terminator came through here, what now? Where'd he go?"

"No idea." Slipping the fragments back into my shorts. "Look around."

We stood at one end of a cavernous concrete hallway—brightly lit and painted a dull green, with steel doors lining both sides. A train of hand carts were pushed against one wall. We were the only people in sight, but that was unlikely to remain true for long.

"This must be how they move things in and out of the exhibit hall," I said. "It's a perfect exit point. We need to find out where the statue was taken."

Hi ran a hand through his frizzy brown hair. "To the parking lot somehow? That'd be the obvious place."

"Maybe." But for some reason, I didn't think so. "I bet security's extra tight down there. Would the crooks really try to move the T-800 openly, like they owned it? Seems awfully risky."

Footfalls sounded from down the corridor.

"Heads up!" Hi whispered. "We need to keep moving."

He began walking purposefully toward an approaching Yellow Shirt.

A middle-aged Asian staffer with a stern expression and an official-looking clipboard moved to intercept us. His mouth opened, but Hi beat him to the trigger.

"Dave just radioed that the service elevator is on the fritz." Hi casually twirled the staff badge hanging from his neck. "What's the next best way to reach the garage level?"

I felt a stab of panic. *Please don't be Dave!*

The man's brow crinkled in confusion. "There's nothing wrong with the lift. I just rode it up here." He hooked a thumb over one shoulder. "See for yourself."

"That Dave." Hi shook his head in mock exasperation, moving purposefully down the hall corridor. "Thanks, bro."

"No problem." The man shrugged, then pushed through the door leading to Stacey's domain.

"Why do we need the service elevator?" I hissed, hurrying to keep pace.

"Act like you belong somewhere, and you will." Hi zoomed by the service elevator without breaking stride. "The key is to *look* like we know where we're going, and never hesitate. Ask a question first. Put the other person on the defensive. Always make it seem like you're in the middle of something important."

"Huh." At times, Hi was a genius.

We encountered two more staffers in rapid succession. Hi bombarded each with questions as we strode by, looking busy and mildly irritated. Fortunately, the deeper into the building we went, the less scrutiny we received. We were nearing the end of the hallway when I spotted more broken glass.

"Hi!" I snagged his arm, pointed. "Look. Right in front of an exit, too."

He peered back down the long corridor. "We've come a pretty long way, Tor. That glass might be totally random."

I dropped to my knees, picked a loose shard off the concrete floor, and set it to my left. Then I removed a floor-mat fragment from my back pocket, being careful not to confuse the two. Finally, I dug a piece I'd taken from the display case from my front pocket and placed it to the right of the other two samples.

"Or not." I shoved my nose within inches of the three fragments. "Glass has several distinctive properties. Not like a fingerprint, but unique enough to determine if shards came from the same broken pane."

I examined the sliver to my right. "We know the exhibit hall case was made of tempered glass. We need to figure out if either or both of these other two samples match it."

"Tempered?" Hi's leg worked as he kept watch down the corridor. Though a quick thinker, he'd be hard pressed to explain why I was on all fours, face to the concrete.

"Strengthened." I kept my focus on the three shiny bits before me. "Tempered glass is chilled rapidly as it cools, compressing the surface area. The process makes it more resistant to breakage. The glass composing the display case was likely also laminated—heat-sealed with thin layers of plastic between several panes of tempered glass. That makes it very tough to break. But when it *does* shatter, the glass cracks into a million tiny pieces. That's what we found onstage."

I picked up each fragment in turn. Held it to the light. Spun it in my fingers.

"I need a microscope," I muttered. "Straight eyeballing is so imprecise."

"Hey, genius." Hi tapped his temple. "Aren't you holding a bag of science tricks?"

"Yes!" I pulled out Tempe's packet and located the cheap magnifying glass. "*Perfect.* Good thinking, Hiram."

"It's what I do."

I pored over each shard again. Then once more, until I was sure.

"The observable properties are indistinguishable." I grinned up at Hi, then pumped a fist. "All three fragments appear identical in color, size, shape, thickness, and texture. We'd need a full lab work-up to be dead certain—fluorescence comparison, curvature analysis, assessment of optical and refractive properties, chemical composition—but right now I'm prepared to say that these shards originated from the same pane of glass."

"I didn't follow most of that, but fine. How'd a fragment get all the way out here?"

I rose and dusted off my shorts. "Locard's Exchange Principle."

"Picard?" Hiram's eyes went Frisbee round. "You mean Jean-Luc? Like, from *Star Trek*?"

"Edmond *Locard*." *Honestly.* "He was a pioneer in forensic science. French. Locard said that a perpetrator always brings something to a crime scene, and inevitably takes something from it as well. It's the basic principle of forensic science: 'Every contact leaves a trace.'"

Hi nodded thoughtfully. "So our perp unknowingly carried these fragments all the way down here. Leaving a trail like Hansel and Gretel."

"Yep. On his clothes. In his shoes. Inside the T-800 as he wheeled it away." I shrugged. "It doesn't matter *how* the jerk transferred trace evidence. Only that he did."

I picked up the sample fragments and placed them in their respective pockets. "Shards this tiny can get everywhere, and be shed for long periods after leaving the scene. Our thieves carried at least a few all the way down this corridor. To *this* door."

"Fine work, Dr. Tory. That means we need inside here." He tried the knob. The door swung open easily. "Ha! Who needs Shelton?"

We slipped through and closed the door behind us.

"Holy moly!" Hi put a hand to his chest. "I've died and gone to heaven."

The shadowy chamber was the size of a large classroom. Metal racks lined three walls, with several long tables running down the center, creating aisles. A rectangular window split the far wall, overlooking a grass field nestled between the convention center and shimmering San Diego Bay. A door in the far corner accessed an outdoor staircase that descended to the common below.

Hi was transfixed by what the racks and shelves contained.

"Good morning, sunshine!" He grinned ear to ear.

An astonishing array of wicked-looking medieval weapons filled the room. Hundreds of them. Swords. Maces. Axes. Spears. A dozen others I couldn't begin to identify.

The collection was both mind-blowing and inexplicable. What was all this stuff for?

Hi lifted a sinuous dagger from the closest rack. "Meh. Too light. Probably made of plastic." Setting it down, he knelt beside a broadsword one space over. "*Now* we're talking. This guy's a real head-chopper."

Then Hi frowned as he gave the blade a closer inspection. "Boo. The edge is blunted. These are prop weapons. Damn good ones, though."

A name was taped to each rack space. Some were normal: Steve Kirkham. Others were comically invented: The Blood Duke of Astorca. Half of the racks stood empty.

"This stuff must belong to the role-playing guys." Hi hefted a bronze helmet topped with an iron spike. "I heard they have mock battles or something."

There was a sudden clanging outside, followed by screams of pain.

We shared a startled look, then hurried over to the window.

On the field below, a dozen medieval warriors were attacking a makeshift castle wall. They brandished a variety of weapons, and wore armor of varying quality. Though howling energetically, many appeared to be in less-than-peak physical condition.

A smaller group was defending the barrier. The two sides hammered at each other, bellowing loudly, but moving at a careful speed. As each combatant was touched by a blade, he or she fell dramatically to the ground, thrashed about in agony, then lay still.

I covered my mouth in surprise, then chuckled through my fingers. "It's some silly war game. A mock battle. This is unbelievably—"

"Wonderful," Hi breathed.

I was astounded by the number of spectators. Elaborate, antiquated tents ringed the battlefield, which had been divided into quarters. Crude wooden stands had been set at intervals to provide for a better view. Surrounding it all were troubadours, wenches, barbarians, and other costumed players, congregating in fluid groups to watch, eat, flirt, and surreptitiously check their cell phones.

"A freakin' Renaissance fair!" Hi shook his head slowly. "But for comic book weirdos. It's like *300* out here. Who knew?"

"These people have been here awhile," I mused, gazing down at the sprawling encampment. "Probably since the convention began, but certainly by early this morning. How could someone sneak an iconic, life-sized robot out this way unnoticed?"

As we watched, the wall's defenders repelled the last of the attackers. The surviving warriors hooted and screamed, banging weapons against shields and slapping one another's backs. The raucous celebration carried all the way to where we watched.

I snorted. "Camelot held. Hooray."

A new group took the field, squaring their shoulders to face a second company forming up diagonally across the grassy expanse. A rare moment of quiet stretched, then dozens of horns began blaring. With bloodcurdling screams, the two groups charged forward at full speed and began whacking at each other.

I couldn't help but roll my eyes. "They do this all day?"

"All weekend," Hi confirmed. "This is serious business, Brennan. Stop hating."

"No, no." Feeling a twinge of guilt. "Good for them. Seriously. I'm glad they have such an . . . enthusiastic hobby. A passion. Whatever . . . this is."

I turned to face the equipment room. "But I'm at a loss. The T-800 isn't here, and I don't see how anyone could've moved it out."

"Should we look for more glass?" Hi sounded dubious.

"Might as well. You take the left side, I'll take the right."

We separated and circled the room, eyes searching the floor, the racks, the tabletops. Came up empty. We traded zones to double-check, but still found nothing.

Hi's shoulders rose and fell. "I guess we've run out of haystack needles."

I was about to agree when I noticed something over his shoulder. "Hi, check it out."

I slipped past him to inspect a corner rack. A sign declared the space to be the exclusive domain of Lord Mace of the Wolf Brotherhood and Bearer of Oathbreaker, the Sword of Despair.

*Please.*

The shelf held only three items: a ratty blue gym bag, a staff ID badge for someone named Frank Connors, and a half-used roll of duct tape.

*Blue-green* duct tape.

"That could match the ransom note." I was comparing the roll to my pilfered tape sample when it hit me. "Wait. Connors. *Connors!* RoboCop said someone named Connors was on his setup crew. But the guy didn't show up this morning."

I arched one brow. "Apparently the missing employee was into *war games.*"

"I'd say the brawl outside qualifies." Hi broke out his happy dance. "Oh man, we're so good at this! Let's toss his bag."

My fingers itched to do just that, but I resisted. "We can't. We don't have the right."

Hi looked at me curiously. "Hardly the worst of our crimes today, Tor."

But I was firm. "I'm not the NSA. We need more than a name and a roll of tape before riffling someone's personal belongings."

"Bo-ring," Hi sang. "That's not how Batman gets it done."

I made a decision. Quickly formed a plan.

A little crazy, but hey? I was improvising.

"Let's find Connors first." My eyes dropped to my watch. "We don't have much time. Text Shelton and Ben and have them meet us by the tourney field outside."

Hi began typing, then stopped. "Wait. Why are we going down there?"

I flashed a wicked smile. "Because you're going to infiltrate the—" my eyes flicked to the labeled rack, "—Wolf Brotherhood, and find Frank Connors. Check him out up close."

Hi's face went still. "I'm gonna do *what* now?"

"Today's your lucky day, Hiram. You get to be a knight."

# CHAPTER 5

"This armor smells like a goat's Porta-John."

"You'll be fine." Though, admittedly, I concurred with Hi's assessment.

Hi was wearing a gray tunic and head-to-foot silver chain mail, complete with a helm shaped like a vulture's head. He struggled down the steps, legs bowed, panting with exertion. I was legit concerned he might tumble all the way to the lawn below.

"I'm going to roast inside this tin can," he whined. "Why are you torturing me again?"

"We need to locate Connors." Reaching the bottom of the stairs, I shaded my eyes to look for Shelton and Ben. "After that . . . I'm not sure. The evidence points to him as our guy, but we've got nothing tying him to the crime. You need to find something."

Hi flipped up the visor of his ridiculous helm. "That's it? Find something?"

"You're the great improviser. Get close to him. See if he's acting strangely."

Hi gave me an exasperated look. "The dude dresses like Robin Hood, and is spending his convention bashing strangers with a fake

broadsword he named Oathbreaker. But I'm supposed to see if he's acting strangely. Got it."

We passed a quartet of minstrels having a smoke break, then skirted
a cluster of rainbow-colored pavilions. In moments we'd reached the
heart of the medieval festival. I spotted Shelton and Ben standing beside
a pretzel vendor. Waved.

"If Connors is our guy," I said quietly, "he must be watching the
clock, right? Checking his PayPal, or whatever. The ransom deadline is
less than an hour away."

Shelton's voice cut through the din. "What in the name of Grayskull?"

Catching sight of Hi, Ben broke out laughing. He now wore a brand-
spanking-new Hellboy T-shirt and shorts with the Warner Brothers
logo. "Nice look, Stolowitski. I'd have paid money to see this."

"You want me to start smiting?" Hi lifted his weapon—an ax blade
mounted on a long pole, topped by a spike with some kind of metal
hook on the back—and shook it at Ben. "I'm not sure what this is,
exactly, but I'll clobber you with it."

"It's a halberd." Shelton couldn't wipe the smile from his face. "Swiss
weapon, from, like, the fourteenth century. Fun fact: Vatican guards still
carry them on the job."

"Awesome," Ben quipped. "Why does doofus have one? And whose
armor is that?"

"Don't know," I admitted. "Let's hope the owner doesn't notice we
borrowed it."

I winked at Ben. "Nice look yourself, by the way."

"Best I could do." But his face burned scarlet.

"Rifle a gym bag?" Hi muttered. "Oh no! *That* would be wrong. But
steal some dude's entire Crusade Warrior costume? That's totally cool."

I ignored him. My ethical standards may *seem* arbitrary, but they're
not. We'd return the armor as soon as we'd finished with it. You can't
return someone's privacy.

*Fine. I'm ridiculous. But it works for me.*

"Just get close to this Connors guy," I repeated. "See if he's the one."

"How?" Hi stamped a chain-mail-covered foot. "What, he's just going to tell me he committed a felony?"

"I don't know. Use your—"

"You there!"

I nearly jumped from my skin, head whipping to a red-faced court jester jogging toward our group. He didn't look happy.

"Heads up," I warned, crossing my fingers that this wasn't Vulture Head's owner.

Hi flipped down the visor on his helmet.

"Gerald the Terrible?" the man intoned, eyes on Hi, blue-and-yellow bells trembling on his floppy purple hat. "I thought you'd reposed to the inn for mead and bread? You'd best hurry if you want to partake in the melee!"

"Err." Hi raised a hand awkwardly. Shrugged. "Um. Yeah."

The jester waved impatiently. "Come! Your company hath already assembled in the north corner of the battleground. You're attacking Skull Crusher's fortress. In *two* minutes."

"Right." Hi didn't move. Hitched up his stolen tunic. "Good."

Exasperated, the jester grabbed Hi by his chain mail and hissed in a sharp Boston accent, "You need to get out there *now,* Jerry. Run, or everybody's gonna be wicked pissed!"

"Is Frank Connors playing in this game?" I asked quickly.

The jester glanced at me in annoyance, resuming his regal brogue. "*Lord Mace* is defending Skull Crusher's fortress, milady. And he'll be most vexed if the *battle* is delayed."

"Of course." I tried a flirty smile. "And which one is Lord Mace, good sir?"

The jester stared as if I'd farted. "The one holding mighty Oathbreaker, of course!"

"Oathbreaker?" Ben scoffed. "What are you talking about?"

"The Sword of Despair," the jester answered testily. Then he stepped closer and whispered, dropping the stage speech, "Frank's the gigantic dude with the big red sword. Look, if you're gonna hang out back here, you need to get the basics down. We try not break character."

"Got it," Ben deadpanned, "my liege."

He winced as I kicked his ankle. "Understood, good jester. Our gracious thanks. Have a glorious battle."

There. That seemed perfect.

The jester snorted. "Work on it. Now come *on*, Jerry."

The peevish little fool marched Hi across the lawn to a group of men and women wearing similar chain mail. At his arrival, his fellow warriors began working themselves up, bashing weapons together and pounding one another's armor. Several welcomed "Gerald the Terrible" by thumping the side of his helm. Hi's knees wobbled as he struggled to keep his feet.

"Oh man." Shelton reached for an earlobe as we hurried for a better view. "This is *not* going to end well."

Ben couldn't stop chuckling. "He's going to get skewered."

A horn sound, triggering a roar from the opposite side of the field. A slightly larger group of warriors charged, howling like madmen, waving nasty-looking weapons above their heads. They flew toward Hi's company.

The defending fighters quickly formed an organized battle line.

One that did not include Hiram.

He stood ten paces in front of the defensive formation, arms slack at his sides, facing the avalanche of screaming humanity alone.

"Oh, damn." My hands rose to my face. "He froze."

Several defenders shouted at Hi, waving him back, but our friend didn't budge. He remained paralyzed, halberd drooping as the stampede of angry barbarians thundered closer.

"Hiram!" Hands now cupped to my mouth. "Run!"

I don't know if he heard, or if his self-preservation instinct finally kicked in. In any case, Hi dropped his weapon and fled before the attacking tide.

Not soon enough. Fake swords clashed up and down the line. Hi stepped on his own pant leg and went down in a rattling heap. As he attempted to rise, a behemoth wielding a five-foot scarlet broadsword thumped him across the helm.

"Ooh!" All three of us at once.

"That hurt," Shelton mumbled.

The battle ended quickly, with Hi's squad getting trounced. His companions lay strewn across the ground in various depictions of feigned violent death. The victors whooped and yowled, high-fiving in a most unknightly manner.

"Well," I said with a sigh, "at least that's over. Maybe he can . . ."

I trailed off as the obvious became clear.

The victors retreated across the field, still pumping their fists. Hi's company circled up in a tight bunch, bickering in angry tones that carried all the way to us. A man in an eagle-shaped helmet dragged Hi to his feet. His helm had been spun sideways, and it took two additional warriors to twist it back into place.

"I think *they* have to charge now," Ben said.

I flinched. "Yikes."

Abruptly, Hi shook off his helpers and retreated a step. Dropped to one knee.

"Quit now, Hiram," Shelton urged under his breath. "You're gonna lose your head."

Hi's portly frame shook. He dropped to all fours, shoulders heaving. Then, as two of his teammates rushed over, he bounced nimbly to his feet and jogged to the group. Hi waved off the offered assistance, his chest rising and falling as if he were breathing hard.

I felt an electric tingle crawl my skin.

"Oh crap!" All three of us at once.

"How about that?" Ben's eyes widened with surprise. "Who knew doofus had the stones."

Hiram was flaring.

"I'll kill him," I hissed. "Twice."

"Come on, Tor." Shelton shifted uncomfortably beside me. "He *is* wearing a helmet. And you did throw him into a freaking sword fight."

True. But still.

Ben's hand squeezed my shoulder. "Help him."

"What?" I stepped back. "How?"

But I knew.

You see, my friends and I have a secret.

Months ago, the four of us were infected by a canine supervirus. The vicious little pathogen was created in a secret lab, during an illegal experiment, and somehow made the leap to human carriers. We caught it while freeing the original test subject, my wolfdog, Cooper.

We were sick for days, then had to battle our own bodies as canine DNA infiltrated our human double helixes. When the dust settled, my friends and I had been forever altered, down to the core. We became a pack. We have the wolf buried deep inside.

And sometimes, the wolf comes out to play.

We don't know what will happen next. Primal canine genes now lurk inside our genetic blueprint. At times we lose control. Lose ourselves.

But our condition is not without certain . . . benefits.

"Watch his back." Ben caught and held my gaze. "Send him signals. You're the only one who can."

"You're as crazy as he is!" I spat. "I don't even have my sunglasses."

Ben arced a hand at the crowd. "Look around you, Tor. You don't need to hide your eyes. Not here. Half the jokers at this convention are wearing goofy contacts. I'd help Hi myself if had the ability. But I don't. Only *you* can link to our minds."

Crap. He was right.

In this crowd, glowing yellow eyes would get me applause, not suspicion. My biggest worry would be people wanting to take my picture.

Shelton tugged my elbow. "Help him, Tor. You can pull it off."

I looked back at Hi. Recalled the hammer blow he'd taken to the head.

*I did send him out there.*

"Blargh." Deep breath. "Fine."

Eyes closed. Gates open.

**SNAP.**

I trembled as the power burned through me.

Fire. Ice. Lightning bolts traveling my spine.

Raw energy unfolded inside me like a flower. Blasting my senses into hyperdrive.

My eyes opened. Gleamed with molten yellow light.

I *flared.* Hard.

The feeling is indescribable. The battlefield shifted into crystalline detail. I heard the slightest clink of armor, the faintest tickle of a lute string. My nose erupted with a mixture of heady scents. Boiled leather. Cut grass. Hot dogs. Sweat. I felt the slightest puff of breeze on my arms, could taste yesterday's rain on the wind.

Every muscle in my body burned with caged energy. Intensity. Focus.

Yet I'd never felt more exposed. More acutely aware of a crowd around me.

But Ben was right. Though several people looked directly at me, their eyes didn't linger. A girl in a Wonder Woman tank with yellow eyes was barely noteworthy in a fantasy land of costumed knights, superheroes, and comic-book characters. When it came to sensational, in this crew I just didn't rate.

A wave of screams rolled from the battlefield.

"It's on," Shelton warned.

I spotted Hi lurking near the edge of his group. This time, however, he'd dropped into a battle crouch, halberd up, one foot bouncing impatiently.

I only had a moment.

Closing my eyes, I visualized a glowing line connecting me to Hi.

It immediately sprang to life in my subconscious. Surprised and pleased, I wrapped the fiery cord with my thoughts. The cord became a tunnel. I drove my conscious mind inside, firing down its length.

*Hiram.*

*—I'm gonna whack that big bastard with this goofy ax if it's the last thing I do. Think you're so tough, Mister Stupid Medieval Death Jackass? Well, Hiram's got a surprise for you, ninja style! It's about to get REAL out here in the Dork Wars, you smug—*

*HIRAM!*

Hi jumped, then spun to face me.

*Tory? What are you—*

The horns sounded. There was no more time.

Sweat dampened my hairline as I sent. *I'm with you. Be careful.*

The horns died. Hi's company began loping toward their foes.

I dropped to a knee, my entire concentration on strengthening our link. Finding that final level of completeness. I *pushed,* somehow, willing the last mental barrier to crumble, and found myself looking through Hiram's eyes.

"Wow," I murmured. "I'm in. All the way, this time."

Shelton and Ben shifted anxiously, but didn't speak. Despite their urgings, I knew the telepathy made them uncomfortable.

Hi was bounding full-speed across the grass. He could barely see anything—the visor's vertical slats severely limited his forward vision, while the helmet's sides blocked his periphery. I backed out of his eyes, sensing I could help more from my own vantage point.

*Worry about what's in front of you,* I instructed. *I'll watch your back.*

*Okay.* Grim determination flowed through our link. *This sucks, by the way. Thanks for the terrible assignment.*

The attackers reached the defensive line.

All hell broke loose.

The fighting splintered into individual duels as sweaty warriors tattooed each other's shields. Occasional breakthroughs forced the touched combatant to drop theatrically in a mock agonizing death.

Hi was on the right, trading blows with a short, fat dude in what appeared to be a bearskin. Moving with flare-induced dexterity, he slipped inside his opponent's guard and fake-gouged his belly. The man fell with a bloodcurdling wail. Hi dropped his cumbersome halberd and grabbed his victim's sword, a better weapon for close-in fighting.

A knight in plate armor appeared over Hi's shoulder, weapon raised.

*Behind you! Spin left and low.*

Hi reacted instantly, dodging a falling ax as it swished through the space he'd just vacated. Then it was a simple matter for Hi to poke the man's back.

*TWO!* Hi thundered inside my head.

*Watch out. Dive right.*

Once again, Hi moved on command, narrowly avoiding another blow. Rolling to his feet, he drew a surprised *ooh!* from the crowd. There was a smattering of applause.

Hi turned, found himself face-to-face with the titanic red-bladed demon.

*You!* I felt Hi's lips curl into a snarl. *I owe you something, pal. Come get it.*

*Easy, tiger,* I cautioned. *Your back is clear.*

Most of the combatants were down, leaving ample space for single combat.

"Dare you defy Lord Mace!?" Connors screamed, holding aloft the massive scarlet broadsword. "Fool! You shall taste the bite of Oathbreaker."

"This freaking guy." Ben shook his head.

"Too much *Lord of the Rings*," Shelton agreed. "He's gone mental."

I stayed focused, nestled inside Hi's mind like a hitchhiker.

*Watch his hips.*

*I'm watching that freaking head-smasher!* Hi sent back.

*He's going to feint,* I warned. *Concentrate on his torso. You can't fake with that.*

On cue, Connors jabbed left, then spun in a tight circle, swinging Oathbreaker as hard as he could. Hi barely avoided the arcing blade. A murmur of excitement rippled through the crowd.

*Okay. So.* Even flaring, Hi was breathing hard. *Pretty sure this guy is trying to kill me.*

*Hi. Do this.* Unable to explain in words, I sent him an image from my brain.

Lord Mace was circling left, forcing Hi right. Following my instruction, Hi leaped forward, tucked into a ball, and then popped up close to his opponent's shield arm.

*Stick him in the side!* I mentally squealed.

Hi struck like a cobra, chopping at the unprotected flank.

But Lord Mace had the answer. Sidestepping deftly, he dodged the strike, then bashed Hi in the face with his shield. Roaring manically, Connors shoulder-charged Hi to the ground. Oathbreaker landed on his chest a second later.

The crowd *ooh*ed a darker note. Then roared with approval.

*Ouch.* Hi lay sprawled on his back. *That didn't work, Tor.*

*Sorry!* I cringed. *Didn't know you could hit with the shield thingie.*

As Hi lay dazed on the grass, Lord Mace stood over him, shaking his weapon in triumph.

Suddenly, Hi stiffened. *Tory. Look.*

*What?* I stepped back into Hiram's eyes. He was staring at his enemy's boot.

Coarse brown fibers curled from its metal rivets.

*Gotcha.*

# CHAPTER 6

We met Tempe in a dimly lit control room.

Three tiers of sleek modular workstations dropped, stadium style, to a window-wall overlooking the exhibit hall floor below. Each station was jammed with hard drives, monitors, microphones, and other high-tech equipment used to keep an eye on the convention.

Tempe was huddled with a small group on the second level. Officer Flanagan was there, along with the stone-faced woman in the navy pants suit, the T-800's owner in his ridiculous Hawaiian shirt, Jenkins the Joker, and a security technician.

Video was playing on one of the screens. No one looked happy.

I hurried to join them, the boys trailing at my heels.

"Did you arrest Connors?" I asked.

Tempe nodded, face troubled.

"Mr. Connors has been temporarily *detained* at Dr. Brennan's request," Flanagan answered. "But I've discussed the situation with Director Ahern—" Flanagan glanced at Pants Suit, "—and we've decided to cut him loose."

"What?" I couldn't believe it. "Did you check his bag? It was in the . . . knights' locker room."

Ahern's voice was ice cold. "We searched Mr. Connors's possessions, as we are permitted to do by contract with any vendor operating at the convention. There was nothing of interest."

She snapped her fingers at Jenkins, who'd found time to wipe off most of his face paint. The boy read from a folded piece of paper in a quavery voice. "Two empty sandwich bags, an empty water bottle, iPod with earbuds, and a box cutter. Duct tape, too, but that was next to the bag, not inside."

"Any vendor here can obtain tape of that kind." Ahern pursed her lips in disgust, then turned to stare down at the stage. "We hope Mr. Connors will be understanding of our mistake."

I followed Ahern's gaze. Connors was sitting on a folding chair beside Officer Palmer, arms crossed, a self-satisfied smirk on his face. He had an enormous head, with close-cropped, spiky brown hair, a pug nose, and small, angry eyes. Connors still wore his bulky chain-mail armor, but thankfully not the sword.

Connors drilled Officer Palmer with a disdainful sneer, which clearly made the gangly officer uncomfortable. He didn't appear worried in the least.

*Not good.*

"The glass," I said quickly. "It led us to the armor room, where we found tape identical to that used on the ransom note. Then Hi spotted brown fibers caught in Connors's boots. Did you compare them with King Kong?"

"We did." Tempe turned to Hawaiian Shirt. "Mr. Fernandez?"

"The hairs match, no question." The man seemed anxious, his fingers tugging at the hem of his bongo shirt. "But Connors helped position Kong last evening, and claims he wore the same shoes. He also says he overslept this morning. Jenkins says that Connors cut out early last night as well. He's out of a job—I won't abide shirkers on my team—but there's nothing pointing to him as the thief. Or anyone else, for that matter," he finished wearily.

"But that's why we're here, right?" I looked to Tempe for support. "To check the surveillance video and see who moved the T-800. It *has* to be Connors. No one else fits the evidence."

"What evidence?" Flanagan scoffed. "Come see for yourself."

The officer nodded to the security technician, who began typing. He had a long greasy ponytail, black fingernails, and letters tattooed across each knuckle. Ouch.

The screen reset. Shelton, Hi, and Ben crowded close behind me to get a look.

"Here's the main floor at six a.m." The tech tapped another key.

The exhibit hall appeared, still and silent. The shot panned back and forth, taking five-second intervals to cover the bottom third of the massive chamber. The stage was visible during each pass. The T-800 stood menacingly between Kong and Shrek, as intended.

"Badass," Hi whispered.

"Play it from here at four-times speed," Ahern instructed.

The image fast-forwarded. A handful of workers appeared, scurrying down the aisles at comic speeds. The tech halted the video just as Jenkins arrived.

"I got there right at six thirty," Jenkins said nervously. "On time. This is me waiting for Connors. At six forty-five, I gave up, and started setting the curtains up by myself."

"Move it along," Ahern said. The tech sped up the scene. As a group, we watched Jenkins linger impatiently, then begin rigging a massive curtain array that eventually enclosed the entire stage. At precisely 6:58 a.m., he tied off the last rope and left.

"That's it, folks." The tech spun his chair in a lazy circle. "Nothing else until the reveal at ten a.m. By then the robot was gonezo." He sped the tape to 8X. Each pass of the camera took only an instant as the room filled with workers, security, and, eventually, excited conventioneers.

The curtains never parted.

At the 10:00 a.m. mark the tech slowed the tape to normal speed. We watched Jenkins appear in his Joker costume, followed by Skipper as RoboCop, who pumped up a gathering throng before pulling the curtains with a dramatic flourish.

Only problem: Shrek was chopped up, and the T-800 was gone.

I didn't get it. "I don't get it."

"Join the gang." Flanagan sighed. "The damn thing just disappeared."

"It certainly did not," Fernandez hissed, tugging at his thick white hair. "It must've been taken in one of the moments when the camera panned away!"

"The intervals are less than five seconds." Tempe shook her head. "I could maybe see the thief sneaking *on*to the stage without being recorded, if he knew which camera to avoid. But to get the T-800 *off*-stage, then all the way to an exit? It doesn't seem possible."

"Well, it didn't just vanish!" Fernandez snapped.

"Of course not." Tempe peered through the window at Connors. "I still think he's our guy. Maybe Connors snuck under the stage and popped the hatch, then took the robot apart and removed it."

"Impossible." Fernandez shook his head vehemently. "The T-800 has over 500 parts, and most are welded together. You couldn't dismantle the Terminator without destroying it."

"I know." Tempe gave him a sympathetic look.

Fernandez's face went sheet white. "You think my machine is already destroyed?"

Tempe took a deep breath. "We have to consider the possibility."

"Then why break the case?" Hi wondered aloud, surprising everyone. "Or slash up poor Shrek?"

"To send a message, of course." Ahern made no effort to hide her irritation. "The bastard wants everyone to know what he'll do if he isn't paid. And the police can't even trace the account."

"In two hours?" Flanagan chuckled without humor. "That's way too small a window for all the parts involved. This guy knows what he's doing."

"The manufacturer assured me that case was unbreakable," Fernandez seethed. "Yet no one heard a thing? No one found an implement? I tell you, this must be a conspiracy!" His eyes darted around the room, as if considering a whole new possibility.

Flanagan sighed, stroking his bristly mustache. "In any case, we've got nothing to hold Connors on. I'll have to cut him loose."

"Let him go?" Fernandez raised his wristwatch helplessly. "The deadline is forty minutes from now!"

"Sorry." The officer shrugged. "I've got no legal basis to hold him."

I listened with a sick feeling in my gut as Flanagan radioed down to his partner by the stage. The younger officer nodded, then said something to "Lord Mace," who rose and stretched dramatically. Connors glanced directly at us, flicked a mock salute, then began sauntering away.

The queasy feeling amplified. "Connors knows where we are."

Tempe nodded. "He probably knows where the cameras are, too."

"Well, this has been a debacle." Director Ahern rounded on me. "On to the next matter. Care to explain how you accessed several restricted areas of this convention center?"

I was saved by a sharp voice.

"Wait."

Surprisingly, it was Shelton.

He was watching the screen, where the surveillance tape was still looping. "Don't let Connors go yet! There's something weird going on here."

"You sure?" Tempe whispered.

Shelton nodded rapidly, his thick lenses gleaming in the monitor's reflected light.

"Officer Flanagan?" Tempe called. "Please hold Mr. Connors for one more minute. We may have something."

Flanagan frowned, but radioed down to Palmer, who hurried to stop Connors and direct him back to the chair. Lord Mace's posture conveyed pure outrage, but he complied.

"What is it, son?" Ahern was at the end of her patience.

Shelton looked to the tech, who hadn't moved from his chair. "May I?"

The man frowned. "You know how to use this, dude?"

"The Yamaha 5500 series? No problemo."

The tech grunted, but stood, allowing Shelton to slide into his seat. He rewound the tape, then watched intently for a full minute. The rest of the group gathered behind him with varying degrees of enthusiasm.

"There." Shelton froze the frame.

Flanagan's brow furrowed. "There what?"

"The curtain." Shelton toggled back a few frames, then forward. "It moved."

I saw it, too. "Good eye, Shelton."

My finger tapped the screen. "Up high, above the rope. Watch that fold." As the camera panned one direction, the left edge of the curtain overlapped the right, but as the lens swept back, the sides had switched position. Then the fabric rippled, ever so slightly.

"Okay. The curtain moved." Fernandez rubbed his chin. "So what?"

"So we check it out." Tempe was already striding for the door.

○     ○     ○

It took ten minutes to locate a ladder. Another five to maneuver it through the crowd, and ten more to return the curtains back to their original position. Fernandez was sweating through his aloha shirt, eyeing the clock as it ticked toward noon.

I'd overheard his phone call making financial arrangements.

If push came to shove, he'd send the money. And pray.

"Jackpot." Tempe motioned me up onto the ladder with her. I

scampered up the rungs carefully while Jenkins and Officer Palmer braced us below. Tempe was inspecting a section of curtain ten feet above the stage floor. "Check it out."

Just shy of the edge, three holes sliced through the plush red velvet.

"It *was* a gun." My eyes shot to the back wall of the display case. "But how are there no bullet holes?"

It hit me in a flash. "Unless . . ."

I spun awkwardly, peering back across the exhibit hall. Calculating in my mind.

*That T-shirt booth. Five rows up, maybe six.*

Tempe followed my gaze. Then her eyes popped. "Of course."

"Given the angle," I blurted, "I'd guess somewhere near that T-shirt emporium."

"Five rows up, maybe six." Tempe's eyes twinkled. "Want to check it out?"

"Um, *yeah*."

We scurried down the ladder, nearly knocking each other off in our haste. Stepping to the floor, I noticed Connors watching our movements. The smug look was long gone.

"Keep an eye on him," I said to Flanagan, who nodded tightly, taking a step closer to the suspect.

"We'll need the ladder over there." Tempe pointed to the far wall.

Jenkins and Palmer exchanged pained glances, but hauled the twelve-footer across the convention floor, fighting the relentless foot traffic. Eventually we reached a massive T-shirt display. A variety of shirts rose twenty feet in a grid, like a giant checkerboard. Altogether, ten rows of twenty shirts each hung from hooks nailed to a thick wooden backboard. Employees retrieved the higher offerings using long, hooked poles.

While Director Ahern placated the furious booth operator, we positioned the ladder at the foot of the display. Then Tempe and I climbed up, past the first five rows, stopping every rung to glance back over our shoulders.

"Tempe, I see it!" I was face-to-face with a rack of yellow He-Man T-shirts.

There. Right below the DC Comics logo. Three singed holes.

Drawing level, Tempe gently pushed the hangers aside. Found three slugs buried in the wooden backboard.

"You were right," Tempe said. "The bullets were fired from *inside* the case. Which almost certainly makes the robbery an inside job. Jenkins or Connors."

"Or Skipper," I added, though I thought it unlikely.

We clung to the ladder a moment, each lost in thought.

"But how'd they get the T-800 out of this hall?" Tempe muttered.

A gong went off in my head. I nearly slipped from the rungs.

"He didn't."

# CHAPTER 7

"Okay, young lady. Everyone is waiting."

Director Ahern's tart words sent a shiver down my spine.

But I *knew* I was right.

I'd led everyone back to the stage. Hadn't shared my theory, not even with Aunt Tempe.

I wanted to be sure.

And, being honest, was enjoying the drama.

*Unless I'm wrong. Oh God, don't let me be wrong!*

"Go on," Tempe encouraged, the ghost of a smile tugging at her lips. Did she guess? "Your show, Ms. Brennan."

My knees shook as I climbed to the platform, walked to the middle, and faced the gaggle of irritated officials. Behind them, a sea of conventioneers had stopped to watch.

Suddenly, *I* was a Comic-Con attraction.

*Just lay it out, piece by piece.*

"We found three slugs embedded in woodwork across the hall." I pointed to where the rack of He-Man shirts hung, then spun to face the wreckage behind me. "Additionally, three bullet holes were found in the curtain covering the shattered pane. This glass was laminated and heat-tempered, making it extremely difficult to break. That's why it was used for the display case in the first place. Therefore, it's clear that our thief somehow gained entry to the case, and shot his way *out,* not in."

Director Ahern raised her hand sarcastically. I chose to treat it as an honest request.

"Yes, ma'am?"

"All of the broken glass fell *inside* the case," she argued. "How could that be, if the shots were fired from within?"

"A common mistake," Tempe answered with a rueful head shake. "One I unfortunately made myself. Glass flexes when struck by bullets, then snaps back, causing shards to spray in the direction from which the shots were fired. The fragments can fly up to fifteen feet *toward* the shooter. This explains why all the debris ended up inside the case."

"But that case was sealed last night, with all three characters inside." Skipper glared at his underlings—Jenkins stood alone, fidgeting nervously, while Connors sat, stone-faced, under the watchful eye of Officer Flanagan. "Those two were the only workers with access. Jenkins had the sole key to the hatch in the stage floor."

"I never went back inside!" Jenkins raised both hands, voice pleading. "I locked the hatch after Connors bailed last night, and didn't open it again. Not even this morning, when that jerk failed to show for setup. You saw the tape—I just arranged the curtains and left."

Connors said nothing. Watched me like a hawk.

"What you've said was obvious upon locating the bullets," Fernandez groused, eyeing me with ill-disguised impatience. "But we still don't know where my robot is."

"And we're almost out of time." Skipper, green-faced as he held up his watch.

"I've got three minutes to make the transfer or I lose my investment." Fernandez shot a black look at Connors. "I can't allow that to happen. I won't. I'll have to pay."

"Cheer up." I spoke with more confidence than I felt. "I don't think the T-800 is in any danger."

Connors shifted in his seat. Leaned forward. I didn't miss it.

*Nervous, big boy?*

I stepped inside the glass enclosure and approached the mutilated troll. "Why was Shrek hacked to pieces?"

"To send a message," Flanagan replied slowly. "As Director Ahern said, the perp wants us to know he'll destroy the robot if not paid."

Ahern, Skipper, and Fernandez nodded in unison.

I turned to Fernandez. "How much is Shrek worth?"

"What, the replica?" He stroked his snowy beard, considering. "Almost nothing, actually. A few thousand dollars at most. He's just a prop once used in a Thanksgiving Day parade."

"So why would you care if *Shrek* was destroyed?" I scooped a piece of green foam rubber from the floor. "He's nowhere near the Terminator's value."

"Perhaps the thief didn't know that?" But Ahern's eyes had narrowed.

A *eureka* expression crossed Tempe's face. "Oh, that's clever," she whispered.

Heads swiveled her direction, but Tempe nodded toward me. "Tell them."

Before I could, stupid Hiram stole my thunder, bouncing forward and shouting, "Shrek wasn't vandalized. He gave birth!"

"What?" Flanagan rounded on my chubby companion. "Son, this is serious—"

"Hi's right." I ripped a chunk from the mangled troll. "Shrek wasn't chopped up to send a message. He was sliced open because the person hiding inside needed out."

Everyone froze.

Except Connors. The big man rose. Arched his back.

*Got you, you oaf.*

"I don't . . . why would . . ." Confusion was plain on Fernandez's face.

Officer Flanagan rounded on Skipper, Connors, and Jenkins. "Inside job. The suspect *knew* that figure was hollow, got inside undetected, and waited."

"This is fascinating, but pointless." Director Ahern slammed a fist into her open palm. "The T-800 is gone. We don't know how it was removed. We don't know where it is!"

"Of course we do." I crossed to King Kong and rapped his belly with my knuckles. "It's right here. Inside this big, misunderstood ape."

For a few seconds, everyone was struck dumb. All but Tempe, who chuckled.

Behind the officials, the costumed crowd murmured excitedly.

*Sweet Lord in Heaven, I better be right.*

"It's a theatrical costume." Shelton had both ears in his hands. "A giant monkey suit."

"Operated from within." Ben nodded appreciatively. "Meaning Kong is hollow, too."

"Mr. Skipper?" I fought to keep my voice steady. "How is Kong opened?"

"Zipper." Skipper's face was slack with shock. "In back."

It took me a moment to locate the black tab at the base of Kong's foot. I yanked upward, my heart hammering in my chest.

*Please oh please oh please oh please . . .*

The zipper rose to chest level, then jammed. Kneeling, I shoved the furry sides apart.

Came face-to-face with an evil metallic grin. Red eyes glared at me with hatred.

"Whaa!" I leaped backward.

Then, face burning with embarrassment, I forced the zipper higher.

More hands joined mine—Jenkins and Skipper magically appeared behind me, panting with relief. Soon we'd parted the suit enough to drag the T-800 out into the light.

The crowd roared. Applause thundered from the costumed horde.

Skipper squealed with delight as he examined the robot for damage. Fernandez was gasping, tears glistening in his eyes, shaking every hand he could find.

Connors took a small step away from the distracted cops.

Bumped right into Ben. "Going somewhere, Lord Mace?"

Shelton pointed both index fingers at Connors. "This dude had monkey fur all over his boots!"

Officer Flanagan placed a hand on Connors's shoulder. "Why'd you do it, boy?"

Connors face was granite. "I didn't do anything. Good luck proving it."

*Damn.*

I looked to Tempe. Her face mirrored mine.

We'd solved the crime, but nothing tied to our suspect. Just some glass, tape, and a few stray costume hairs. Connors could explain away each with little effort.

"The gym bag!" Hi slapped his leg as if he'd just solved a riddle. "I get it now."

Flanagan gave him a questioning look.

"Provisions." Hi winked at Connors. "I get you, Lord Mace. Packed a few sandwiches and some tasty *agua* for your stay in Troll Town? Snuck inside last night, before Jenkins locked the hatch? No wonder he couldn't find you. And you were still inside this morning, until the curtain went up and you used the box cutter to slash free. Well played. Almost."

Connors sniffed. "Nice story. Did my box cutter shoot three bullets through the glass?"

Tempe crossed to the gym bag, which was sitting on a chair by the stage. She'd somehow acquired a pair of tweezers. Squatting, she began to inspect its exterior. Her fingers darted, plucking something from a seam.

"Care to explain this?" Tempe held aloft a small bit of shredded green foam rubber. "There are tiny pieces of Shrek all over your bag, Mr. Connors. Yet you haven't been onstage since the robbery occurred."

"Oh snap!" Hi made explosion hands at Connors. "You just got Picard-ed!"

"Locard," I corrected, smiling coldly at the hulking suspect. "He's right, though. All of the trace evidence points to you."

"That stuff has been flying everywhere," Connors said defensively, but a sheen of sweat now glistened his brow. "You can't prove I cut him open. You can't prove *anything*."

"He's got a point," Flanagan said softly. "Without the gun, or any bullet casings . . ."

*If only we'd found the gun in his bag.*

Skipper and Jenkins finished setting the T-800 back on its dais. They exchanged a nervous laugh, like two little kids who'd somehow dodged a certain punishment. The crowd surrounding us gave a lusty cheer.

As they dusted the Terminator, I noticed a black plastic box attached to its hip.

"Mr. Skipper?" I waved for his attention, pointed. "What's that?"

"It's the weapon holster." He flipped it open absently. "We don't bring the . . ."

His voice cut off. Skipper gaped into the box.

I knew what he was seeing.

"Officer Flanagan?" Tempe had been paying attention. "I think they found something on the machine."

Flanagan nodded for Palmer to watch Connors, then climbed onstage and peered over Skipper's shoulder. Pulling a handkerchief from his pocket, he reached down and removed a .45 caliber handgun from the T-800's holster. Then, surprisingly, he carefully set the gun down and reached back inside, retrieving a long black cylinder.

"Gun and silencer," Flanagan announced. "Excellent. And I think I see casings in there, too. Maybe we'll find some prints after all."

"Silencer!" Hi smacked his hands together. "*That's* why no one heard the shots. Brilliant. And he would've gotten away with it, if it hadn't been for us meddling kids."

Shelton punched Hi in the shoulder. "C'mon, man. *Scooby-Doo?*"

"I saw the whole gang walk by here earlier," Hi shot back, rubbing his arm. "Dead serious. Their Daphne needs work, though."

Officer Palmer grinned at Connors. "We'll just check the registration on that piece, hey, friend?"

Connors shrugged, unfazed.

*Crap. It's not going to be registered to him.*

But Tempe had the answer. "I suggest you bag the suspect's hands. Paper is best."

"Bag his hands?" Palmer gave her a strange look. "Why?"

"That gun was fired three times within the last four hours." Tempe looked Connors squarely in the eye. "Gunshot residue likely transferred to the shooter's hands. A simple swab should give us the answer."

Connors's eyes widened. Then narrowed. "I'm not doing any test."

He took a half step backward, was met by Palmer's restraining hand. "Should I cuff him, boss?"

Flanagan nodded as he descended the stairs. "Frank Connors, you are under arrest for—"

He got no further.

Connors turned and sucker-punched Palmer full in the stomach. The lanky officer dropped to his knees with a silent wail as the air exploded from his chest. Then Connors shoved Ben aside and barreled into the crowd before anyone could react. In moments he was lost in the shuffle.

"After him!" Flanagan shouted, tripping on the last step and tumbling to the ground.

Palmer rose with a sickly wheeze and gave chase, as Director Ahern screamed and waved her arms. Staffers converged, then a wave of Yellow Shirts went scrambling down the packed aisle in Connors's wake.

"Oh my." Fernandez pawed at his chest, staggering, face scarlet beneath the shaggy white beard. Tempe dashed over, steadying the elderly man and easing him to the floor. Skipper and Jenkins jumped from the stage, then looked at each other, unsure what to do. Flanagan hurried over to assist Tempe, barking into his shoulder radio.

Ben scrambled to his feet, his face a thunderhead. "I'll kill that bastard!"

"Wait!" Shelton jumped on Ben's back an instant before he bolted in pursuit. "I know where Connors is going."

That got my attention. "You do?"

"What?" Hi sputtered. "Where? How?"

Ben shrugged Shelton off his back, but turned to listen.

"What's the one thing we know Connors won't leave here without?" Shelton whispered.

"Of course!" I felt a rush of adrenaline. "Good thinking."

"I want to catch that jerk," Ben spat. "Personally."

I glanced at Tempe. She and Flanagan seemed to have Fernandez in hand. Director Ahern was waving at a pair of EMTs hurrying through the press of bodies as Skipper and Jenkins helped clear a path. I heard several debates as to whether the whole episode was being staged.

No one was paying us any attention.

"Okay." Deep breath. "Let's bag this jackass."

We snuck off as quietly as church mice.

# CHAPTER 8

Connors crept into the silent equipment room.

Forgoing the lights, the big man wasted no time as he beelined for his rack. He hefted Oathbreaker with a satisfied smile.

I slipped from the shadows a dozen paces behind him. "Hey, Frank."

Connors spun, dropping into a fighting stance.

I winked. "Had a feeling *Lord Mace* wouldn't abandon the Sword of Despair."

"You're a very stupid girl," he hissed. "Get lost, or you'll meet this blade personally."

"Tut-tut," Hi chided, stepping out of the darkness at the opposite end of the aisle. "Threatening an unarmed girl, Lord Mace? What would the Brotherhood say?"

"You think I won't bash the both of you?" Connors's head whipped back and forth, eyes narrowing, his whole body quivering at the prospect of impending violence. "You're quick, fat boy. But not quick enough."

Connors took a step down the aisle toward me.

"Hiram and I will take a pass," I said airily. "Unfortunately, we've already spent our strength for the day."

Ben ghosted to my side, eyes blazing with golden fire. Startled, Connors pivoted, eyes darting back down the aisle toward Hi. Shelton's gleaming irises stared back.

"*These* guys, however, have plenty of punch left in them," I said softly. "You probably shouldn't test them."

"Stupid parlor tricks!" Spittle flew from Connors's mouth. "Do you think I'm an idiot?"

"Yes, actually." Ben cannoned forward and shouldered the lummox in the chest.

Caught by surprise, Connors flew backward onto the concrete floor. Shelton swooped in and slammed an iron helm over his fat head. Then Ben's foot connected with a thunderous clang, spinning the big man sideways.

"Booyah!" Shelton fired two shooters at Connors's prone form. "Pow-pow, yo! That's why you don't mess."

Connors lurched to his feet, tree-trunk arms flailing. One elbow caught Shelton in the shoulder, careening him into a nearby rack. Then he kicked out blindly, catching Ben's shin and dropping him to the floor.

Connors tore off the helmet. "Pathetic cretins! You will never defeat Lord Mace!"

He spotted Hi, who heroically dove under a table. Oathbreaker slammed its surface as my friend scurried into the next aisle.

Regaining his feet, Ben shoved Connors halfway down the aisle.

Connors stared in surprise. I doubt many people had knocked him off balance before.

But he'd never tangled with a flaring Viral.

Ben stalked forward, eyes burning with yellow light.

"Y-your eyes," Connors stammered. "I've never . . . what's that . . ."

"Silly knight," Ben hissed. "We're the *real* Wolf Brotherhood."

A look of horror filled Connors's face. Abruptly, he flung the helm at Ben, forcing him to dodge. Then he charged, knocking me to the ground and disappearing out the door.

"Crap!" I sprang to my feet. "After him!"

As one, we fired in pursuit, out the door and down the stairs to the field below.

I was sure he'd flee to the battlefield, but Connors surprised me by racing along the outer wall of the convention center. After bullying through a line of Hello Kitty freaks, he vaulted a security fence and bolted toward the marina.

"After him!" Ben tore after Lord Mace, making no effort to conceal his flaming eyes. Several girls dressed as Power Rangers stopped to applaud. Shelton was a step behind, with me trailing as best I could.

Hi fell behind, wheezing and sweating. "I requested no sprinting."

Connors raced down a concrete quay bordering the waterfront. Spotting a couple at an access door to one of the marina's secure docks, Connors bashed into them, waving his ridiculous sword, then snatched up their pass card and opened the gate. He slammed it shut behind him, then jogged down the pier out of sight.

The couple ran toward the hotel in a panic. Ben reached the security gate and tested the handle. It wouldn't budge. He shook the bars in frustration.

Shelton arrived at Ben's side just before I did. "Can we climb over?"

Hi was still twenty yards behind, moaning in agony.

"No. There are spikes on top." Ben glanced to the side. "But this fence only extends ten feet each way. It's only meant to block off the dock."

Shelton grabbed an ear. "So?"

Ben smiled grimly. "Time to get wet."

He hurried to where the fence ended, took a breath, then leaped into the placid water eight feet below. Shelton and I watched him swim over to the dock and drag himself up.

"Come on!" Ben wiped saltwater from his long black hair. "It's easy."

"Jump into that?" Shelton's golden eyes narrowed with distaste. "You don't swim in a harbor! We could get tetanus. Or rabies. Something bad."

"Quit whining." I vaulted down after Ben, disturbing a family of ducks sunning by the water's edge. Ben helped haul me up onto the dock. I heard a splash behind me. Moments later Shelton sputtered up and over the side.

Shelton spit out a mouthful of ocean water. "Damn, I lost my flare."

"Oh, great!" Hi called down from the quay, red-faced and sweaty. "Wonderful. The hotel pool's not good enough for you guys?"

But he launched himself over the railing anyway. "Cannonball!"

Sopping wet, Shelton and Ben dragged him from the water.

"We have to be careful," I cautioned, surveying the dock. It stretched fifty yards ahead of us, both sides packed with pleasure boats of all kinds. "Connors had a gun before."

Ben was still flaring, but Lord Mace was the size of an ox. We needed to utilize our numerical advantage.

With Ben in the lead we crept down the dock, scanning each slip as we passed. In moments I spotted Connors hastily untying a twenty-foot yacht named *My Second Wife*. Nice.

"How'd he get a boat like that?" Shelton whispered.

"He's stealing it, dummy." Ben looked to me. "Plan?"

"What, seriously?" I snorted a nervous laugh. "Distract him. Then someone whack him with something heavy, and hope he falls down."

Shelton grabbed both ears. "Not good, guys."

"No, wait!" I waved the boys close. "How about this?"

○     ○     ○

*My Second Wife* had been backed into a slip with its stern facing the dock. Connors was kneeling on the vessel's bow, his back to the pier, grimly untangling a knotted line.

I snuck aboard, then crept up three steps to the flying bridge. Connors was visible on the foredeck below me.

"Hey, Frank," I called down from above. "Where you headed?"

He flinched, then glared up at me, eyes filled with pure hatred. "You just don't know when to quit, do you?"

Connors moved for a slender, foot-wide walkway along the boat's port side, which allowed access to the stern. He found Hi there, wielding a long hooked pole. "Come at me, bro. I bet your balance sucks, since you're the size of a tanker truck."

Connors growled, then reversed himself and hurried to the starboard side of the vessel.

Found Shelton blocking that way with a spear gun. "Feeling lucky, dude?"

Connors stepped back, frustration painted on his face. "You kids are done. I'm through playing games." He stepped to the center of the bow, grabbed a crossbeam, and began hoisting himself up toward the flying bridge. Toward me.

"No way to stop me now, little girl." Connors slapped one hand over the railing. "Which one of you wants to drown first?"

Then he noticed Oathbreaker's tip, an inch from his eye.

"You were saying?" Then I whirled the broadsword overhead. Slammed the flat of the blade down on his fingers.

Connors fell back with a yowl, landing hard on the bow and shaking both hands in pain.

He failed to notice a dark shape slip from the water onto the deck behind him.

Ben, eyes glowing, lifted the boat's anchor.

Connors rose, furious eyes locked on me. "You never should've touched my sword."

The anchor took him in the side of the head.

I winced. "Night-night, Lord Mace."

○   ○   ○

Palmer opened the back of a squad car. Connors, in handcuffs, grunted as the young officer "accidentally" smacked his head against the doorframe in the process.

"Oops." Palmer slammed the door with a satisfied smile.

I hoped Lord Mace's headache lasted a week.

I returned my attention to Flanagan, who'd just finished reading us the riot act.

Schooling my face, I tried to look chagrined, nodding in the right places, expressing contrition for our reckless behavior. But the truth was, I couldn't help feeling a bit smug.

We'd tracked a suspect, foiled a robbery, and even run the bad guy down.

Pretty solid day's work.

Tempe walked over to where the four of us were sequestered on a stone bench, dripping wet, trying to hide our smiles. She sighed. "I've no idea what to tell your parents."

"As little as possible?" I suggested.

"Undoubtedly. How'd you track him down?"

"The weapon." I gestured to the giant scarlet broadsword tucked under Flanagan's arm. "No way Connors was leaving without mighty Oathbreaker. It's his whole identity."

Tempe shook her head. "You know we have to give statements at headquarters tomorrow."

"I figured."

"Connors claims Ben and Shelton are possessed."

"Crazy."

Tempe seemed about to say more, then shrugged. "Good work, Tory. All of you. They wouldn't have solved this one without your help. Fernandez would've paid the ransom."

I felt a stab of concern. "He okay?"

Tempe nodded. "Just a little too much excitement. He'll be fine."

"You were great, too, Aunt Tempe." I was attempting to cover the fireball of pride burning inside me. The boys stayed quiet, drying contentedly on a warm San Diego afternoon.

A gentle breeze blew across the marina, stirring my hair into tendrils. The sun hung at its apex as gulls chirped all around us, dive-bombing the surface of the bay in search of food.

The day simply couldn't get any better.

"My iPhone is toast." Hi shook the waterlogged device, then shoved it back into his damp pocket. "But if I recall correctly, the *Game of Thrones* panel starts in an hour."

Shelton smiled ingratiatingly at my aunt. "Think Director Ahern could score us some more VIP passes? We missed *Bones* while saving the day."

Tempe snorted. "I'll ask. I'm not sure where she stands on you guys. You broke about a hundred rules."

Ben flashed a rare grin. "Tell her she can keep the sword."

"Will do. Hang tight." Tempe headed over to the cluster of suits, leaving us alone.

I looked from Hi to Shelton to Ben. Didn't know what to say.

Decided nothing was needed. Instead, I stuck out a fist.

Three more appeared. Banged mine.

Then I leaned back on the bench, lacing my fingers behind my head. "Not bad, boys. Not bad."

# SPIKE

# CHAPTER 1

I was staring into the abyss.

Giant, brimming, sky-blue wells of horror, only moments from unleashing a torrent of mascara-infused tears.

"I already looked in there!" Whitney moaned, wrapping her arms around her chest and stomping a foot peevishly. Her snow-white wedding dress shimmered in the afternoon sunlight that poured into the dressing room. Perfect blond tendrils bounced precariously atop her head. "I'm telling you, Tory, it's *missing*!"

I dropped her Louis Vuitton bag to the floor, struggling to keep my annoyance in check. "Okay, Whitney. But I'm sure it's around here somewhere. We double-checked everything before we left the island."

Whitney's hands seized the sides of her gown. Then she flinched, releasing her grip and frantically smoothing the delicate white silk with her palms. She'd been a live wire all morning, from the moment I'd first spied her at dawn, practicing her walk down the aisle.

"Can you describe it for me again?" Voice calm. Gaze steady. Afraid that if I looked away, she might crumple to the floor.

My soon-to-be stepmother's eyes bugged. "It's *blue*, obviously!"

"Yes, Whitney, I know your 'something blue' is, in fact, blue." Deep breath. Neutral expression—like one you'd use on a stray dog of unknown temperament. "Perhaps a little more detail?"

"It's a garter," Whitney huffed, hands fluttering uselessly. "My mother's, from her own wedding. Robin's-egg blue with white embroidery."

I nodded, remembering the tiny item. "You had it at home, when we inspected your bag before leaving." *For the fourth time.* "So it must've been here when you unpacked. We just have to track the thing down."

"Unless it was stolen," Whitney muttered darkly, a frown pinching her delicate features. "I was in the ladies' room before, and that hairstylist left in an *awful* hurry."

"Devin didn't steal your garter." I was now well past irritated, but trying to cover it. "She had to go touch up the other bridesmaids." Oh, how I wished I was with *them*, even though I had nothing in common with Whitney's gaggle of beautiful frenemies. But the maid of honor has ironclad personal-assistant-to-the-bride duties on the big day, and right then, they consisted of me locating a six-inch hoop of missing taffeta.

We were alone on the second floor of the Williem Carter House, one of the most exclusive wedding venues in Charleston. Both the service and reception were being held there. A National Historic Landmark, the home boasted museum-caliber art, a stunning ballroom, and two cozy garden courtyards. It was the height of refinement and charm. Whitney Blanche DuBois—a Southern debutante to the tips of her manicured toes—wouldn't have had it any other way. Even I had to admit the place was perfect.

However, at that moment, the palatial residence was hiding an apparently crucial element of Whitney's ensemble, and she was verging on hysterics. So I was down on my knees—in a sea-green bridesmaid's dress and three-inch heels—peering under a collection of ornate couches, bookcases, and coffee tables for a stupid, useless, confounded blue garter that no one but my father would ever see anyway.

*Ew.* I fast-forwarded past *that* unpleasant thought, probing the carpet with my fingers. My quarry continued to elude me.

"We'll simply *have* to postpone," Whitney babbled, collapsing heavily onto a divan. "You'll tell the guests. And Kit as well, the news should come from you. I'll speak to the Magnolia League photographer, although *of course* Agnes Taylor will use this as an excuse to cut my spread from the fall publication. She's been against its inclusion from the beginning! The caterers will howl, but I don't see any way—"

"Just hold on." I sat back on my heels, palms up in a calming gesture designed for spooked horses. "Take a breath. We don't need to postpone the wedding. Let's just retrace our steps a bit. Find this stupid garter."

"It is *not*—"

My hands chopped sideways. "Of course not. Poor choice of words."

I rose and began pacing, chewing my bottom lip, my blue-green eyes slipping out of focus as I reviewed our progress that morning. After the . . . *events* of last year, my irises had never returned to their former pure emerald green. People noticed the change from time to time, but not in a particularly startled way. "It happens" was the phrase I heard most often.

Not usually from ingesting a covertly manufactured antiviral serum created in hopes of reversing a catastrophic DNA mutation—one granting infected subjects extrasensory canine superpowers—but whatever. *It happens.*

Whitney stared at the ceiling, looking hopeless. "We left home, had brunch at the hotel, then came straight here," she said glumly. "I had *everything* in my travel bag. But the garter has simply vanished!"

Something clicked. "Didn't you pay for brunch?"

Whitney nodded impatiently. "*Overpaid*, if you ask me. Runny eggs, scorched toast, plus the mimosas were—" She cut off abruptly as I arrowed for the window.

In the courtyard below, guests were already being seated. I spotted Hi and Shelton, both looking uncomfortable in their tuxes as they ushered friends and family members to the rows of white folding chairs facing the altar.

As I watched, Hi awkwardly extended an elbow for Madison Dunkle, which she took, even though she'd clearly arrived with Jason Taylor. Those two had been dating for several months, and the odd match seemed to be working. Maddy would never be my favorite person in the world—too much shady history between us for that—but I was happy they'd found each other. Unsure of decorum, Jason followed on their heels as Hi led Maddy to a pair of open seats on the groom's side.

Just behind them, Shelton was attempting to shepherd Jason's mother, Agnes, down the aisle, but Mr. Taylor rebuffed him with a friendly wink, escorting his wife himself. Shelton trailed them for a few steps, then shrugged and turned around, leaving the detective and his wife to find their own seats. Professional ushers my friends were not.

The next pair stifled my amusement.

Chance and Ella.

*Why did we invite them?*

That wasn't fair. For all the trouble Chance Claybourne had caused over the last few years, he'd also come up big when we'd needed him most. Chance's quick thinking was one of the only reasons I was attending my father's wedding at all, instead of banging my head against a cage door in some top-secret government lab.

Still.

His betrayals ran deep. Chance had created most of my problems in the first place.

And Ella Francis . . .

She was my best girl friend. Even now. She'd apologized more times

than I could count, and I knew she meant every one. Ella had backed me
in the end, too, when the chips were down.

But, still.

The knife wounds in my back were still healing.

I could close my eyes and smell the charred ruins of our clubhouse.

*It is what it is.*

Chance stopped abruptly, as if responding to a sixth sense. He
turned. Looked straight up at the window.

My breath caught, and I ducked away like an idiot.

Had he felt me watching him? No. How could he, with his powers
snuffed out?

Yet my nerves were thrumming like guitar strings.

Chance remained irritatingly beautiful, seemed to grow more darkly
handsome by the day. More than a few local debs gave Ella the stink eye
when spotting them out together, though she was no less captivating
than he was. With her three-foot cable of lustrous black hair, and dancing, mischievous eyes, Ella was the prettiest girl I knew in real life. Small
wonder Chance was hooked. Let the haters hate.

*Not me, though. I made my choice.*

"Tory?" My head whipped to Whitney, who'd sat up and was eyeing
me curiously. "Did you find it?"

"Not yet, but I will." Feeling foolish, I swung back to the window.
Chance and Ella were strolling down the aisle, unescorted. They grabbed
a pair of seats on the bride's side.

*Interesting.*

Random, or deliberate?

Shrug. Trying to divine answers from the actions of Chance
Claybourne has never been a profitable business. Not for me, at least.

Then I spotted my original target, and my heart swelled.

Ben Blue. *My* Ben.

He looked miserable in his penguin suit, but that doesn't mean bad.

His shoulder-length black hair was pulled back into a ponytail, exposing his tanned face and sharp brown eyes. Ben was supposed to be ushering like Hi and Shelton, but he'd planted himself by the guest book, smiling uncomfortably as people paraded by, his natural shyness winning out.

Ben sensed my attention as well. He squinted up at my window, then smiled—the open, unguarded version reserved only for me. My stomach did a backflip.

Benjamin Blue.

My boyfriend. Mine.

It was weird. It was wonderful. It was still hard to believe.

*This is the worst day of my life*, Ben sent, the sour thought at odds with his quirked lips. *I feel like a movie theater host.*

Ben's irises grew muddier as his voice sounded inside my head.

His reaction was easiest to cover. Add blue to brown, you get more brown.

*Classier than that*, I sent back, my own eyes brightening to a crystal-clear blue, with only flecks of green remaining. *Maybe an upscale steak-house? Anyway, you look very handsome.*

*I look like a jackass. When do I get to see you?*

*Soon. I cannot wait to escape this room. Whitney is a Bridezilla.*

*We can disappear. This building must have some fancy hiding places.*

Ben's emotions were streaming up at me, and I blushed. Could he read me as easily?

Not that I minded sharing my feelings. Not with him. Not anymore.

*Just in time for him to leave.*

I pushed the painful thought away. Hoped he hadn't caught it.

Ben had graduated from Wando High in the spring, and had been accepted at Warren Wilson College in Asheville. In less than a month he'd be moving to the Appalachians to pursue a degree in environmental science. I was insanely proud of him. Rotten timing, for sure, but we'd make it work. I'd drive the four hours up I-26 every weekend if I had to.

"Tory?" Whitney squeaked, insistent. "What are you doing? We have a *problem* here!"

"One sec!" Averting my eyes, though in her current state I doubt she'd have noticed their sudden blueness. A far cry from when they'd blazed with golden fire.

*Is Whitney being awful?* Ben sent, his speech weaker in my mind since we'd broken eye contact. *I bet she's being awful.*

That's how it worked now, with all four of us. No more mind-wrenching snaps. No explosions of overwhelming sensory perception. No inrush of visceral power. Everything came smooth and easy, though slightly muted from our previous highs.

We were connected all the time, our flaring effects dulled from a roaring fire that was hard to ignite—and extinguish—to a low simmer that never fully dissipated.

No more tells, either. Just an ocular flush of blue when we communicated.

It'd been almost a year since that morning in the woods. Our current condition had developed slowly, then stabilized. This . . . *icing* effect felt like a new normal, but who knew what the future might bring? I'd learned—repeatedly—that *I* never did.

Something buzzed inside my head. I glanced at Hiram, who waved. He'd picked up our conversation and, of course, had to chime in. *Old ladies smell weird. FYI.*

I rolled my eyes. *Noted.*

Shelton stomped over to stand beside Hi, shading his now-bluish eyes as he scowled up at my second floor perch. *I'm doing twice the escorting as these two fools put together. I should get a bonus.*

*This is* supposed *to be an honor,* I scolded, mock-stern. *Now get back to it. I need Ben.*

*I bet you do,* Hi deadpanned. What can only be described as kissing noises echoed in my skull, followed by Shelton's laughter.

*Doofuses.* I hoped my scarlet cheeks were too far away for Ben to notice. Unlikely, since we could all see like eagles. *Can you check on something for me?* I asked him.

*Of course,* Ben replied.

*The cloakroom by the entrance. See if there's a gold clutch inside Whitney's black coat.*

*A what now?*

I snorted. *A slim, flat handbag. If you find it, bring it up here on the double.*

*Will do.*

I slowly turned to face Whitney, my irises fading back to aquamarine. She was slumped sideways across on the divan, one arm thrown over her face.

"I signaled for Ben to get your coat." Mostly true. "Could the garter be in your clutch?"

Whitney popped up like a champagne cork, her face electric. "Yes! It is! I put it there for safekeeping! Tory, you're a genius!" She swept forward and crushed me in a bear hug.

"Just doing my job," I wheezed.

Whitney drew back to arm's length, tears sparkling in her eyes. "I'm so happy to be joining your family, honey. I'll be the best stepmother you could hope for! You'll see!"

"Yeah." I coughed into a fist. *She tries hard. Never forget that.* "It's gonna be . . . great."

A soft knock. Whitney released me with a small cry, her expression scandalized. "No one can see me yet!" Lifting her dress, she fled into the bathroom.

"Good lord." Shaking my head, I walked over and opened the door.

There he was. Ben.

My stomach did another double axel.

*Soooo cute.*

Ben held up his prize. "I really hope this is a clutch."

"Bingo." With a relieved sigh, I snapped the gaudy thing open. Whitney's garter was neatly folded inside. "Congrats, Blue. You're the hero."

One of his hands found my waist. "Doesn't the hero usually get a reward?"

I grinned wickedly, tapping him on the chest. "Naughty boy. It's not *our* wedding day."

"Close enough." Pulling me in.

Our lips met, and all other thoughts fled.

For a hot second only.

Then Hiram's voice hissed inside my skull.

*Tory, we've got a problem! Get down here ASAP!*

# CHAPTER 2

They were all clearly dead.

Every flower, every centerpiece.

Wilted petals. Broken, flaccid stems. Murky brown water filled the bottom of each crystal vase, soiling the white rocks artfully placed within. The same horror repeated throughout the ballroom.

I gasped, a hand shooting to my forehead. "What happened to the lilies?"

We stood at the entrance to the ballroom, surveying the carnage. The reception was scheduled to begin immediately after the outdoor church service, but now the decorations were only appropriate for a gothic rave. All the dying plants gave me the chills.

"I came in here to stash my mother's purse, and found *this*." Hiram's nose crinkled in a grimace. "It even *smells* bad. Like the Walking Dead crashed your dad's wedding."

"This makes no sense!" Shelton was tugging an earlobe. "I saw this room like forty-five minutes ago, and everything looked great. They even had those Mag League snobs in here taking pictures. The place was perfect."

"Where are the stupid florists?" I spat. We were the only ones present at the moment.

"They left a while back," Ben said disgustedly. "I saw them go. The head guy told your aunt Tempe that everything was all set up."

"Oh boy." I covered my eyes. "What do we do?"

Whitney had designed and planned everything, forgoing a full-time wedding coordinator. Despite the hundreds of tiny details involved, she hadn't wanted anyone else "in the way" at her nuptials. While no one doubted her ability to handle the task—Whitney was *born* to dream up and execute extravagant events—her dictatorial micromanagement had left a leadership vacuum here on the big day. Kit's mother, Harry, was supposed to be coordinating the vendors, but she'd proven hopeless at it, so Aunt Tempe and some of the other ladies were helping out.

Hi blew out a breath. "I'm no flower scientist, but I'm pretty sure they're supposed to last longer than a half hour. Methinks you're entitled to a refund."

"Like that'll do us any good." I thought of Whitney, still nervously prepping upstairs, and my stomach dropped through my shoes. "You guys, Whitney will *not* be able to handle this. She's a mess already. When she sees Stephen King's floral arrangements . . ."

Hi snorted. "That actually might be funny. We could YouTube it."

He yelped as Ben smacked the back of his head.

"We have to fix this." I pressed my fists to my forehead, thinking. "Should we call the florists back? I don't have their number, plus their shop is all the way in Mount Pleasant. And they won't have a truckload of backup centerpieces just lying around, anyway. Or even the same flowers."

"A different place?" Ben suggested doubtfully. "Somewhere close? Or maybe we could snag the flowers for the outdoor service, and swap them in here?"

Shelton shook his head. "In front of all those people? Everyone would freak. And then the actual wedding would look like trash."

"Shoot!" I stomped a foot. "No one can fix this in time. Two hundred white lilies don't fall from the sky!"

"No," Hi said seriously. "They grow in the ground."

I gave him a nasty look, but Shelton's clap grabbed my attention.

"That's it!" He smiled wide, then pointed to a door on the opposite side of the room. "There *are* flowers outside. Hundreds of them!"

Ben frowned. "You're the one who said we can't swap the arrangements."

"No!" Shelton was bouncing on his balls of his feet. "Not the courtyard! I'm talking about the botanical garden on the other side of the building! Flowers grow in the ground, just like Hi said!"

My eyes rounded. "We raid their flower garden! That's genius!"

Hi shook out his sleeves, then tugged on his cuffs. "Let's all remember that this was *my* idea. Sometimes brilliance strikes like lightning, whereas—"

Ben smacked Hi again, but kept his focus on me. "What types of flowers do they have back there?"

I shook my head, nerves returning as I strategized the best course of action. "Whatever they are, we have to make it work."

Shelton's enthusiasm abruptly dried up. "I'm guessing the manager won't love us destroying their award-winning garden. That's for real, by the way. This place won awards."

Wince. Shrug. "We'll pay them back. Kit will. I'm sure."

"So what's the plan?" Ben asked.

I took a calming breath. "Ben, go tell Kit what happened. Get his permission to raid the garden—tell him it's the only way to keep Whitney from imploding. Then meet me back there."

"And if he doesn't say yes?"

"Get him to!"

Ben nodded, trotted for the door.

I turned to Shelton. "I need you to round up Tempe and Harry. Tell them what happened, and then bring them to the garden with whomever else they want to include. Someone has to decide what to pick for the new arrangements. I don't have a clue."

Shelton clicked his tongue. "Great. Round up some old ladies at a wedding and get them to commit vandalism. No problem at all." But he hurried to carry out my instructions.

"I assume you want me to go have a snack?" Hi suggested hopefully.

My hands found my hips. "I saved the best for you, Mr. Brilliant. I need you to clean all this up. Every dead flower has to go, every vase needs to be rinsed out and scrubbed. The rocks, too. I'm counting on you."

Hi groaned. "Maybe we should reconsider this whole thing." He waved a hand at the morbid lily centerpieces. "These arrangements have a certain . . . serial killer . . . charm."

I gave him a flat look. "Get moving."

As Hi trudged to the closest table, bemoaning his fate, I ran a hand across my face. The plan could work, but we had to move fast. I was about to track down the house manager—to calmly inform him that we intended to devastate his flowerbeds—when Hi's voice echoed across the ballroom. "Tor! Come here a sec!"

I spun, annoyed. "What is it, Hi? I have to go."

Hi was holding the first centerpiece, an odd look on his face. "Something's not right."

Curiosity won out, and I hurried over to him. "What do you mean?"

Hi shoved the wilting arrangement at my face. "Smell this."

I batted dead lily petals from my eyes, glaring at Hi. But then I noticed it, too. A faint chemical aroma, wafting from the vase water. Shoving my nose closer, I inhaled deeply, irises washing blue as my sensory powers amplified the odor.

My nose wrinkled. The smell was harsh. Bitter. "What *is* that?"

Hi shrugged. "Water mixed with . . . something. Maybe a fancy preservative?"

I looked around at all the dead flowers. "Then why are they all dead? *Super* dead."

I took another whiff, concentrating on the bouquet of aromas emanating from the vase. Once upon a time, I was better at this—I could've told you what lake the water came from—but I could still sense that something was off.

"I'm not certain," I said slowly, "but part of this mixture smells like rubbing alcohol. There's more, too. Another chemical. Acrid. It burns my nostrils." I took a step back, shook my head to clear it. "All I can think of is . . . *weed killer.*"

Hi snorted, pulling dead stems from the liquid. "Basically the last two things you'd use to keep plants alive. Stupendous job, florists! Prepare for a really bad review on Yelp."

"Seriously." Yet the hairs on my arms were standing. How could such an obvious mistake occur? What kind of bonehead would place flowers into a solution that would kill them within minutes?

The door opened, driving all other thoughts from my mind. Shelton slipped inside, followed by Aunt Tempe and Harry, Kit's mom. She's also technically my grandmother, but we hadn't spent much time together. Harry's an odd bird, to say the least.

The two women froze, ogling the flower massacre.

"What in God's name?" Harry's dyed-blond curls quivered as she stared in disbelief. "Who designed this look, Tim Burton?"

Tempe shook herself, strode quickly to my side. "Okay. Disaster. Do we have a plan?"

I nodded, standing a bit straighter. Tempe had that effect on me. "Every flower in here is toast, but there's a botanical garden on the grounds. I sent Ben to alert Kit—it might get expensive when we gut the flowerbeds to replace the centerpieces."

Tempe closed her eyes a moment. Then, oddly, barked a laugh. "Clinical and effective. Good thinking. If the manager doesn't have us arrested for destruction of property, that is."

I cringed. "I was just going to get his permission."

Tempe shook her head firmly. "We pick first, ask permission afterward. Fortune favors the bold, right?"

Roses.

Red. White. Pink. Yellow.

Working swiftly and silently, we plucked dozens of delicate buds, then smuggled them into the ballroom undetected. Hi kept lookout by the door as Harry assembled the arrangements. In thirty minutes, the chamber had a brand-new look.

*A damn good one, if I do say so myself.*

Whitney would notice the changes instantly, of course, but no one else should. Harry had done a masterful job. As Tempe slid the last centerpiece into position, I breathed a sigh of relief. Crisis averted, with minutes to spare.

"Okay everyone, let's go!" Tempe was tapping her watch.

"Things are happening!" Hi called from the door. He'd cracked it an inch, was peering out at the guests in the courtyard. "Kit just walk-ran down the aisle. He looks like he's freaking out. And there's a green-dress girl circling the audience. She looks mad."

I winced. "Searching for the maid of honor, no doubt."

"Go." Harry made shooing motions with her hands. "Y'all are in the wedding party. The service starts in five, and they must be frantic. I'm done here. Tempe and I will be on your heels."

The boys straightened their tuxes, then hurried out to join Kit by the altar. I was halfway through the door when Tempe caught me by the hand.

She gave my shoulder a squeeze. "Nice work, Tory. You saved the day."

"Just glad it worked out." But I felt a warm flush of pride. *Booyah.*

As I stepped from the ballroom, the frantic bridesmaid spotted me and practically ran in my direction. I plastered on a smile. The day was saved. Whitney would understand. But as I was being literally yanked toward the building—and scolded by a complete stranger for good measure—an unsettling thought occurred to me.

All those centerpieces destroyed, because of an incredibly stupid blunder.

But what if it wasn't a mistake?

What if the flowers had been murdered?

# CHAPTER 3

I put one foot in front of the other.

Slowly. Stately.

Wobbly.

I'm not an ace in heels.

Whitney's train slid down the aisle before me, a tidal wave of white silk whispering along the red carpet. Though maid of honor, I was to follow directly behind her as she entered, a dictate of DuBois family tradition. No doubt a relic of their cherished debutante past, allowing the bride-to-be a final, glorious one-upping of her sister or closest friend.

*Don't be ugly. Whitney means well. Mostly.*

Step. Pause. Step. My floor-length dress made each stride a challenge, but I was determined not to pull a Jennifer Lawrence. When *she* trips in front of everyone, it's adorable. I'd look like a circus clown.

My hastily assembled crisis team had scrambled back into their respective positions. Problem solved, but I still couldn't understand how such a ridiculous mistake could occur. Those florists were in for some sharp words. I'd make sure Kit demanded a refund.

Beyond Whitney, I could see Kit grinning like a dope as he stood before the raised wooden altar. The priest, Dr. Allen, was on his left. Whitney's younger brother Eric, in from Chicago, stood to his right. Whitney had suggested that Eric be Kit's best man. Kit being Kit, he'd agreed without complaint.

*My God, it's really happening.*

At the end of this walk, that ditzy woman would become my stepmother.

*Blargh.*

I squeezed my lids shut. Snapped them open. Glancing around for a distraction, I spotted my friends' parents in a row to my right. Tom Blue looked sweaty in his ill-fitting rented tuxedo, but he smiled and nodded as I paced by. We'd gotten to know each other on a personal level in the months that Ben and I had been dating. A well-read man, he was thoughtful and polite, prone to quoting famous literature when making a point. Ben's ears burned every time it happened, but I was a fan. I love it when life—when *people*—surprise me.

*Unless they're trying to kill me, of course.*

But I was all done with that.

Ben's mother, Myra, sat next to Tom, in a lovely cinnamon dress that matched her eyes. I'd never sensed any bad blood between the elder Blues—honestly, I wasn't even sure they were officially divorced. That topic I studiously avoided. Ben would say more when he was ready. It wasn't my place to pry.

Beyond Myra sat Shelton's parents, Nelson and Lorelei Devers, holding hands, eyes glued to each other. Shelton said they *loved* weddings. Watching them now, I guessed they liked to relive their own. Farther down the row, Linus Stolowitski was patting the shoulder of his wife, Ruth, who'd buried her nose in a handkerchief. Linus gave me an apologetic shrug, but I smiled. Ruth's an emotional lady, no question. Ask Hi anytime he gets on her bad side.

Another pace forward. The next row held less pleasant guests.

Dr. Mike Iglehart sat in the closest chair. He dodged my glance as if burned by it, and well he should. Chance had divulged that Iglehart had been his secret spy at LIRI, but I'd decided to keep the information to myself. Kit liked to think the best of everyone at the institute, and the Iglehart problem was fully neutralized. No need to shatter my father's illusions.

Still. What a jerk.

The rest of the row was filled with classmates I was less than thrilled to see. Ashley Bodford sat with her parents, looking bored yet beautiful in a jet-black dress that matched her hair, eyes, and heart. Beside her, Courtney Holt sat with perfect posture, her cream-colored dress way too close to white, not that she'd understand why that mattered. The clingy, low-cut garment set off her blond hair, and that's all she cared about.

I hated that they were invited, but, *naturally*, their parents were close friends of the DuBois family. So they got to attend my father's wedding despite having tortured me daily for the better part of two years. My glance hardened to a glare, but they didn't notice.

*Easy, tiger,* Hi sounded inside my skull. *Don't forget—police are in da house!*

My gaze flicked back to the altar, a high, wide platform of polished oak, cunningly fit together to appear as a single unbroken piece. A carved wooden arch graced its apex, woven with garlands of white flowers. Whitney had had the entire thing flown in from Ireland for the service, and it'd taken several hours to reassemble the night before. Anything for her ladyship.

Hi, Ben, and Shelton stood atop the bulky platform, in a line with the other groomsmen. I was genuinely touched that Kit had chosen *my* best friends to fill out his wedding party. Having them close by made the whole day easier for me, which was likely his intention.

On the opposite side of the archway were the bridesmaids, their makeup-coated expressions a mixture of happiness, envy, and boredom. Squinting, I could easily picture Ashley and Courtney in their vapid company.

*Parasites*, I sent back to Hi, still riled by unwelcome faces in the gallery. *I wouldn't mind if a few chairs collapsed. Into a volcano.*

*Haven't mastered that trick yet.* Shelton smoothed the sleeves of his tuxedo jacket, ducking his head to hide his smile. *When I can do more than talk in your dome, I'll let you know.*

*I wouldn't worry about these cops.* Ben was scowling at Captain Carmine Corcoran, who was hitching his pants beside the courtyard entrance. *That moron couldn't guard a cheeseburger unless there was a press conference involved.*

I lowered my head, stifling a laugh as I kept my sapphire eyes from view. *Kit's idea. He thought an official presence might keep the paparazzi away.*

It hadn't worked. A gaggle of photographers was lurking just beyond the courtyard wall, hoping to get lucky. I'd spotted at least one snapping shots from a nearby roof.

As director of the Loggerhead Island Research Institute, Dr. Christopher Howard was—distressingly to my father—one of the prominent citizens of Charleston. Add in the wealth and prestige of the DuBois family, plus the infamous Chance Claybourne in attendance as a guest, and this wedding was officially an Event in the city. Despite Corcoran's preening, I was glad for the extra security. His team of off-duty cops had bounced a dozen crashers already.

*The people discovered Hiram Stolowitski would be here,* Hi trumpeted inside my head. I watched him buff his fingernails on a silk lapel. *TMZ coverage was inevitable.*

Red sparks in my mind, followed by inarticulate squawking. Ben had struck a third time.

*One of these days*, Hi griped, *I'm charging you with assault.*

*I'll alert my attorney.* Ben's eyes found mine, and the skies cleared.

Benjamin Blue, now a serial smiler.

Who'd have thunk it?

We continued down the aisle, passing rows filled with LIRI staff, local dignitaries, and Bolton Prep families. Madison gave me a friendly nod, Jason a grin. His mother sat in the chair beside him, wearing a small frown as she muttered about the pollen count. Whitney nearly missed a step. As president of the Magnolia League, Agnes Taylor's opinions on style were local gospel. Whitney would've crawled through a sewer pipe to make a good impression.

Mrs. Taylor was a substitute teacher, and, being the nosy type, stayed in-the-know regarding school gossip. It wasn't clear what she thought of Madison and her son being together, but her face was pinched in a scowl. Jason pretended not to notice, his fingers interlocked with his girlfriend's. Though Maddy smiled prettily, I noticed her knuckles were white.

Kit's family manned the front row. Harry sat between Tempe and Kit's father, Howard Howard—don't ask about the name—who was followed by Tempe's daughter Katie, her ex-husband Pete, and some others I didn't know very well. I ignored the opposite side of the aisle, jam-packed with DuBois family members and their countless friends and social connections. A decent-sized crowd, all told, though I knew Whitney had agonized over whom to invite. And delighted in several snubs.

*Last chance to blow this up.* Hi kept his face straight, but his voice swirled singsong in my brain. *You could still fake a seizure. Or grab the rings and bolt.*

*Don't think I haven't considered it.*

We reached the foot of the altar. I looked up, saw my father's beaming face. His palpable joy burned away my cynicism.

*Can't do it, folks. I'm going down with this ship.*

*Bah.* Shelton made a covert dismissal with one hand. *Twelve months, then you're out of there. Just make, like, a yearlong Advent calendar or something. Count the days.*

True. I didn't like thinking that way—it wasn't fair to Kit, who'd taken me in when I'd had nowhere else to go—but facts *were* facts. After one more year at Bolton, I was off to college. Whitney would become a summers-and-holidays-only problem.

I glanced at Ben, who was studying his boxy black shoes. A strange cocktail of emotions was seeping from him, before closing off abruptly. I kept my own fears from flowing back.

I didn't know yet where I'd go to college, but it almost certainly wouldn't be in Asheville like Ben. I'd already applied to Wake Forest and Vanderbilt, which weren't too far, but the other schools on my list were all a plane ride away. And, given that I was a shoo-in for valedictorian—everyone else knew it, so there was no point denying it myself—I'd have good options.

*Options away from Ben. Some far away.*

He looked up then. Gave me a sad smile.

I jerked my eyes away. Missed a step and nearly went down. I realized Whitney and her father had stopped moving. With infinite dignity, the elder DuBois placed his daughter's hand in Kit's.

*It's real. My God, it's real.*

Tears gleamed in my father's eyes. His happiness filled me, too.

Whitney's head whipped around. She gave me an exasperated look. "*Tory!*" Suddenly, everyone was looking at me. I was supposed to be doing something.

"Oops, sorry!" I dropped to a knee and smoothed Whitney's train, then hustled up the altar's three steps to my spot on the left, facing the assembly.

Wood groaned beneath my feet, the ancient platform dipping a fraction.

I shuffled a step to keep my balance.

Accidentally locked eyes with Chance.

He was sitting in the second row on the DuBois side, black hair slicked back, his dark eyes dancing with amusement. Chance's tuxedo clearly wasn't a rental, a classic James Bond number with a silk tie and cummerbund—he'd once said that vests were for bartenders. Ella sat beside him, looking gorgeous in a sleek lavender cocktail dress.

Chance smirked. Nodded. Ella's smile, at least, seemed genuine.

*So much has changed.*

Dr. Allen mounted the first step, turned to bless Kit and Whitney as they stood together at the foot of the altar. I wobbled in my heels as the platform shifted slightly.

Chance could get under my skin without even trying. Our alliance had been pressure-forged like a diamond, but there were times when I still didn't know what to make of him. Were we friends? *Good* friends? Frenemies?

*We're no longer pack, that's for sure.*

Did he know that my friends and I had evolved a second time?

That some powers still flowed on Morris Island?

I couldn't say, but I fervently hoped not, for everyone's sake. If experience had taught me anything, it was this: the fewer people who knew my secrets, the better.

Chance and I had barely spoken in the months since our escape, a necessary cooling-off period for both sides. Plus, though Ben had mellowed considerably since we'd started dating, any mention of Chance resurrected his scowl. Understandable.

My heart lurched. I felt eyes on the back of my head.

No, more personal. *Inside* my head.

I pivoted slowly to avoid notice. Spotted Ben glaring at Chance, and making very little effort to hide it. They hadn't been in the same place since Ben and I got together, but today had been unavoidable.

I detected a flurry of sendings from Shelton and Hi, trying to put out the fire.

Ben ignored them at first. Then he noticed me watching.

*I don't like how he's looking at you.*

*Ben, this is my father's wedding. Tighten up.*

Ben flinched. Taking a deep breath, he gave me a nearly imperceptible nod, schooling his face to stillness. But I could feel his anger burning white-hot.

*We need to keep those two apart*, Hi sent, feeling a need to state the obvious.

For his part, Chance seemed indifferent to Ben's ire. He patted Ella's hand, whispering something in her ear that evoked a laugh. Over her shoulder, his gaze found mine again.

Something hid there. What, exactly, I had no idea. Interest? Mockery? Challenge? Maybe all three. Then the window shuttered as Chance snapped his trademark wink.

Which I hated.

He wasn't hitting on me. I didn't think. But casual flirtation had masked deceptive agendas in the past. I'd been hoping we were beyond that. Now? I couldn't say.

*Just how he likes it. Damn him.*

Dr. Allen mounted the last two steps, strode to the archway, and then turned to address the congregation.

A tiny vibration tickled my heels.

*Uh, guys?*

I glanced across the platform to see Shelton, brow furrowed as he squinted down at the wooden slats beneath his feet. *You hear that? Something sounds . . . off.*

*What is it?* I asked. Though our powers had migrated to being nearly equal in most aspects, we each still possessed an area of greater acuity. Shelton could hear like a bat. If he said something didn't sound right, I paid attention.

*I'm not sure.* Shelton said, straining to listen. *But every time someone moves, there's a . . . a scraping . . . or . . .*

Ben looked down at his feet. *The platform is wobbling. I felt it when Tory stepped up, but it got worse when the priest stepped up.*

Dr. Allen's voice rang out, beginning the service.

Hi nodded toward Kit and Whitney at the foot of the altar. *What happens when they join us up here?*

Shelton discretely tapped a heel against the polished oak flooring. *It's a grinding noise, like sandpaper. Wood on wood, maybe. I . . . uh . . . guys, I think it's getting worse.*

Dr. Allen intoned a blessing. The audience repeated his words.

Kit and Whitney mounted the first step.

Suddenly, I heard it, too—a faint tearing, grating sound from under our feet. I thought the noise emanated from the center of the platform, beneath the carved archway. Right where the happy couple was supposed to stand and make their vows.

Kit and Whitney ascended the second step.

The scraping intensified. I felt a sickening vibration in my toes.

The bridesmaid on my left quirked her head. Glanced down at her feet.

*The floor's trembling over here*, Hi sent from the opposite side of the archway.

Kit and Whitney reached the top of the platform.

I watched in horror as the entire structure bowed beneath their added weight.

A sharp crack. Then another.

The reports released me like a starter's pistol.

"Wait!" I shouted, waving my hands as I bounced forward. Startled, Whitney stumbled backward, only her grip on Kit's arm saving her from face-planting in the grass. Her momentum dragged them both down the steps and off the platform.

Steadying themselves, they stared back up at me in shock.

I'd come to a stop in the center of the platform, directly before a wild-eyed Dr. Allen.

Beneath me, wood groaned audibly.

The floor dipped, suddenly bouncy and insubstantial.

"Everyone off the altar!" Matching action to words, I hot-stepped for the safety of solid ground, worried with every footfall that the whole thing would implode and take me down with it. Hi, Shelton, and Ben bailed immediately as well.

The rest of the wedding party stood frozen like statues. Even Dr. Allen.

"I'd hop to it," Hi advised, pointing to several drooping planks in the center of the altar. "Unless you *want* to be on that thing when it collapses."

His words did the trick. With a curse, Eric DuBois leapt from the platform. Then herd instinct took over: the others raced down like lemmings, groomsmen shouting incoherently, bridesmaids struggling for balance as they navigated the narrow steps in their heels.

As he crossed the center of the altar, a section of flooring separated beneath Dr. Allen's feet. He tripped and fell forward, and only Ben's quick reflexes saved the day. He caught the elderly priest's arm and helped him safely down to the grass.

We formed a ragged, panting line at the foot of the altar.

Shouts erupted in the gallery. Whitney's head whipped side to side in a panic.

"What's going on?" Kit hissed, staring at the unstable platform.

Ben shed his jacket, jogged around the altar, and knelt in the grass. Hinges squeaked as he opened some sort of hatch on its backside. Before anyone could question what he was doing, Ben wiggled through the opening and disappeared.

"Wha . . . wha . . ." Whitney seemed unable to form a coherent thought.

No one else tried.

Seconds ticked past, and the crowd grew restless. Mrs. Taylor began grumbling loudly to another member of the Magnolia League, and Whitney's face crumpled.

Then Ben's voice carried from beneath the woodwork. "Found the problem! Somebody get my dad!"

"What's the deal?" Hi yelled, as Tom Blue circled the altar and, with a sigh, got down on his knees and shimmied under the structure.

"The pins fell out!" Ben shouted, a note of incredulity in his voice. "The central joins aren't locked into place. We're lucky this thing didn't fall apart, but it's an easy fix. Shove them back in and we're good. Give us five minutes."

"Uh, thanks, Ben!" Kit called, then he turned to address his guests. "Slight mechanical issue, folks. Won't take a second to fix. Don't worry, we're still getting married!"

Chuckles from the gallery. Rueful shrugs. Kit hurried to a member of the wait staff, and, moments later, trays of champagne flutes began circulating the thirsty crowd. The delay became a cocktail break. Everyone relaxed.

Shelton and Hi sidled over to my side, consternation plain on their faces.

"The pins *dropped* out?" Hi scoffed. "Who put this together, Stevie Wonder?"

A cold feeling swept over me. "Weird, right? And right after the flower thing inside . . ."

"What do you mean?" Shelton froze in the process of cleaning his glasses. "You think somebody did that stuff on purpose?"

I didn't have a chance to answer. Ben popped up behind the altar, followed more slowly by his father. The pair wiped grass from their pant legs as they swung back around the platform, wearing matching grins.

"Done!" Ben said proudly. "Easy, honestly. Two pins just needed to be reinserted."

"Everyone take your seats!" Kit waved the wedding party back to their places. I stepped up slowly, testing my weight. But the Blues were right—the footing was firm and true.

Thank goodness we'd noticed in time. Another disaster averted.

The cold feeling returned.

*I don't believe in coincidence.*

In the center of the altar, Whitney smoothed her dress, breathing deeply as she attempted to regain her composure. Kit squeezed her hand, planted a kiss on her cheek.

Everyone was back in position. The next few minutes passed in a blur. The priest spoke. Whitney spoke. Kit spoke. Rings appeared, vows were made, for some reason they poured pastel sands into a vase together.

*I now pronounce you husband and wife.*

My father and Whitney kissed to thunderous applause.

It was done.

*Sweet sassy molassey.*

Hugs. Backslaps. The happy couple floated down the aisle.

*I have a stepmother. This is not a drill.*

I began mentally listing Whitney's good points, starting with how much Kit loved her, and how devoted she was to him. I almost forgot to take Eric's arm as we followed them down the wedding gauntlet.

This wouldn't be so bad.

Right?

Right?

Ahead of me, Whitney let out a squeal of delight, hugging my father close. "We did it!"

A sigh escaped.

I smiled. This time it wasn't *too* forced.

No, it wouldn't be so bad.

Things change, and this wasn't even a bad one.

My father's face. Tears of pure joy, manfully contained.

As they passed into the building, their interlocked hands flew up in celebration.

Not so bad at all.

*Welcome to the family, Whit.*

# CHAPTER 4

Dinner was about to be served.

The ballroom was decked out in linen and silk, with a square of sparkling hardwood at its heart. Gleaming silver utensils flanked fine china and crystal water goblets. Elegant hand-printed menus adorned each place setting. A string quartet was playing in one corner.

I snagged my personalized card as I entered, though I knew which table was mine. Whitney had dubbed the seating arrangement "the hardest thing" she'd ever had to do. Apparently half her family couldn't stand the other half, and there were *literally dozens* of VIPs requiring pride of place.

The tables were round, arranged in staggered rows. Mine was up front, of course, with Aunt Tempe, Harry, and some of Whitney's family I didn't know. My new stepmother had ignored my not-so-subtle hints that I'd have preferred a secluded table in back with my friends. Oh well. At least Ben was sitting with me. I'd insisted on that much.

A sweetheart table for the bride and groom sat on a dais at the very front. Whitney took her seat, beaming, though her smile faltered a bit when she noticed the replacement centerpieces. She said something to Kit, who whispered a lengthy response, eyeing his new bride nervously as he held her hand. Whatever he said seemed to mollify her. It didn't hurt that the new flowers looked fantastic.

Whitney glanced my way. Gave me a grateful nod. I waved back. *It was nothing.*

Her smile returned as she looked down on the mass of people like a queen on her throne. No one could mistake whose day it was.

"Your dad looks comfortable," Ben said sarcastically. Kit was squirming in his chair under all that scrutiny. "I assume *he's* the one who wanted to eat dinner perched on a pedestal like a canary, in full view of a hundred and fifty people?"

Kit drummed his tabletop, nearly knocking over a glass in the process.

"I bet he had no idea." I shot Ben an amused glance. "Like it would have mattered. This isn't his show, and everyone here knows it."

"At least *that* dais looks sturdy," Ben joked, fiddling with his ponytail. He didn't wear his hair back much, but I was digging it. "We don't need another structural emergency today."

"I know, right?" I leaned in close, speaking fast. "I can't believe what almost happened out there. Don't you think it's weird that the platform was defective?"

"Not defective," Ben corrected. "It wasn't assembled properly."

"Even worse!" My face scrunched in disbelief. "How could the set-up crew mess that up? The pins are literally all that holds the altar together, right?"

Ben hesitated. "I wasn't going to bring it up, but yeah, it's . . . bizarre. It's not like that structure is particularly complicated, it's just large wooden pieces connected by metal pins at the joins. I can't see how you'd possibly miss any when constructing it, and I can't see how they'd just fall out, either. It's almost like . . ."

He trailed off, but I finished the sentence. "Like someone *pulled* them out."

Ben lowered his voice. "Who'd want to sabotage a freaking altar?"

I shrugged. "Maybe the same person who'd kill a room full of flowers."

Ben sat back, eyeing me. "You think someone's trying to ruin this wedding." He didn't pose it as a question. Then his face clouded. "You know, only *two* pins were out of position. Both were in the center, right beneath where the priest was standing. That's why the thing didn't crater before, when the wedding party climbed up. But if Kit and Whitney had taken one more step . . ."

"Boom," I finished. "Game over for Whitney's Irish fantasy service."

He nodded. "We got lucky."

I clicked my tongue. "Unless those pins were targeted. By someone who knew *exactly* which ones to remove."

Ben gave me a skeptical look. "So that the platform would only collapse when the happy couple stepped onto it? Seems pretty far-fetched. That'd take an impressive feel for physics, Tor. Weight. Tensile strength. Load-carrying capacity. All that stuff."

Good point. But I couldn't shake the feeling that the flower and altar glitches were connected somehow.

Before I could respond, a bell chimed. Everyone took their seats.

"Talk more later," I whispered as Ben pulled out my chair. "I might be crazy."

He raised an eyebrow. *We could move to this channel. And you're never crazy.*

"It's okay, really." Then I sent, *Too many people around for telepathy. It'd look pretty strange if we just stared at each other the whole meal.*

Now Ben's eyebrows bounced up and down. *Staring at you is fine by me.*

I snorted, startling the DuBois relations sitting close by. Plastering on a smile, I nodded to our dinner companions, then pretended to hunt for my napkin. *You see?*

After drink orders were taken, Ben and I built an invisible wall around ourselves. Harry and Tempe were all the way across the table—impossible to speak with anyway—and I'd spent an entire week schmoozing various DuBois clan members. Not tonight, thanks. Our tablemates took the hint, and we were quietly left alone.

The first course was lobster bisque. As the noise level increased, it began to feel like a private date between the two of us. "Do you speak again?" Ben asked, spooning up the last of his appetizer.

"No, thank God." I blew a stray hair from my mouth. "My toasting duties were completed at the rehearsal dinner. Only the best man speaks tonight."

Another DuBois wedding quirk, but fine by me. One heartfelt speech extolling Whitney's virtues was all I could manage. Her tearful hug last night had left makeup stains on the shoulder of my dress.

Salads arrived, followed by filet mignon. Ben and I grimaced as Best Man Eric stumbled through a drunken, rambling toast no one could follow. The guy barely even knew Kit. Shrimp came last, disappearing in seconds. Then coffee. The band started up, and my foot began tapping on its own. Caffeine will do that.

Ben and I were holding hands under the table, a habit we'd recently developed that I had no intention of breaking. I was about to ask him more about Warren Wilson's science program—we didn't discuss his leaving much, but we'd have to face reality soon enough—when a shadow fell across the table.

I glanced up. Ben's grip tightened, then his hand fell away.

"Sorry to interrupt." Chance didn't look sorry in the slightest.

"Then don't." Ben deadpanned, but with a hostile undercurrent.

Chance dismissed Ben completely, in that way only he could manage. "May I have this dance?" He extended a hand gracefully, as if he spent most evenings patrolling swanky tuxedo parties picking up girls. Who knows? Maybe he did.

Ben went rigid. I was about to decline when Ella clapped Ben on the shoulders. "Come on, thundercloud. These two need to chat, and I won't sit out another song." Caught off guard, Ben allowed himself to be tugged away from the table. A second later, he was out on the dance floor, looking miserable as Ella grooved effortlessly beside him.

"Well then!" Chance smiled rakishly, bending closer and whispering in my ear. "There doesn't seem to be a problem now. Shall we?"

I nearly refused out of pique, but took a deep breath instead.

Chance obviously wanted something. I wanted to know what.

*He isn't my enemy. He may even be an ally.*

"Tactful as always, Claybourne." Taking his hand and rising.

"A gift."

Chance led me onto the hardwood, away from where Ben was awkwardly trying to keep up with Ella. He nodded toward the bandleader. Instantly the song changed, a slower tune filling the room.

My eyes rolled. "Oh, very nice."

Chance wrapped an arm around my waist, pulling me in. "Easier to talk this way."

We moved in rhythm, our heads nearly touching. I wasn't able to see his eyes, but his voice crawled straight into my ear. "How have things been, Tory?"

"Fine. Wonderful, actually."

A pause, then, "No . . . external complications?"

I tensed, but responded quickly. "Nope. None."

He pulled back to look at me, his tone low and insistent. "Are you certain? No rooftop watchers? No suspicious visitors to your little island? Nothing at all?"

"Nothing, Chance. They're gone." I swallowed. "I hope."

Chance nodded, seemed to relax a bit. We resumed our dance. "Same. Claybourne Manor has been positively . . . *tame* since you four stopped happening by."

I snorted. "If by 'tame' you mean nobody's had to jump off the roof, then I'll take it."

He chuckled, spinning me in time with the music. "I've had several less-than-cordial discussions with my security team about that, believe me."

We fell silent for a moment. I tried to spot Ben, but couldn't pick him out of the mass of swaying bodies. I knew more was coming. Chance already knew that our pursuers had called off the chase. Whatever he really wanted to discuss, we hadn't gotten there yet.

"And you?" he asked suddenly.

"Me what?"

"Nothing going on . . . inside?"

I felt a jolt. Tried to cover it. "You know what happened, Chance. You were there."

He didn't respond at first, and we took another turn around the crowded floor. But I was beginning to sweat. Did he suspect my powers weren't actually gone? Then I went cold. Was he experiencing the same thing?

I decided to go on the offensive. "And you?"

He cocked his head slightly. "What about me?"

"Any lingering . . . feelings?"

Chance watched me for several heartbeats. I couldn't get a read on him. Then, "Not a ripple. It seems my work was entirely successful. Same goes for the rest of the red-eyed pack, I looked into it. None of the old magic remains. Being Viral has been snuffed out entirely."

"Good." I turned away. "Same here."

Chance stopped dancing. "Are you *sure*, Tory? Have you really tried?"

I glanced around, voice dropping to a hiss. "*Of course I did*. It's gone, Chance. Done."

He watched me intently, for what seemed like an eternity. Then he sighed, drawing me in again. "I suppose it's for the best."

"You think?" I whispered sarcastically. "Losing our powers was the only thing that saved our lives! We'd be locked in cages otherwise."

Chance nodded unhappily. "I know, I know! But I can't help missing it, and I was Viral for a much shorter time than you. Surely you have regrets?"

Regrets? How could I? I'd recently become something else. Something more.

*But I'm not telling you that.*

"There's no point looking back," I said curtly. "Done is done."

I could tell Chance didn't share my opinion. To keep him from prying further, I said the first thing that popped into my head. "You and Ella seem to be getting along."

A wicked smile creased his lips. "Jealous? *Ouch!*"

I removed my heel from his foot. "Oops! Sorry."

He breathed a throaty chuckle. "Guess I deserved that."

"And more."

"So how is Benjamin?" Chance asked dryly. "Still rooting around in creeks?"

"He's been accepted into a prestigious environmental science program," I responded primly. "One of the best in the country. At a *college*. Perhaps you've heard of such places?"

Chance sniffed. "They seem cute, but I have a company to run."

I gave him my most level look. "You don't work there anymore, Chance. It was all over the news. The Board kicked you out after discovering those bills you ran up in Special Projects."

His expression soured. "Curing *us* was one of those expensive projects, thank you very much." Then he snorted derisively. "Whatever. I still own the stupid place. Let those suits handle the boring daily details."

We swung another turn. This was a long freaking song.

"Why *don't* you go to college?" I asked, genuinely curious. "You're too smart for your own good, and I'm sure you could buy your way in to wherever you felt like going."

Chance shrugged. "Maybe I will." The rakish grin returned. "Or I could cut out the middleman, and simply buy a university. Give myself all sorts of degrees. You might be onto something, Brennan."

I was about to scold him when I spotted Ben, still manfully escorting Ella in circles, his head swiveling as he scanned the crowd. He located me just as the music finally ended. I tried to disengage, but Chance led on as another slow song began to play. Ben glowered, the old frown sliding into place as Ella gathered him up again.

"Before you run off, I just want to be sure."

Chance forced me to meet his eye. He was very close. And damn good-looking.

"Sure about what?" My thoughts bounced like a tennis ball—from my relationship with Ben, to rejecting Chance, to the dark secrets we all shared. "I don't like games, Chance."

"There's *nothing* left of your flare power?" he asked, watching like a hawk. I got the distinct impression he didn't believe me the first time. "No lingering trace? Not a shred of the old abilities?" Chance moved closer and whispered, "Or anything new?"

I swallowed, but held his gaze. "It's gone, Chance. You've got to move on."

His eyes narrowed. He opened his mouth to speak again, but a strong hand clamped down on his shoulder, spinning him around.

"May I cut in?" Ben growled.

Chance's composure slipped a notch as he glared at Ben. Then he smirked. "By all means." He stepped back. Ben took my hand. Chance watched as Ben led me away across the dance floor.

"Thanks for the lovely dance!" Chance called. Then, quieter, "I'll be seeing you."

I tried not to wince. What did *that* mean?

"Jackass." Ben was scowling full throttle.

"Be nice." I nuzzled in close. "How was your twirl with Ella?"

"Humiliating." Ben released my hand and began tugging at his collar. "She moves like a ballerina, and I'm a frozen caveman." Then he blanched. "Not that—"

"Shut it, Blue." Resting my head against his chest. "I've seen her dance, too."

Ben put his mouth to my ear. "She had a lot of questions."

I nodded without looking up. "Chance, too."

He lifted my chin so I could see his face. *Should we worry?*

I shrugged. *What's the point?*

But I remembered the look in Chance's eyes.

Did he believe me? Was he suspicious we were hiding more? Was *he* hiding more?

The last thing we needed was Chance Claybourne on our scent again.

But ultimately, what could we do?

*Blargh.*

Business as usual.

The song ended, and we clapped politely with the other guests. A jaunty, bouncy tune came next. I squeezed Ben's hand, putting Chance out of my mind.

This was my father's wedding, damn it. I was going to have fun.

"One more?" I begged, rabbit-pecking his cheek.

Ben's smile was sickly. "Sure. You know me. Dancing. Love it."

A half hour of busting moves later, Chance was the furthest thing from my mind.

# CHAPTER 5

The cool evening air was refreshing.

I stepped from a covered porch, scanning the now-picked-over flower garden. A quarter of the rosebuds were gone, sacrificed to Operation Emergency Centerpieces. I felt terrible about the damage, but we'd had no other choice. Better a plundered garden than a suicidal bride.

Upon seeing our handiwork, the house manager had nearly fainted on the spot. Only Kit's promise of full reimbursement—plus a hefty donation to the building's annual arboretum fund—had smoothed his ruffled feathers.

I sat down on a stone bench. Heard a rustling in the bushes at the far end of the yard.

No need to call out.

Cooper already knew I was there.

*Sister-friend.* Coop emerged from the shadows wearing a wide doggie grin. I reached out and rubbed his head. He nuzzled my other hand, sniffing out the treat I'd brought for him. *Food?*

*I wouldn't forget about you.* I unwrapped a half-portion of filet mignon. Held it up for him to see. *Kit says you're being spoiled.*

I tossed the meat in a short arc. Coop caught it easily, then settled at my feet and began gnawing his prize. *Food is shared. Keeps pack strong.* The wolfdog radiated contentment as he scarfed down the expensive steak.

I smiled. *Try telling him that.*

Coop paused. Cocked his head. *Can't tell eldest. Can't hear. Nor his mate.*

*I know, buddy.* I stroked his scruffy back as he resumed eating. *Be thankful for that.*

Coop and I could communicate almost perfectly since . . . *whatever* . . . had happened when I swallowed Chance's antidote. But some things—like sarcasm—simply didn't translate. Our minds were too different for stuff like that.

I noticed a shallow cut on his snout. *What's this?* I asked, tracing the wound with a finger.

*Devil animal.* Coop gave me what I took to be a plaintive look. *Allowed to bite?*

Sighing, I shook my head. *Sorry, boy. Banjo belongs to Hi now. You two have to find a way to get along.*

*Foul beast.* Cooper bared his teeth. *Pretends friendship, then attacks. Then runs!*

I chuckled, scratching behind his ears. *Banjo's a cat. That's what they do.*

The music inside cut off. A slurred voice began droning into the microphone—no doubt an unplanned toast from an over-served guest. I was glad to be outside, away from all the hoopla. Chirping crickets sounded better to me than the raucous cheers in the ballroom.

A door opened, and one of the singers stepped out for a smoke. I sighed, nodded politely as he wished me a good evening. My moment of solitude had lasted less than a minute. But one look at Cooper—a nearly full-grown wolfdog, topping one hundred and twenty pounds—and the man beat a hasty retreat, shooting me a wide-eyed glance as he stumbled back inside.

I snorted, though I couldn't blame the guy. He probably didn't expect to find an apex predator roaming the swanky grounds. Coop's inclusion on the guest list had nearly cost us the booking, but I'd made Kit hold firm until the owners agreed to allow our "dog" the run of the garden during the event. I was extremely glad they hadn't asked for a picture first.

Coop nudged my arm with his wet nose. *Pack comes.*

A moment later Hi and Shelton ambled outside, with Ben a short step behind. Spotting Cooper and me by the bench, Hi boasted, "I told you so," as they moved to join us.

"The band ignored your request for a reason," Shelton said to Hi, tossing me a half-wave as he unbuttoned the neck of his tuxedo shirt. "Nobody wants to *hear* 'YMCA,' much less dance to it. It's an objectively terrible song."

"The Village People are a wedding staple!" Hi removed his jacket, raked a hand through his sweat-dampened brown hair. "Plus, I know how to read a room. That crowd was primed for some funky disco action."

Shelton shook his head. Pointed to Ben without looking.

"Disco sucks," Ben said.

Shelton nodded. "True story."

"I'm surrounded by barbarians." Hi glanced over at Cooper crouching in the grass next to me, and his brow formed a V. "Tell that mutt of yours to stop harassing my sweet angel. Banjo's been in a terrible mood all weekend."

"Your psycho cat is the problem." Then I sent, *And tell him yourself.*

"Cujo over there started it." Hi jabbed an index finger at the wolf-dog. *I saw you chase my darling kitty-cat into the dunes this morning. Quit being a bully.*

Coop growled deep in his throat. *Deceitful creature. Ambushed me.*

"Coop has scratches on his face," I snapped. "Your stupid cat likes to jump out of the bushes and slash him, then bolt into the woods. One of these days, she's getting chomped."

"She better not!" Hi warned, crossing his arms. "I didn't rescue Banjo from homelessness just to serve her up as wolf chow. Feline rights, yo. Cats matter, too."

Whatever my response might've been was preempted by the sound of breaking glass, followed by high-pitched laughter. A guitarist strummed a few chords, then the whole band picked back up.

"Reception's picking up steam." Ben absently kicked a pebble. "Long night ahead."

Shelton plopped down onto the bench beside me. "If it's all the same to you guys, I might just hang out here for a while. People in there are acting like fools."

"Not me, gents." Hi elbowed Ben, catching a dark look in return. "I know *you're* spoken for, but this party is a target-rich environment. I wouldn't want to let the ladies down. Player's gotta play."

Shelton covered his eyes. "You need to stop."

"Seriously." Ben knelt and scratched behind Coop's ears.

Outside the garden wall, a car door opened and shut. Seconds later an iron gate rattled less than a dozen yards from where we were gathered. The bars swung open and a man in a white chef's uniform entered the garden. He closed the gate quickly and hurried toward the building.

Coop lifted his head, tracking the stranger's progress. Then he yapped sharply, popping to his feet with hackles raised.

The newcomer nearly jumped out of his skin. He backpedaled a few steps, eyes darting, trying to pierce the gloom.

"Coop!" I scolded, grabbing his collar and pulling him back.

It must've been an odd scene to the late-arriving chef. While my friends and I could see perfectly well in the moonlight, to him we were four teens skulking in a dark garden. With a sizeable wild animal, no less.

"Kids and a freaking wolf," the man muttered in astonishment, but his body relaxed. He was tall and bulky, with close-set green eyes and bushy red hair poking from beneath his chef's hat. The name BIGGS was stitched on to his pure white smock, which was fully buttoned up, as if we'd interrupted him mid-shift. Gathering himself, the man nodded our way, then strode briskly for the door and disappeared inside.

Coop barked again. Hauled me a step closer.

*Easy, fella.* I was surprised. It wasn't often Coop menaced someone.

And yet . . . something about the cook's reaction felt . . . off. Like he was relieved it was only us, despite the presence of a riled-up half-wild canine.

Was he avoiding someone? Everyone?

My earlier suspicions flared back to life. Dead flowers. Missing altar pins. And who was this random chef, showing up way late and sneaking in through a secluded garden gate?

The bulk of Corcoran's security team had disbanded after the service, when the guests moved inside. Only the captain and two handpicked officers remained to "keep an eye on things." And stuff their faces with free gourmet food, of course.

Coop gave a last snarl and settled back down. But I'd learned to trust his instincts.

I straightened, began chewing my bottom lip. "Huh."

Ben's head rose. "What is it?"

I scratched my cheek, thinking. "That guy was acting kinda weird, wasn't he?"

Hi glanced at his watch. "Dinner ended almost an hour ago. If he's on tonight's catering crew, he missed the job. Maybe he's hoping no one will notice."

I frowned. "Could be."

Ben was now eyeing the door. "But you don't think so."

"It's just . . ." I shook my head, unsure.

I looked at Coop. *That man? Was there something wrong?*

Coop's head tilted, as if he struggled with how to respond. *Smell . . . off. Smell trouble.*

The others heard our exchange. Frowning, Shelton removed his clear-lensed glasses. He could see perfectly now, but had no idea how to explain that to his parents. "Lots of things going wrong at this wedding, huh?"

"Yep." Hi gave me a significant look. "If we're laying it out there, I'm still baffled by the liquid in those vases. How could a florist accidentally use chemicals that *kill* flowers?"

Ben cleared his throat. "Yeah. So. I've been thinking about the pins." He glanced up and met my eye. "I can't see how they could fall out on their own. The whole point of their design is that they *don't* fall out."

"You know, now that I think about it . . ." Shelton pointed a hesitant finger at the door the mystery cook had entered. "Weren't the caterers wearing uniforms with blue stripes?"

My pulse sped up. The newcomer had been dressed in white from head to toe.

"That actually seems right." Hi tapped his chin, making a show of considering Shelton's words. "You think the guy's working for HYDRA? Or is just drunk and lost?"

Snap decision. "Let's go see."

Popping to my feet, I headed for the door. The boys exchanged mental shrugs before rising and following. Cooper leapt to join me, but I placed a hand on his furry head.

*Sorry, boy. Out of bounds. Wait here.*

He whined, but stayed put. *Call if need.*

Inside the door, the reception was straight ahead, but a covert scan of the ballroom failed to turn up our mystery chef. I ducked back out before anyone noticed me. "He's not in there, which isn't surprising."

Hi pointed to our left, down a short hallway. "Only one other way to go."

I nodded. The corridor led to the kitchen, which was empty for the moment. I paused in the doorway as doubt began creeping in. What was I doing, really?

Footfalls in an adjacent room. I looked to Ben, who shrugged. "Why not?"

We entered a small staging room connected to the ballroom by a pair of swinging doors. Music and laughter leaked through the cracks, but I only had eyes for our chef. The big man had his back to us as he hovered over Whitney's triple-tiered wedding cake.

I put a finger to my lips, edging closer for a better look. The man was smoothing the cake's frosting with a flat-bladed implement. He held something in his other hand I couldn't see. As I watched, he glanced at a notepad lying on the cake's rolling cart.

Nothing about this felt right.

"Hey!" I called out.

The man flinched, then spun around, keeping both hands hidden behind his back. He seemed to recognize us after a beat. His gaze darted to the kitchen door, then the doors leading to the ballroom. He blew out a shaky breath, once again looking relieved. "Yes?" he snapped in an annoyed voice.

"What are you doing in here?" I squinted at the notepad. Something was scribbled in cursive on its face.

Biggs noticed my glance. Eyes widening, his right hand shot out, ripping off the top sheet and crumpling it in his fist. The notepad tumbled to the carpet, ignored. "Just, uh, relaxing the frosting mixture," he stammered, eyes once again darting between the doors. "We don't want it to, um, harden before the cake is served. Pretty basic stuff."

His back was ramrod straight. Beads of sweat darkened his temples.

All my alarms were sounding at once.

Something was wrong.

*Check him out*, Ben sent, as if he'd read my thoughts. He may have.

I stepped closer to Biggs than most strangers find comfortable. Leaned forward and inhaled deeply, drinking the man's scent. I detected the acrid stench of deception immediately.

*He's lying.*

Biggs reared back, watching me warily. "Did you just—"

The ballroom speakers squealed. Someone made an announcement.

Biggs seemed to forget I was there, eyeing the doors, an artery pumping in his neck.

I stepped sideways to get a look at the cake, a three-level monstrosity of pink curls and raspberry script, topped by a chocolate bride and groom. Beside it, a metal bowl half-filled with brown liquid rested on the cart. A pastry brush and plastic icing smoother sat beside it.

Biggs had been retouching the cake.

And from the looks of things, doing a crap job of it.

"Why is the icing smeared?" I demanded. The top and middle tiers looked uneven, as if the frosting had been massaged with significantly less skill than the original application.

*I don't like this. What's he doing? The cake looks worse.*

The boys tensed behind me.

Biggs must've sensed the change in atmosphere. He stepped backward, his left hand still tucked out of sight.

"What's in the bowl?" Hi pointed at the cart. "Weird place for a finger bath."

Biggs glared, then sniffed imperiously. "I don't have time for this."

He started to turn away. Found a hand on his shoulder, stopping him.

Ben winked at the chef. "Make time."

Biggs shrugged Ben off with a sneer. But despite the bravado, dots of perspiration lined his brow. His left hand remained maddeningly out of view.

"This cake looked better before you messed with it." Shelton spoke softly, as if making a casual observation. "You sure you were supposed to?"

I pointed to his closed fist. "What's that note about? Why'd you ball it up?"

Biggs didn't answer. I could sense his confidence leaching away, despite his size. The four of us had him surrounded, and it was making him uncomfortable. "I . . . I . . . uh . . . I have to prepare the cake for service now." He made a shooing gesture with his fist. "You'd better run along now. Go on."

No one moved.

"Okay, fine." Biggs spun and dropped something into the bowl, then scooped it with one hand, shielding the rim so we couldn't see inside. "Guests aren't supposed to be back here. I'm going to get my boss." He shouldered through our circle—and the kitchen door—before anyone had a chance to stop him.

We exchanged glances.

"That was interesting," Hi said. "It's like we caught him with his pants down."

"Maybe we did." Shelton was inspecting the cake. "Dude really jacked this frosting up. It's not crazy noticeable, but he smashed some of the ridges when he smoothed the icing. Look at the bottom tier. See how it's supposed to look?"

Hi licked his lips. "Still looks delicious. Maybe I should take a small taste, just to—"

"Don't even think about it," Ben warned. "Whitney would have a heart attack. Whatever that guy was doing, thankfully the damage isn't too bad."

True.

But something was definitely fishy.

Just then, three cooks bustled in from the ballroom, laughing and exchanging jokes. Seeing us around the cake, they smiled. "Soon!" promised a woman with twinkling brown eyes.

I barely heard, eyes glued to her uniform.

Specifically, to the royal blue piping on her pants, hat, and smock.

I scanned the other two cooks. They were dressed identically to the first woman.

Biggs wasn't wearing the same uniform.

A cold feeling formed in the pit of my stomach. I spun.

*Shelton, find that jerk. See where he goes and what he's doing.*

Shelton ran a hand across his face, but hurried out. *Can't even go to a freaking wedding . . .*

Oblivious to my anxiety, the three caterers unlocked the cart's wheels and began wheeling the cake toward the double doors. They hadn't noticed the damage to the icing. As they disappeared into the ballroom, I felt a twinge of panic.

*Hi, follow the cake. Just . . . keep an eye on it.*

*That I can do.* Hi slipped through the doors behind them.

Ben and I were alone. He grabbed my hand, worry lines creasing his forehead. *What is it?*

I shook my head as a shiver swept through me. *I don't know.*

But my instincts screamed in warning.

# CHAPTER 6

Applause thundered inside the ballroom.

The wedding cake had arrived, and another speech was taking place.

I knew what came next. Cutting. Pictures. Whitney and Kit hand-feeding each other like dorks. Tiny plates being distributed amongst the guests.

I broke out in a cold sweat.

The bowl. The liquid. The brush. Smeared icing.

Biggs had done something terrible, I just knew it.

*I let them wheel that sucker out of here, without saying a word.*

*Should we stop it?* Ben asked. I must've inadvertently broadcast my thought.

I wavered, unable to decide. Was I being paranoid?

I didn't *know* anything. Biggs had definitely messed with the cake, but what if he really *was* supposed to be there? It's not like I had the freaking catering staff memorized. Maybe being a suspicious jerk just came naturally to him.

No. I trusted my gut. This felt all wrong.

I reached out with my thoughts. *Shelton, where did Biggs go?*

His response was faint. We couldn't see each other, and were almost out of communication range. *We're in the men's room. I found him inside, but he didn't notice me. Right now he's washing the bejesus out of that metal bowl.*

"Not good," Ben grumbled, eavesdropping on our communications.

I wholeheartedly agreed. *Hi, you have eyes on the cake?*

*Affirmative. It's parked near the dance floor, but they haven't touched it yet. Kit's mother is blabbering about horseshoes or something. I think she's drunk. Tempe's trying to pull her aside. Oh man, the cake looks delicious.*

*Don't let anyone eat a piece. Not yet.*

Hiram's reply was laced with annoyance. *How am I supposed to do that?*

*Use your imagination.*

Shelton's voice cut into our headspace. *Biggs trashed the bowl, and then flushed the note! That's weird, right?*

My stomach dropped. Worse and worse. *Don't let him leave the building!*

*What? HOW?!?*

*Improvise!* I had no idea either.

"You think he's trying to *poison* people?" Ben asked me in a sharp voice. It was almost jarring to hear words spoken out loud.

"I don't know!" I was suddenly pacing. "Should we barge in there and stop the cake ceremony? We'll look like lunatics. No one would understand, and I can't prove anything!"

Ben winced. "Whitney might burst into flames."

My eyes fell on the notepad lying on the carpet. I rushed forward and grabbed it.

"What's that?" Ben said.

A blank sheet stared up at me. I flipped through the rest of the pages. More of the same.

"Nothing." Then an idea struck me. "Unless . . ."

In the corner of the room was a small table with a desk lamp. I raced over and switched on the light. Held the notepad close to the bulb. Angled it slowly. "Ben, look!"

When tilted *just* so, I could see faint characters indented into the top sheet.

I stared at the marks until my eyes watered, but even with my enhanced vision I couldn't make anything out. I handed the pad to Ben, but he had no better luck.

"Damn it!" Ben growled. "Whatever was written here, he really didn't want us to see it."

"But we can!" I blurted, eyes rounding. "I need a pencil!"

Ben gave me a puzzled look, but he'd learned when to hold his tongue. A quick survey of the staging room turned up nothing, so he ran into the kitchen. I heard drawers being yanked open, followed by a triumphant "Bingo!"

Ben raced back in with a weathered number two pencil covered in bite marks.

"Gross." But I snatched it from him anyway. "It's sharpened, at least."

I placed the pencil tip flat against the top sheet of the notepad. Softly, carefully, I began sliding the graphite back and forth across the indentations on the page.

Ben scratched his temple. "Care to explain?"

"If I do this correctly," I said, tongue wedged between my teeth, "the graphite will darken the paper *around* the indentations without reaching inside them, leaving the valleys white."

He was already nodding. "Revealing on *this* sheet whatever's been pressed into it by the handwriting on the page above." Ben squeezed my shoulder, sending a surge of warmth through my body. "Tory, that's brilliant."

"Hold the applause. We haven't found anything yet." But internally, I preened.

Shelton's voice arrowed into my brain. Still faint, and panting like he'd run a marathon. *Okay. So. I ran two brooms through the bathroom's door handles and . . . and . . . well . . . Biggs is currently locked inside there. He's . . . he's . . . uh . . . he's pretty mad about it. But the door seems to be holding up.*

Ben looked as shocked as I felt. *You imprisoned him in the men's room?*

*YOU TOLD ME TO STOP HIM!* Shelton mind-shouted, his voice jagged as a live wire. *What was I supposed to do, politely ask him to wait in the lobby!?!*

*No. Right.* I tried to sound reassuring, though my arm hairs were standing on end. *Good job.*

Then to Ben: *Oh my God. If I'm wrong about him, we're in serious trouble.*

*I heard that!* Shelton yelled. *I knew this was crazy! I'm now officially a kidnapper.*

*Speeches are done!* Hi sent from the ballroom. *Whitney is waving a giant knife.*

"Crap." I couldn't rush my shading work without compromising the results. *I need five more minutes, Hi. Stall them.*

*You've got sixty seconds*, he replied tersely. *Whitney's jabbering right now, but she'll be ready to slice and dice at any moment. Hey, if everyone else takes a piece, there's no reason why I can't have one, is there?*

Ben slapped his forehead. *It might be poisoned, you moron!*

*All life is risk.*

I jumped as Shelton burst into the room. "Biggs is pounding the bathroom door!"

Ben covered his face. "He's probably a bit upset. I'd be."

Shelton's hands flew up. "What were my other options!? Tackle him? Hogtie him in the handicapped stall? He washed the bowl, flushed the note, and was about to bail. There was nothing else I could do except just let him go!"

"Everyone zip it!" I finished the last pencil strokes and gently blew excess graphite from the page. Two cursive lines were now legible.

> *Two parts per thousand into the icing*
> *Ipecac commercial syrup—1/14 extract roots/rhizomes*

"Oh mamma," Shelton moaned. "There *is* something in the frosting!"

"But what?" Ben said. "Some kind of syrup? That doesn't sound bad."

*Time's up!* Hi's voice was as tense as barbed wire. *They're cutting the cake together.*

My mind blanked. I stared at the notepad without any idea what to do next. The second line was a total mystery. What the heck was commercial syrup?

*Whitney and Kit have the first slice*, Hi reported.

"Ipecac commercial syrup," I mumbled, thinking furiously. "Made from . . . plant roots?"

"I feel like I've heard of that before," Shelton muttered.

My head whipped to him. "What? Which word?"

"Ipecac." Then Shelton snapped his fingers, eyes rounding like dinner plates. "I remember now! My cousin Dudley! One time when we were kids, he drank a bunch of Windex on a dare. My grandmother found out, started screaming for that stuff. Ipecac. The word stuck with me. She had some in her medicine cabinet."

I was practically bouncing up and down. "Why would Biggs put *medicine* in . . ."

My eyes popped as the answer hit me. *Ipecac.*

*Forks are out!* Hi sent. *Repeat: forks are out! The photographer is lining up a picture!*

I took a running step toward the double doors. Realized I'd never make it in time.

*Hi, you have to stop them!* I sent urgently.

*I think that ship has sailed, Tor.*

*Do whatever it takes! The frosting is spiked!*

*What am I supposed to do, freeze time? I'm not an X-Man!*

*HIRAM! This is SERIOUS! STOP THEM!*

Raw panic from Hiram. *How the heck am I—*

*JUST DO IT!*

*ALL RIGHT ALREADY!*

Adrenaline flooded the bond. Shelton, Ben, and I shuddered with the force of it.

Shelton reached for his earlobe. "What's he doin—?"

Something crashed in the ballroom. Followed by screams.

A voice boomed through the double doors. "Somebody stop him! He's crazy!"

"Ho boy," Ben breathed.

Shelton winced. Removed his glasses.

I shook my head, bereft of speech.

As one, we barreled into the reception.

# CHAPTER 7

Flustered guests had formed a circle on the dance floor.

Someone was lying facedown in the middle of it.

"Well," Ben began, but didn't follow up.

Shelton swallowed.

I pinched the bridge of my nose. "He didn't have a lot of alternatives."

Hi was sprawled out on the hardwood, covered in crumbs and icing. The rolling cart was upended to one side. Plates and forks littered the parquet around him. He'd clearly thrown himself onto the cake, knocking everything over in a desperate attempt to prevent it from being eaten.

"HIRAM!" Kit was still holding his fork, mouth hanging open, his face a rare shade of purple. Whitney stood beside him, dumbstruck, gripping a now-empty plate. Everyone was staring at my friend, clearly unable to comprehend why this insane teenager had thrown himself atop a perfectly good wedding cake.

"This will be difficult to explain," Ben whispered.

Shelton giggled involuntarily. "That's an understatement."

I rushed over to Hi, who'd rolled onto his back and wasn't moving. "Are you okay?"

"I even got the slice in Whitney's hand," he mumbled through a layer of icing coating his face. He rose to an elbow, wiping sugar from his eye sockets. Sighed. I could tell he was trying to come to grips with what he'd just done. He lay back down on his back. "I'm gonna need some help smoothing this one over, Tor. Plus a gurney. I broke my everything."

"My . . . my . . . *wedding cake!*" Whitney stifled a sob, her hands shooting toward the wreckage on the dance floor. "It's ruined!"

Best Man Eric elbowed a path through the crowd, red-faced and struggling for balance. "You're dog-meat, pal!" he slurred. "You ruined my sister's big day!"

He reached for Hi, but I shoved him sideways. "Back off! I'll explain."

But how? All I had was the shadow of a note, and a wild hunch.

*Plus a red-haired chef imprisoned in the men's room.*

Lightning raced down my spine.

I felt every eye in the room. Stunned gazes, quickly growing angry.

Then Ben was at my side. Inside my head, steadying me. *Take it slow. Step by step.*

Shelton snaked around Eric, positioning himself protectively over Hi. My skinny friend watched Whitney's brother warily. "You need to step back, dude."

I took a moment to marshal my thoughts. *Start strong.*

"This cake was poisoned!" I said loudly, eliciting horrified gasps.

There. Good.

Kit's mouth worked, but no sound emerged. Whitney glanced at the smeared plate clutched between her fingers, then squealed, dropping it like a snake. Shattering china sparked a fresh round of exclamations.

"Tory!" Kit shook his head roughly, as if chasing away a bad dream. "Why would you say such a thing?"

Captain Corcoran preempted my response.

Which, admittedly, I hadn't quite formed yet.

"Did the girl say *poison*?" Corcoran began maneuvering his bulk through the circle of onlookers, projecting so everyone could hear. "Tory Brennan, are you accusing someone of . . . *attempted murder*?"

Shelton's eyes found the ceiling. *Man, I can't stand this guy*.

*Feed him the cake*, Hi suggested, still lying over most of it.

*Slow*, Ben repeated, catching my eye and holding it. *Step by step*.

I sucked in all Ben's confidence I could absorb. Gave his hand a quick squeeze. Then, clearing my throat, I addressed the ring of glowering faces. "The icing on this cake was spiked with something dangerous. Hi learned at the last moment, and did what he could to stop you guys from eating it. Everyone should be *thanking* him. You just dodged a bullet."

A tremor rippled through the crowd. Hissed denials. The band huddled together onstage, shaking their collective heads. They'd probably seen it all, but not this.

My gaze darted from face to face, assessing the impact of my words. Chance and Ella had wormed to the inside of the group and were eyeing me strangely. Beside them, Tempe and Harry wore matching frowns of concern. Madison and Jason together stood with his parents, while Ashley and Courtney were huddled a step behind them, whispering and hiding smiles. *God, I hate those two*.

But people were listening. I had a shot at this.

Corcoran crossed his arms. Glared down from his high horse. We'd never had a great relationship—or even a good one—but he knew better than to dismiss me outright. "Whaddya mean, *spiked*?"

I pitched my voice to reach everyone. Not that it was difficult—at that moment, despite the dozens of guests, you could've heard a mouse sneeze in that ballroom.

"A few minutes ago, an unknown individual was tampering with this cake." I spoke formally, aiming to be as precise as possible.

"The man was dressed like a chef—with the name Biggs embroidered on his chest—but his uniform didn't match the ones worn by tonight's catering staff. My friends and I caught him mixing an unknown liquid into the icing. When we asked him what he was doing, he stormed away, but my friend Shelton caught him cleaning out a metal bowl in the men's bathroom. Then he threw it away."

Furious whispers. A tense-faced server sprinted toward the kitchen, likely to retrieve the head caterer.

I caught Kit's eye. Registered his complete bewilderment.

Whitney's shoulders were trembling. "Why would anyone *do* such a thing?"

"Just hold on!" Corcoran held up a hand before giving me a hard look. "You saw a cook fixing the wedding cake, and just assumed he was up to no good?" The captain crossed his arms, displaying his skepticism to the rapt audience. "Sounds like your imagination may've gotten the best of you. And this poor cake, unfortunately."

Choking back my irritation, I held up the notepad. "When we found him, the suspect was referring to something written down on this pad. Instructions of some kind. He balled up the page when we confronted him, and later flushed it down the toilet. But we were able to recover the message by shading the sheet directly beneath it. See for yourself."

The crowd stirred. Ella and Chance exchanged a glance. What were they about?

As I handed the pad to Corcoran, I noticed Tempe nodding, which gave me confidence.

"*Two parts per thousand into the icing*," the captain read, frowning through his mustache. "And what's this here about . . . ip-e-cac syrup?" He sounded the word out slowly, then rubbed his chin. "I swear, everything you kids touch never makes any plain sense. And how are we supposed to locate this mystery chef? Biggs, you said? Sounds made-up to me."

I glanced at Shelton, who gulped, but nodded.

"We know where he is." Keeping my voice level. "He's been . . . detained."

Corcoran's eyes shot to me. "Detained? By whom?"

Ben stepped between us. "He's locked in the men's bathroom. We were just coming to find you."

Before anyone could react, Eric DuBois stepped forward and grabbed my arm. "Are you saying that someone put *ipecac syrup* in the wedding cake?"

I nodded. "In the icing. We think."

Eric grew wide-eyed. "Oh jeez."

Ben clamped a hand on to Eric's wrist. Met his eye. Shook his head.

Eric released me with a shrug. "That's bad news," he said to Whitney, who was standing stone still and blinking like an owl. "Remember when I ate those urinal cakes as a kid? Mom made me drink that stuff. It makes you puke something fierce."

My eyes darted to Tempe, who'd paled. I spoke over the murmuring crowd. "He's right. For years, ipecac syrup was a household medicine."

"So it's not poison?" Hi had propped his elbow again, but otherwise made no effort to rise from the dessert-pocalypse he'd created. "We can eat the cake?"

I shook my head. "Ipecac syrup makes people throw up. Immediately. It tastes very sweet, like concentrated sugar, but get some of that junk inside you and it's coming out. Period. But doctors stopped recommending it because its side effects are worse than the benefits. It can kill you."

"What?" Eric looked incredulous.

"It's true." All heads swung to a grim-faced Tempe. "For decades ipecac syrup was used to induce vomiting. Pediatricians used to advise parents to keep some in their homes in case of accidental poisonings, but current guidelines strongly advise against it. In fact, you're supposed to dump any remaining ipecac syrup down the drain. There's little evidence it actually helps in poisoning cases, and overdoses can be fatal. They don't even make it anymore."

Corcoran held up a finger, spoke as slowly as the ponderous wheels of his reasoning. "So . . . whoever wrote that note . . . was trying to . . . *kill* . . . all these people?"

Shouts erupted, but Tempe jumped in before the panic could spread. "I highly doubt it. Ipecac was a trusted medication for years. I bet whoever did this just wanted to give everyone a really terrible night."

Whitney stomped a foot. "*My* night!" She was seconds from releasing the waterworks.

"Sabotage," Kit growled, clenching his fists. "When I find this bastard . . ."

"Find him?" Someone said with a laugh. Chance stepped into the limelight, amusement twinkling in his eyes. "Isn't the culprit currently imprisoned in a toilet?"

Corcoran flinched, then sprang into action. "Johnson! Vorhees! On me!" He tossed the notepad at me, clamping a hand on Shelton as his remaining subordinates hurried to obey. "This young man will tell us where the suspect is."

"Sure," Shelton agreed, eyeing Corcoran apprehensively. "No problem. Since I clearly did the right thing by locking him up in the bathroom, right? The legal, not-in-any-way-criminal, correct call. Right?"

Corcoran huffed impatiently. "We'll see."

Whispers spread like wildfire as Shelton told the cops where Biggs was. I blocked them all out. Something Corcoran had said was bothering me.

"*Whoever wrote that note,*" I muttered, testing the phrase in my head. Then it hit me.

*Not just the cook.*

The boys shot me puzzled looks as Corcoran's team hurried from the ballroom.

*Spiking the cake*, I sent. *It can't be Biggs working alone.*

I grew excited and nervous at the same time.

*Think about it! Biggs wouldn't write such a simple note to himself. Someone else did!*

I glanced down at the notepad. The cursive script was neat and tidy. Flowery.

Distinctly female-looking, though I'd been wrong on that count before.

*An accomplice?* Hi rose awkwardly, wiping cake debris from his ruined tuxedo. The other guests gave him a wide berth. *Seems overly complicated, don't you think?*

*Not if you want an alibi.* Ben was scowling like old times. *Throw people off your scent.*

I stared at the floor as pieces of evidence clicked together in my mind. *The note lists an active ingredient, ipecac syrup, and gives specific instructions on how to administer it. It's very precise. Whoever wrote this was familiar with the substance. Knew the exact proper dosage.*

My head rose. I scanned the faces surrounding us, my thoughts streaming freely for the boys to hear. *This morning, someone killed flowers using a toxic mixture. Later, the altar nearly collapsed just as Whitney and Kit stepped onto it. The precisely correct pins had been pulled.* I spun in a slow circle as I sent, inspecting the crowd. *Then we caught Biggs messing with the cake, carrying specific instructions on how to insert a dangerous substance into the frosting.*

I stopped as a familiar face came into view.

*Someone wanted this wedding to be a disaster*, I said.

*Someone vindictive*, Hi agreed.

*Petty*, Ben added.

*And carrying a major grudge*, Shelton finished.

Anger ignited within me. *Now who'd want to do a thing like that?*

Mike Iglehart was lounging at the back of the circle, a strange smile on his face.

*Iglehart.*

My blood boiled at the sight of his smug little grin.

*He* hates *Kit*, I sent, *Chance told us so. And he's got an advanced degree in chemistry!*

Hi nodded like a bobblehead. *He's a veterinary PhD. Does boatloads of lab experiments. Knows biology, chemistry, and physics. Even medicine.*

Shelton whistled. *Everything you'd need to pull off these moves.*

Ben stared daggers at the wormy scientist. *Want me to grab him?*

I pounded my thigh, stymied. *We have no proof.*

Iglehart abruptly noticed our attention. The self-satisfied smile vanished. With a lurch, he began edging backward, angling toward the exit, no longer looking so entertained.

Kit turned to speak with me and noticed the direction of my glare. His frown deepened as he spotted his coworker sneaking toward the door. "Mike?"

Heads turned in Iglehart's direction. He straightened quickly. "What?" he demanded loudly, blinking and fidgety under all that scrutiny. "Why are you staring at *me*? I had nothing to do with this!"

"Nothing to do with what?" Hi asked innocently.

"With anything!" Iglehart backed up another step. Those standing near him inched away, leaving the twitchy little man isolated. "Stop twisting my words!"

Kit looked at me. I shrugged, still glaring at Iglehart. "Biggs probably had an accomplice. He wasn't here this morning when the flowers arrived, and didn't attend the service. Plus, who wrote that note?"

"You think it was *all* intentional?" Kit hissed, evidently considering the prospect for the first time. I nodded.

"All what?" Whitney demanded. We hadn't noticed her listening.

Kit blanched, then took his wife's hand and patted it gently. "The lilies, honey. We talked about how they died so quickly this afternoon, and had to be replaced. Then the altar nearly fell apart during the service. It's all very . . . suspicious."

The crowd had been listening, and now held its breath in shocked silence. Whitney looked as if each of Kit's sentences had been a physical blow. Biting her bottom lip, she pointed dramatically at Iglehart. "And this scoundrel may be involved?"

"No!" Iglehart squawked. "I'm an important scientist!"

"This freaking guy." Hi snorted. "His mother obviously didn't hug him enough."

"*Is* it him?" Ben whispered to me out of the side of his mouth.

I shook my head, unsure. Frustrated. I *knew* Iglehart hated Kit, but that didn't prove he'd tried to poison everyone. "Biggs may be the only one who can ID his accomplice."

I watched the kitchen door. What was taking Corcoran so long?

"What about the ipecac syrup?" Hi asked suddenly.

"Nothing left," Shelton said sourly. "Biggs cleaned out his bowl before he dumped it."

"No, wait!" I punched Hi's shoulder in excitement. "You're a genius!"

"Ow!" Hi rubbed his arm. "Don't hit the genius."

"Biggs came through the garden gate empty-handed." I grabbed Shelton's scrawny arm. "What did he have with him in the bathroom?"

Shelton eyed me skittishly, hoping to avoid any follow-up blows. "Just the crumpled-up paper and the bowl. Nothing else that I saw."

Hiram's eyes bulged. "His uniform didn't have any pockets!"

Ben nodded, catching on. "So the ipecac was already *inside* the building when Biggs arrived. He knew where to find it, must've located a bottle of the stuff before we followed him into the staging room."

"The notepad as well," Hi added. "He picked up both. Quickly, too, since we weren't far behind him."

"We know he flushed the note." Ben frowned. "But not the bottle?"

Shelton shook his head firmly. "And he didn't trash it, either. Just the bowl."

"Which means the ipecac bottle is *still* here somewhere." Blood rushed to my face as I laid out my theory. "Biggs sneaks inside, locates the notepad and a bottle of ipecac syrup—"

"Probably together," Hi interjected.

I nodded. "Then he fills a bowl and gets to work. But we catch him in the act. So he hides the medicine bottle from us behind his back, then storms out and stashes it before Shelton catches up to him in the men's room." I snapped my fingers. "I bet you *anything* he put it right back where he found it. Probably didn't have time to do anything else."

Hi tapped his temple. "That means the bottle's currently hidden where his accomplice left it in the first place."

"That location might tell us a lot," I said excitedly. "We just have to find the bottle."

Hinges creaked. Every head swung toward the kitchen doors.

Captain Corcoran reentered the ballroom, a trio of shadows at his back.

"Okay," Shelton said cautiously. "So how do we find the bottle?"

I smiled, eyes gleaming. "We use our best nose."

My eyelids slid shut. I sent the call.

Moments later, a gruff voice answered.

*I come.*

# CHAPTER 8

"He's not talking," Corcoran grumbled.

The captain was huddled with Kit and Tempe beside the stage. Biggs stood between the other two officers, at the edge of the dance floor, sneering arrogantly. Guests were giving the big man a wide berth.

The crowd had clumped into chattering groups, observing the bizarre scene with varying degrees of shock and titillation. Ella and Chance were whispering animatedly, their expressions guarded. Ashley and Courtney couldn't keep their mirth in check. Agnes Taylor loudly instructed her husband to gather their things, proclaiming the wedding to be a scandal unfit for Magnolia League participation. Whitney, being comforted by her bridesmaids, nearly crumpled in mortification.

Kit sighed. "What do we do?"

Corcoran moved closer, dropping his voice. Every Viral still heard, of course.

"We've got nothing to hold him on." His tone was laced with frustration, but also carried an undercurrent of anxiety. "No evidence of anything at all, to be honest. We still don't know for sure that the cake is bad. *And those fool kids locked that man in the john!*"

"At the very least he's trespassing," Tempe argued. "We've proven he's not on the catering staff."

"That's the only thing that might save our butts." Corcoran frowned. "He claims he's a wedding crasher looking for a free slice of cake. Can't toss him in a cell for that. Or cage him in a bathroom, FYI!"

Tempe nodded unhappily. "Then let's sweat the rat."

But questioning Mike Iglehart proved no more fruitful. Called forward by Corcoran, the little scientist wasn't happy about it, standing before the captain with his head sunk between his shoulders like a man facing the guillotine.

"You know this man?" Corcoran demanded, motioning to Biggs. The false chef stood with his arms crossed, a statue of brash poise, unmoved by the glares raining down on him.

"Of course not!" Iglehart glowered at Corcoran, but his nervous gaze kept darting to the mass of onlookers. He shrank visibly from the collective scrutiny, much of which came from his LIRI coworkers. The man couldn't have looked guiltier. "I've never been more insulted in my life!" he huffed.

"You know about this ip-e-cac stuff?" Corcoran clearly didn't understand the particulars, or seem in a hurry to learn them.

"I mean, um . . . throughout my career, I've . . ." Iglehart glanced at Kit, who was eyeing him sternly, then slapped his side in frustration. "Yes, of *course* I know what it is!" he spat. "It was a very common medicine. Every LIRI employee here knows about ipecac syrup!"

Corcoran swung to Kit. "You keep some of this stuff on your crazy monkey island?"

Kit nodded. "A little. In reserve, in case we need it for something in the future. As Tempe said, pharmaceutical companies stopped making ipecac syrup in 2010, so I thought it'd be wise to stockpile a few bottles." He looked coldly at Iglehart. "Only senior employees like Mike have access to those stores."

Everyone watched the weasel squirm. Chance and Ella were now whispering with Jason and Madison, while Courtney and Ashley looked as happy as toddlers at the circus. Some people just love drama.

I caught Chance's eye, and he shrugged apologetically.

I nodded. I'd never suspected him. Chance was a lot of things, but spiking a cake to make people vomit wasn't in his playbook. I briefly considered Courtney and Ashley, snickering behind him, but this didn't feel like their style either. They'd have come at me directly somehow, and would want me to know who'd done it. Anonymously ruining my dad's wedding just didn't track.

Tempe had moved to Whitney and was trying to calm her down. My stepmother was close to hyperventilating. After a few moments Tempe glanced back at Corcoran, who continued to hammer at Iglehart. She wore a small frown. I shared her disapproval. The captain was getting ahead of himself in an attempt to grab the spotlight.

As much as I despised Iglehart, we didn't have proof he'd done anything.

Yet.

Which is why I'd called in reinforcements.

*Here.*

The swinging doors nudged open.

A hundred-plus-pound gray-wolf hybrid slipped into the ballroom.

At first no one noticed. Then heads turned. Shouts erupted. A distant cousin of Kit's leapt onto a table, screaming silently as she gaped at my furry friend.

My wolfdog glanced up and bared his teeth, but I could sense his amusement.

*Coop, heel. And stop showing off.*

*Foolish human.*

Dismissing the skittish woman, Coop trotted through a rapidly expanding gap in the circle of onlookers. "Everyone relax!" I shouted, patting his head as he reached my side. "Cooper is very well trained."

"KIT HOWARD!" Whitney recovered enough to jab a finger at Cooper, her face aghast. "The *dog* is inside our *wedding reception*!"

Kit shot me an exasperated look. "Tory! What are you thinking? Coop can't—"

"He can help," I said quickly. "Just give me a second."

The doors swung open a second time. Shelton hustled in, carrying the infamous metal bowl he'd been sent to retrieve. "It was still in the trash," he said breathlessly, "but I watched Biggs wash this out pretty good. Won't the ipecac odor be gone?"

"Let's hope not, or it's my funeral."

Kneeling, I placed the bowl under Coop's nose. The crowd watched with sick fascination as he snuffled the shiny object. All in all, it had been a pretty eventful cake-cutting ceremony.

*Got it, boy?* Stroking Coop's head.

*Faint. Sweet.* He rose.

"Track!" I said aloud, worried people might wonder if I didn't issue a verbal command. "Find the scent!"

*Check* him *first*, I added silently, nodding at Iglehart.

Coop yapped once, then stalked slowly toward our target, testing the air with his nose.

"Get that monster away from me!" Iglehart yelled, but he didn't dare move.

"Why?" Corcoran asked menacingly. "You got something to hide, fella?" The fat captain was definitely enjoying himself.

"Of course not!" Iglehart shot back peevishly, swallowing hard as he tracked Cooper's approach. "But if this mongrel bites me . . ."

Coop reached the man. Halted. Thrust his snout to within an inch of the cringing scientist. The hairs on my neck stood as my friend took a sharp sniff. The room held its breath.

Coop blinked twice. Snorted. Moved past Iglehart toward the buffet tables.

My face soured. *Coop?*

His head swung my way.

*Not him?*

*No scent.* The wolfdog began snuffling the carpet. *Something here. This way.*

Movement in the corner of my eye. Whitney approached in a rush, eyes tight with anger. "*Tory!*" she seethed, trying—and failing—to keep her voice down. Which was pointless anyway, since everyone with a pulse was watching Cooper search the room.

Whitney was too horrified to notice. "This is a *wedding!*" she hissed. "In one of Charleston's finest buildings! *You're not allowed to have a dog in here!*" Then she spun to glare at Kit. "I should *never* have allowed Coop here in the first place!"

Kit's shoulders rose and fell helplessly. "No one's gonna be home all day, and everyone else who lives on Morris is here, too. Who was supposed to feed—?"

"Where's that animal going?" Corcoran barked. Coop had moved beyond the tables and was pawing at a door in the corner.

"That's the cloakroom," Tempe answered.

I looked to Ben, who nodded. He'd been in there earlier, retrieving Whitney's clutch. Before anyone else reacted, Ben jogged over and opened the door for Cooper. Boyfriend and wolfdog disappeared inside.

"This is getting absurd!" Mrs. Taylor radiated disapproval as she strode over to stand before her son. "Honestly!" she sniffed, smoothing Jason's tuxedo jacket with her hands, which he endured uncomfortably. "I've never witnessed such a thing in all my years in the League."

Whitney blanched. Began to tremble.

"A travesty!" shouted Iglehart.

"A lawsuit!" growled Biggs.

Corcoran shuffled his feet uneasily, seemed about to issue an order when we heard a series of machine-gun barks from inside the cloakroom. Ben reemerged carrying a pink leather handbag. Coop was snarling at it as they strode back across the ballroom.

*Scent here. Strong.*

As Ben eased through the mob, all eyes were on the bag in his hands.

"What in heavens?" Agnes Taylor flushed scarlet. "That boy has my purse!"

But something in her tone rang false.

*Oh my God.* Hi stared at Jason's mother, wide-eyed. He'd noticed, too.

Shelton shifted, removing his glasses and squinting in disbelief. *I don't get it.*

*The cloakroom is right beside the men's room*, Ben sent, eyeing me significantly. *It has a second door to the hallway. Biggs had time to stash something in there before Shelton caught up to him.*

A chill ran down my spine. I glanced left. Caught Mrs. Taylor staring at me.

I took a step back, startled.

For the briefest moment, I'd spotted a flash of . . . hatred.

Which made zero sense. Why would Jason's mom hate me? We barely knew each other, had only met on the few occasions I'd been to Jason's house, or when she would substitute teach at Bolton Prep.

I steeled my nerve. Looked again.

Nothing. Agnes Taylor was now glaring at Ben, her face a picture of affronted dignity.

But I knew what I saw. What I felt.

"We need to see inside the bag," I said forcefully.

"Tory!" Jason dropped Madison's hand, wrapped an arm around his mother's shoulders as he gaped at me across the dance floor. "Surely you're not suggesting—"

"No, no! Of course not." *Absolutely I am.* "It's simply the quickest way to dismiss an obvious mistake and move on."

Then I mind-shouted, *Open the purse, Ben!*

*With pleasure.* He unsnapped the clasp with his thumb.

Jason lurched forward, but not before Ben reached inside and removed a brown medicinal bottle. "Ipecac syrup," he read aloud, turning it over in his fingers. "It's also labeled 'Bolton Prep Nurses Office.'" Ben smiled coldly at Mrs. Taylor. "This expired in 2009, FYI."

Dead silence.

Jason had frozen mid-stride, paralyzed by the sight of the bottle.

All eyes swung to Agnes Taylor.

"What?" she blurted testily, fussing with her dress. Her eyes darted to Biggs for a millisecond, then jerked away as if burned. "I found that in the school pharmacy, and was going to dispose of it. I must've forgotten."

Jason was staring at the bottle in Ben's hand. Then, slowly, he turned to face his mother. "But school's out for the summer, Mom. You haven't been to Bolton in months."

Mrs. Taylor shot Jason a warning look before composing her features once more. "I'm sorry. You're right, Jason. I was mistaken." She lifted her chin. "That bottle clearly isn't mine. Someone must've put it in my bag without my knowledge."

*False*, Coop rumbled.

*Lying.* Shelton and Hi. Jinx.

*Definitely lying.* Ben tossed the bottle lightly to the floor. It bounced end over end, rolling to a stop between Mrs. Taylor's feet.

She glanced down. A bead of sweat slipped from her forehead.

I glanced at Biggs. He was breathing hard, staring at the floor and muttering, his former cool long gone. An officer behind him brandished his handcuffs.

Kit looked flabbergasted. Whitney's cheeks began twitching, like she'd been tased. Neither had any idea how to react, or what to do next.

Aunt Tempe leaned forward and caught my eye. She sensed it, too.

Mrs. Taylor was totally full of crap.

Hi spoke suddenly, strong enough for everyone to hear. "Funny story. You've always been my favorite substitute teacher, Mrs. T. Doesn't matter what subject. Chemistry. Biology. Physics. Health. I've learned more about science from you than *anybody*."

Shuffled feet. Embarrassed coughs. No one would meet Agnes Taylor's eye.

Except her son.

Jason was staring at his mother with an expression I can't describe. Then his head swung over to Biggs. "You. What's your real name?"

Biggs flinched, but didn't answer.

"You've got a tattoo on your left arm, don't you?" Jason asked. "A red anchor?"

Biggs blanched. His whole body tensed.

"Don't make me ask twice!" Corcoran warned, ignoring that Jason had actually posed the question. The captain had been watching the confrontation with his mouth hanging open, just like the rest of us.

Biggs seemed about to resist, but the officer behind him rattled his cuffs. The big man's shoulders drooped. With a sigh, he rolled up a sleeve. The nautical tattoo was plain for all to see.

Madison looked at Jason, covering her mouth with both hands. "How . . . how?"

"Okay, what's going on?" Corcoran abandoned a suddenly relieved-looking Iglehart and stomped over to confront the Taylors. "How'd you know about that body ink, boy?"

Jason pressed both palms to his temples, was staring at his mother with a nauseated look. "That guy over there is my idiot second cousin, Jimmy. I've heard my mom complain about him plenty, but we've never actually met." His tone grew angry. "No ex-cons under your roof, eh, Mom?"

Agnes Taylor bowed her head. Then her eyes snapped open, raking the assemblage with undisguised contempt. "Fine! I did it." Snorting harshly, she thrust her wrists at Corcoran. "Arrest me, Captain! Throw me in the slammer for a silly little prank!"

Detective Taylor leapt forward, shamefaced as he edged around his wife. "Now let's hold on a minute! No one's talking about jail, Agnes." He regarded Corcoran anxiously. "Carmine is a reasonable man, and no crime has been committed here."

Corcoran regarded Jason's father frankly. "All due respect, sir, but I think one has been. Messing with food is, like . . . serious business. A misdemeanor, at least. I'm fairly sure."

Tempe cleared her throat. "I'm not a police officer, but remember— this wasn't a harmless prank. An overdose of ipecac syrup can kill. These two nearly poisoned everyone in the room."

Mrs. Taylor rolled her eyes disdainfully. "Don't be so dramatic. The stuff just makes you toss your cookies. I gave it to my son once; I know."

If her words were meant to reassure everyone, they failed miserably. Noses crinkled. Protests erupted. Turns out, people don't like it when you tamper with their diet.

Tempe gave Agnes a withering look. "Putting aside how childish this stunt is—how pathetic it makes a woman of your age look—what you did *was* dangerous. Ignorance isn't an excuse, and that goes double for a science teacher."

"Don't forget my centerpieces!" Whitney blurted, wide-eyed and trembling. "And my altar, which nearly collapsed with the wedding party on top!"

Mrs. Taylor allowed herself a satisfied smirk. "The Mag League has strict standards for its publications. It's not my fault no one double-checked this event for quality."

"But *why*, Mom?" Jason demanded. "What on earth were you thinking?"

"You really have to ask?" Agnes barked an ugly laugh, thrusting her chin higher into the air. "Whitney DuBois has been stalking me for years. A silly, naïve girl from the *wrong* branch of the DuBois tree, and now she thinks she can run the League? I think not!" She thrust an accusatory finger at my stepmother. "I know you're trying to steal my position! Teaching you a lesson was my pleasure."

Silence filled the room like a living thing. Whitney's head dropped. Kit stared at Agnes, slowly shaking his head. "So you decided to spoil her wedding day?" he said softly. "One of the most important days of her life?"

"Don't act blameless here!" Agnes cried. "She's been hounding me for years, trying to poach what *I* built. You encouraged her. You two thought I'd just lie down and accept it? Ha!"

Corcoran blinked. "What in the world are y'all talking about?"

"An election." Kit shook his head in disgust. "Whitney's considering a run for Mag League president next month, and Agnes must've gotten wind of it." My father wheeled on Mrs. Taylor. "Which shouldn't matter in the slightest, since Agnes *can't* run again, according to the bylaws. Someone *has* to take her place. Whitney has every right to put herself forward."

"Don't talk to me about things I know better!" Mrs. Taylor scolded. "Rules change. You two have attempted to undermine me for months, not that I'd let that happen. Your entire family is a nest of vipers. Everything about this wedding is *offensive*. Mucking it up was a public service."

Jason's eyes glinted with frustration. "Just stop talking! I've never been more embarrassed! We're *guests* here, Mother. At one of my best friend's invitation."

"More's the pity for us!" To my complete shock, Mrs. Taylor turned and scowled at me. "That little harlot is no friend of yours. After what she did to you?"

I blinked. "Huh?"

Jason was no less baffled. "What? Tory?"

"Excuse me, did you just call my daughter a *harlot*?" Kit's voice was dangerously flat. My father rarely loses his temper, but I could feel the tethers slipping.

Mrs. Taylor shot forward and tried to take Jason's arm. He shrugged her off, staring at his mother as if he'd never seen her before. "Explain yourself. Now. All of it."

"Tory led you on like a puppy dog, sweetie." Agnes was concentrating on her son to the exclusion of all else. "For almost two years, she had you eating out of her hand, and then what? She starts dating a *dock boy*."

"A what?" I gave Mrs. Taylor a level stare.

"Oh lord." Detective Taylor covered his eyes.

From the corner of my eye, I noticed Tom Blue coughing into a fist. It took me a moment to realize he was laughing.

"Mom!" Jason yelped in a strangled voice. "What is *wrong* with you!? You will apologize *this second*!" He spun to face Ben, his expression scandalized. "Ben, man. I'm so—"

Ben waved off the apology. "No need. Forget it." Was he smiling, too?

But Mrs. Taylor had more to say. "She should've been *grateful* for your attention, Jaybird." Tilting her head, trying to catch her son's eye. "You're a smart, handsome, *successful* boy. From one of the best families in Charleston! But *no*. And now look what's happened. Heartbroken, you've fallen into the clutches of this . . . this . . ." She waved a dismissive hand at Madison.

Madison paled. Her legs began to shake as the focus shifted to her.

For a few beats, Jason merely gawked at his mother, reeling from one blow too many. "*MOTHER!*" he finally spat. "Don't you *dare* talk about my girlfriend like that! Maddy is the kindest, sweetest—"

"Please!" Mrs. Taylor spat, well past caring about appearances. "Madison Dunkle has been a nasty, selfish bully her whole pampered life. I should know, I taught her more times than I can count. People like that don't change. And now she's inside my kitchen, eating from my own table!"

Madison stumbled back a step, sniffing loudly, seconds from fleeing in tears.

My temper boiled over.

"That's *enough!*" I strode briskly to Madison's side and took her hand. She was trembling like a leaf. Ella was a step behind me, snatching up Madison's other hand and fixing Mrs. Taylor with a death stare.

"Mrs. Taylor," I said, clear and cold, "Madison is a dear friend, and here at my invitation. In addition to trying to *poison* everyone, you're being rude." A glance at Kit, who nodded vigorously. "I'm afraid I have to ask you to leave."

Eyes tight with fury, Mrs. Taylor opened her mouth, but Jason's father jumped in before she could do any more damage. "Yes, yes! Very fair. I think that's best for all involved." He turned to Kit, his embarrassment plain. "I'll pay for the damaged cake, of course. But for now, my wife and I will get out of—"

"I'm not sure I can allow that, Detective." Corcoran frowned, mustache drooping. "A crime has likely taken place. And I *definitely* want to talk more with Cousin Jimmy over there. All due respect, but . . . I mean, this is . . . serious consequences . . ."

He trailed off, scratching his head.

Detective Taylor gave his colleague a blistering glare. Though technically lower on the official totem pole, Mr. Taylor ran the city's entire violent crimes division. I wasn't sure who could pull rank. Evidently, they weren't either.

Whitney stepped into the breach. "That won't be necessary tonight, Captain," she said with icy dignity. "I, for one, don't plan on pressing charges on my wedding day, and I imagine my guests all feel the same. If the city has to arrest Agnes, it can easily do so at a later date. She's not a flight risk."

Mrs. Taylor bristled. "Run from you? An up-jumped hussy after my position? Hardly!"

To everyone's astonishment, Whitney laughed. Then she spoke in a stage whisper loud enough to echo. "Honestly, Agnes. You're *embarrassing* yourself. It'd be best for you if you just left quietly. Who needs the scandal?"

Murmurs of agreement filled the air, though scandal was inevitable. Gossip this juicy couldn't possibly be contained. The Howard Wedding Debacle would be on every lip by dawn the following day.

Agnes gave Whitney a haughty look. "You've always been soft, DuBois."

Whitney met her rival's disdain coolly. "Of course, you'll need to resign from the Magnolia League immediately. Crime or not, we can't have such *uncivilized* behavior associated with our honored civic institutions."

*Dagger.*

Eyes widening, Mrs. Taylor spluttered, "How *dare* you! Of all the—"

But Detective Taylor had had enough. "That sounds fine, Whitney," he shouted over his wife's impressive string of expletives. "Very generous of you. We'll be out of your way in two shakes." Hissing furiously, he hurried Mrs. Taylor past Corcoran and toward the exit. At the last second he turned.

"Jason?" Hesitant. "You coming?"

"Not a chance." He turned his back.

"Okay, then." Mr. Taylor bustled his wife out the door.

Jason stole Madison's hand from mine, whispering a quiet "Thanks."

"No problem." I gave him room. This wasn't his fault, and I knew his conscience would be killing him for what his mother had done.

As Corcoran and his team escorted Biggs from the room, boisterous chatter sprang up on all sides. No one knew what to do next—social graces don't typically cover this type of experience. So it was startling when Aunt Tempe burst out laughing.

Whitney gaped as Tempe elbowed her in the side, tears sparkling in my great-aunt's eyes. "Good lord, Whit. This is one *hell* of a wedding story!"

Soft chuckles from the gallery. Whitney shivered, rubbing her arms. Then, incredibly, she began giggling herself. "My God! I mean, have you *ever*?"

A cloud seemed to lift. The chuckles became outright laughter. Seizing the moment, Kit spun and waved frantically at the band. Quickly taking their places, they launched into an upbeat number. Shouts of approval echoed in the chandeliers.

I sighed. *What a night.*

But when I turned, Ben was missing.

I rose to my tiptoes, craning my neck as I searched the suddenly energized crowd. I spotted Ben whispering urgently with Kit. Before I could call out, he bolted across the ballroom and disappeared through the kitchen doors. *Huh?*

Hi appeared at my elbow, stuffing a chunk of cake into his mouth. "Where's he going?"

"Hiram!" I slapped the crumbs from his hands. "That's *poisoned*, remember?"

"Not the lowest tier," Hi countered. "Probably." Wiping icing from his hair, he stuck two fingers into his mouth. Sighed with pleasure.

"Sometimes you just have to gamble, eh, Brennan?"

# CHAPTER 9

The reception was roaring again.

Guests were dancing, back to having fun. Whitney had somehow turned a corner, was now laughing nonstop about the whole affair, exchanging scandalized whispers with her friends. She was enjoying the downfall of her nemesis a bit more than was proper, but I wasn't going to judge. Agnes Taylor tried to destroy her wedding. That's dirty pool in any playbook.

Mike Iglehart was whining about his mistreatment to anyone who'd listen, but no one took him seriously. He hadn't left the party, no doubt enjoying both Kit's sincere apology and the righteous indignation of the wrongfully accused.

Whatever. We *had* screwed him over a little. Enjoy the open bar.

Jason was following Madison around like a baby lamb, looking distressed. Maddy was acting upset, but I could tell she secretly loved the attention. The other Bolton Prep girls had formed a protective circle around her, taking turns giving her hugs and telling her how great she was. It was the most popular she'd been in ages. People are dumb.

Me? I was standing by an empty table, anxiously tapping a foot.

Ben was still AWOL. No one had seen him since he'd fled the ballroom twenty minutes earlier. I'd even sent Shelton and Hi to look for him, but so far they hadn't returned.

Where had he gone, without a backward glance?

What had he whispered to Kit?

My mind cycled through awful possibilities. Had Mrs. Taylor struck a nerve?

Anger smoldered within me at the prospect. *If that harridan screws up my relationship with Ben, so help me . . .*

But he had to know how ridiculous she'd been. With her stupid, classist, snobbish prejudices. I couldn't have cared less about what Ben's father did for a living, or his family's so-called "place" in society. No, that wasn't true. I *liked* Tom Blue's job. I *adored* his family.

Ben was the sweetest, strongest, most loyal person I knew.

I loved him.

*There. I said it. Thought it, anyway.*

My face flushed, but I didn't back away from my feelings. Even if Ben *was* leaving in a few weeks. Even though I might lose him forever to some doe-eyed co-ed in Geology 101.

*I love Ben Blue. I'm ready to tell him.*

*So where is the stupid jerk?*

Dark silk flashed in my periphery. I turned. Chance was standing behind me, his sardonic smile in place. I jumped. Couldn't help it. Dude came out of nowhere.

"Do you mind?" I stepped back and hugged my chest, repressing the shiver of excitement his proximity always gave me. "It's impolite to sneak up on people."

"I've been standing here for thirty seconds," he replied airily, then waved a lazy hand. "While you've been staring at the door." A sculpted eyebrow rose. "Talking to your furry friend again? That was a truly amazing performance by Coop earlier. Almost as if he knew *exactly* what to look for."

"Coop and I can't talk anymore," I snapped, trying to hide my unease at his perceptiveness. For the hundredth time I reminded myself never to underestimate him. "You know that, Chance. He's just . . . well trained."

"So you've said." A statement of fact, not agreement.

I glanced over his shoulder. A few feet away, Ella looked bored as she leaned against a buffet table. She shrugged apologetically. Obviously this wasn't her idea.

"Can I help you with something?" Resuming my vigil. Where *was* Ben already?

Chance didn't speak for a moment, but I felt his eyes on me. Then he sighed. "I hope you'll trust me again one day, Tory. It'd be nice if we *all* could be honest with each other. For a change." He straightened, tugging his sleeves. "Thank your father for the lovely invitation. Our gift is on the table. It's an espresso maker."

I stifled a flinch. What did he mean, if we *all* could be honest?

Was Chance holding back, too?

I turned, but his back was already to me. Chance strolled over to Ella and offered an arm, then escorted her from the ballroom.

*Damn him. Every time I think I'm playing him, I find out it's the opposite.*

*Or is it?*

The kitchen doors swung open, driving all other thoughts from my mind. But it was only Hi and Shelton. They shook their heads in unison as they joined me.

"Ben left the building." Shelton fiddled nervously with his bow tie. "I'm sure he'll be back soon, though. Maybe after what Mrs. Taylor said, he just needed some air or something."

I nodded, but my heart sank. Exactly what I was afraid of.

"Maybe he took up smoking?" At my irritated frown, Hi raised both palms. "I'm just spitballing here. Maybe Ben's a superhero, and there's crime afoot."

Shelton leaned close, whispered, "Have you tried calling him on our *private* network?"

I nodded glumly. "Nothing. He's either out of range or blocking me."

Through trial and error we'd discovered that our telepathic connection wasn't simply an open line. You could close off the pack if you wanted privacy. Mind-linked as I was to three teenage boys—and a giant wolfdog—I was usually grateful for that fact.

Not right now.

Why would Ben go so far away? Why would be choose to shut me out?

My sick feeling increased.

"He used a side gate." Hi adjusted his sagging cummerbund for the tenth time. He'd wiped the frosting from his hair and face, but the tux was a wreck. "Coop tracked him there, but obviously couldn't go any farther."

Coop was back in the garden, to the immense relief of nearly everyone. No matter how well trained I assured everyone he was, your average wedding guest isn't comfortable with a hulking apex predator circling the dance floor. Whitney had insisted that Coop scram, though I'd caught her ruffling his ears as he padded outside.

"What happened to Biggs?" Shelton asked. "Cousin Jimmy, I mean."

"They let him go," I answered, still eyeing the door. "But Corcoran got all his information, and told him not to leave town. Corcoran still doesn't know what to do next. Arrest them both, I say."

Hi chuckled. "It'd be pretty funny to see Mrs. Taylor in stripes."

"She deserves it." I was miles less forgiving than Whitney. "If we'd been a few steps slower, everyone here would've been puking their guts out. She and Cousin Jimmy are criminals, scandalous or not."

"I'm with you," Shelton said. "Wackos. You can't sweep attempted poisoning under the rug, though I bet they try. Did Jimmy kill the flowers, too?"

I shook my head. "Mrs. Taylor got the flowers. Remember, she was inside the ballroom during setup, supervising the Magnolia League's camera crew. She must've gotten to the vases when the florists weren't looking."

"Makes sense," Hi agreed. "But I can't see an old lady crawling under that altar in a cocktail dress. Or maybe I just don't *want* to see it."

"*That* was Jimmy," Shelton said. When Hi and I both looked at him sharply, he tapped his ear. "I overheard some of Corcoran's interrogation while looking for Ben. Jimmy came by here last night and pulled the pins. Mrs. Taylor told him exactly which ones to remove. She knew how to time the collapse perfectly."

Hi whistled. "All that planning, just to embarrass a social rival. Looney Tunes."

My face flushed with anger. "Psychotic."

An intake of breath beside me. I glanced at Shelton, who pointed to the doors. "Look! He's back."

Ben backed into the room carrying something bulky in his arms. It took me a moment to figure out what it was: three large cardboard boxes stacked atop one another. Two men in white aprons followed Ben with identical loads.

"What in the world?" Shelton squawked. "He go shopping?"

"No, no!" Hi smiled, rubbed his hands together in excitement. "I'd know those boxes anywhere. Our boy Benny just saved the day!"

Kit rushed over to assist, a confused Whitney trailing in his wake. The four men set the boxes on a table and began peeling back the lids. Inside were cupcakes. A *lot* of cupcakes.

I beamed. "He replaced the wedding cake!"

Relief. Ben hadn't run from me, or Mrs. Taylor's stupid insults.

He'd thought fast, slipped out, and solved our problem. Like a boss.

Whitney clapped her hands like a schoolgirl. "Oh, Benjamin! They're beautiful! Thank you so much!" She planted a kiss on his cheek.

"Nice," Hi breathed. Then yelped as my elbow found his gut.

Ben spotted me and extricated himself from Whitney. As he made his way over, I noticed something else unusual. Ben had changed out of his tuxedo, but not into his standard black tee and jeans. He was sporting a dark gray uniform of some kind, with a black stripe straight down the middle of the jacket. Military cut. I'd never seen him wear anything like it.

"Just like Richard Gere," Hi whispered, rounding his eyes theatrically.

My gaze flicked to my friend. "What now?" I could tell he was mocking me.

Hi danced away with a sly smile. "You'll see. Later. I got dibs on a red velvet."

My head whipped to Shelton, who was grinning ear to ear. "Thank *God* he's telling you tonight! I'm terrible at keeping secrets."

My eyes narrowed. "What secret?"

Shelton stuck his hands in his pockets and ambled away, whistling merrily.

Exasperated, I turned to find Ben standing right in front of me. He executed a low bow, looking positively bizarre in his fancy outfit. The uniform was tantalizing familiar, but I couldn't place it.

"Replacement desserts delivered, ma'am." Ben smiled, clearly pleased with himself. "Hope everyone likes chocolate."

"Out with it," I demanded.

Ben lifted his hands in surrender. "After Hi destroyed the cake, I remembered that fancy bakery a few blocks over on King. Your dad jumped at the idea, told me to use whatever means necessary. So I jogged over and—"

"Not that!" I poked the buttons on his chest. "What secret are you keeping? And why are you dressed like a . . . like a . . ." Then it hit me. "Like a cadet?"

Ben placed his hands on my shoulders. Looked me square in the eye.

"Because I am one," he said simply.

I shook my head, lost. "Cadets attend The Citadel. You're going to Warren Wilson."

"I'm not." Ben released me. Abruptly stood at attention. Saluted. "I've joined the Cadet Corps. Knob Blue, at your command!" Then he grinned sheepishly, lowering his voice. "Or something like that. I have no idea. I'm not even supposed to wear this Citadel stuff yet. Whitney lent me a uniform for tonight. Her cousin's, I think."

"Wait. What?" I couldn't move. Or breathe. "You're joining the freaking Citadel? Since when? You hate soldier stuff!"

"I like *you*. Love you, I mean," he blurted, as if determined to get the words out. "So I'm sticking around here for a while. If that's okay." Suddenly he was scarlet-faced, and as nervous as I'd ever seen him.

Head spinning.

Heart pounding.

Feet floating on air.

"You borrowed a cadet's uniform from my stepmother?" was all I managed, still trying to process the rest. *Did he really say . . .*

"She's the one who got me in." Ben shook his head, as if unable to believe it himself. "Whitney pulled a few strings so I could stay close to home. She kinda knows everyone in town, FYI."

"Ben . . . I . . ."

I clamped my lips shut, cutting off the weak effort. Tried to gather myself. Finally, I noticed Hi and Shelton a stone's throw away, grinning like crocodiles, pretending not to eavesdrop as they exchanged a fist bump. Kit and Whitney weren't even doing that much, watching us openly with wide smiles.

*Obviously the last to know.*

I grabbed Ben by the front of his jacket. "Ben Blue, you do NOT have to give up your life goals because of me. If you're worried I'm going to bail because you're moving out of state, don't be." *Gulp.* "I love you, too, okay? You don't have to do this."

"Hey, I *love* marching in formation. Rules. Orders. Yelling. Can't wait." Ben swept my hands up in his. "Whatever buys me another year with you is worth it." Then he hugged me close and whispered, "Besides, it's only *one* year. Then we can *both* get the heck out of town."

We were nose to nose.

The music stopped.

Everyone was watching.

*Don't care.*

I pulled Ben in. Smashed my lips against his.

Applause rained down around us. Inside my head, Hi wisecracked that Ben and I had a lousy ship name. Shelton told him to shut it. But I was a thousand miles away.

Ben was staying. My Ben.

We wouldn't have to be apart. Now, or maybe ever.

It was the best day of my life.

My eyes sparkled, as blue as the ocean.

*Love you, Ben Blue.*

*I love you, too.*

Outside in the darkness, Cooper sat back and howled.